LAID

TO rest

The Rebirth

©2024

Dr. Taura M. Turner

SANSSCRIPTS

SansScripts by San'sChild
Memphis

ISBN: 979-8-9897139-2-9
PUBLISHED BY SansScripts
www.SansScripts.com
Memphis
Printed in the United States of America

DEDICATION

In memoria aeterna erit iustus
(For the Righteous Shall Be Remembered Forever)

Sandra Marie Hunt (2/2001)
Walter "Jon Jon" Wells Jr. (3/2017)
Brenda Diane Hunt Wells (1/2021)
Rest in Paradise

And now, abideth faith, hope, charity (love), these three; but the
greatest of these is charity (love).
1 Corinthians 13:13

Table of Contents

THE GREEN FAMILY TREE
MASTERS, MISSISSIPPI

The Green Family Tree

Joe Green (Laura)

Steve Green (Belle aka MaBelle)

Dallas Green (Bertha)

Martha	Mabel	Constance	Lilly	Diane	Sonya	Leona
(Sam Love)	(Lonnie Payne)	(Princeton Johnson)	(Pastor Ken Jeffries)	(Ryce Smothers)	(Reggie Warren)	(Monroe Jackson)
Charity	Morgan	Nicholas	Hannah Grace	Sarah	Jaylin & Kaylin	
Joi (Derrick)	Carmen	Markus		Lisa	Mona & Monique	
Madden				Lionel	Leslie & April	
				Jeremy	Kera & Keith	
					McKenzie & Kensington	

PROLOGUE
CHARITY LOVE

Journal Entry 17... 9-25-2024

Death changes you. It shakes you to your core, rearranges everything you thought you knew about yourself. Death is a thief, stealing pieces of your identity, your rhythm. You breathe differently, walk differently, think differently. It's like stepping into a brand-new world, a world that suddenly demands a new normal. In the aftermath of loss, you find yourself forging new habits and navigating experiences you never imagined—without the ones you love. And with those new habits and experiences come new challenges. But here's the kicker: It makes you stronger. So, which side will you pick, Charity? Will you stand still, or will you move forward?

Today, I've decided: I'm moving forward. In too many ways, I've stood still, convinced I was pushing ahead, but all I was doing was treading water.

Death, as hard as it is, also offers an opportunity for something else: Rebirth. Your new normal doesn't just change the world around you, it transforms you. You find a new strength, a new peace, and, slowly, you start rediscovering yourself. You grow new wings, new ideas, new energy, and you start to move forward. I've been stagnant for too long. Today, I choose to move forward.

Peace out, love in.
—Charity Love

Charity placed her journal carefully on the dark blue nightstand and collapsed back into bed. She glanced at the clock: 4:15 a.m. "My sleep pattern is still off," she muttered to herself. This was the new normal, the latest casualty of losing her mother. Her sleep was fractured now. In bed by 9 p.m., up by midnight, back to sleep by 2 a.m., and then wide awake again by 4 a.m. Another change, another adjustment she wasn't quite ready to accept.

It had been this way ever since her mom, Martha Love, passed away. Charity had made peace with her mother's death; she knew Martha had lived a full, joyful life. But that didn't stop the emptiness that crept in every time Charity thought about picking up the phone to call her. Or just stopping by the house to see her. That simple act—being able to show up at any time—was something she would never take for granted again.

She lingered a little longer, staring into the darkness of the early morning. *Should I try to sleep for a couple more hours, or just get up now?* After a few minutes of thinking about the day. She swung her legs off the bed and padded over to the ornate bedroom window, her feet brushing the cold hardwood floor. Her hair, usually tied up in a messy bun that had long since lost its battle with gravity, was now in an uneven knot halfway to the side of her head. She could never keep a bonnet on all night. Her long pink Mississippi Mud t-shirt, the one she'd won at the state fair two years ago, hung crooked around her waist. It was oversized, but it was comfortable, and she loved it.

To her surprise, tucked among the white blossoms of the tall Southern magnolia in her backyard were two birds, chirping away. "Do birds really chirp this early?" she whispered with a small laugh. Superstition was never her thing, but she had a sense, a feeling, that this was somehow a sign.

She was supposed to visit her mother's grave today, after stopping by her grandmother Bertha Green's house for a family brunch. The whole Green clan would be there—every last one of them. Charity took a deep breath, feeling a surge of energy flood through her. Today, she would get up, clean up, and write before getting ready for Bertha's brunch with the Greens.

Charity and Martha had been close, more like best friends than mother and daughter. Charity had always been a fighter, a giver, and a nurturer. She lavished her love on the Green family, sometimes to the point of exhaustion. But lately, she'd felt drained, running on fumes. It was obvious to everyone, but she kept on going.

Martha's death had broken a link in the Green chain, and the family had struggled to regain their balance. The hole left by Martha was undeniable. But even in the aftermath, the Greens began to rally. Life, they realized, had to go on.

A few hours later, after a long shower and a careful battle to tame her messy bun, Charity finally finished getting herself together. Standing 5 feet, 3 inches tall, she was heavy set with natural curls that she kept in the messy bun most of the time. Checking her appearance in extra-large wall mirror, she took a slow deep breath and stepped out of the house, ready to face the day.

As she drove to the cemetery, the familiar mantra played in her head: *Blessings on blessings.* It was her daily reminder that she was covered, protected. But today, the words felt less reassuring. Her stomach twisted as she parked her car and took out the keys. She had promised herself ten years ago that she would never come back to this place because Martha wasn't here, but here she was.

Stepping out of the car, she whispered under her breath, "Just make it through this moment." The wind whipped past her, and she pulled her jacket closer to her body. She passed grave markers—some fresh, some worn, all reminders of the ones who had come before.
"No crying today, Charity Love," she told herself firmly.

Charity hated cemeteries. Who thought it was a good idea to create these cold, sterile places for people to lie forever? "Just bury me in the backyard," she thought to herself, then caught herself with a quick laugh.

When she reached her mother's grave, she noticed fresh flowers resting on the marker. *Which one of the Green sisters has been here?* she wondered, suspecting it was Constance, the family's resident busybody.

She couldn't help but smile. The Green sisters—the *Seven Wonders of Masters*, as her Great-Granddaddy Joe used to call them—were a force to be reckoned with. The daughters of Dallas Green, a beloved attorney, were as strong and beautiful as they were unique. There was Martha, the engineer; Mabel, the artist; Lilly, the baker; Diane, the quiet but firm accountant; Leona, the distant attorney; Sonya, the NFL wife and mom of multiple twins, and Constance, the chief of the Green Clan, the one who kept everyone in line.

Charity smiled at the thought of her mother's sisters. She was blessed to have so many surrogate mothers after the death of her mom. She loved her family, even if they drove her crazy sometimes.

Her thoughts drifted back to the day her mother passed. Her aunts, all strong women, had fallen apart. One by one, they'd collapsed in the funeral home, overwhelmed by grief. It was a rare moment of vulnerability for the mighty Green sisters.

Charity came back to the present. "Enough procrastinating," she muttered to herself. She needed to talk to Martha today.

Sitting down on the grass in front of the headstone, she spoke as though her mother could hear her: "Hey, Mom. It's been a while since I've been here. Last time I was here, I promised I'd never come back, but today... I just needed to talk. I know you're not here, but I just needed to visit the place where you are laid to rest."

She shifted her weight and propped her arm on her knee, looking out at the grounds. "Have you ever been lonely in a room full of people? I never really felt that until today. I was at Grandma's with the whole family, and I felt... alone. I mean, I was surrounded by love, but inside, it was like I was invisible."

She paused, glancing at the sky, letting the words sink in. "You always told me to slow down, to enjoy life. I was too busy back then, but now, everything feels... stuck."

She sighed, rubbing her hands together, a bitter laugh escaping her lips. "Even Grandma's sneaking around with someone. Can you believe it? Bertha Mae's out here living her best life. And me? I'm still trying to figure things out."

Charity wiped a tear away, but there was something freeing about the moment. "I've been in survival mode, Mom. Ever since you left, I've just been surviving, making sure everyone else was okay. But now... I see it. I haven't lived. Not really."

Charity stood up, pacing in front of the grave, her words coming faster now. "I'm leaving Masters, Mississippi for a while. Maybe just a week, maybe longer. I'm going to close the company, take a break from all of this. I need to write. I need to find myself again."

She took a deep breath, glancing one last time at the cemetery, at the flowers, at the quiet grounds. "I'll be back in town soon, Mom. But for now, I need to go. I need to breathe. I need to live."

With that, Charity wiped her face and turned away from the grave. As she walked back to her car, she felt the weight of her decisions settle in. She wasn't just moving forward with her life—she was reclaiming it. "Goodbye, Masters," she whispered as she slid into her car and started the engine. "I'll see you later."

She was ready for the next chapter.

CHAPTER 1
BERTHA GREEN

"Shit!" Bertha Green muttered as she cut her finger trying to cut a piece of her famous Cinnamon bread that she made each Sunday afternoon. She turned her gaze upward. "Oh, Father, forgive me!"

Bertha was a righteous woman of God. She'd rarely cursed in all her eighty years of living. The birds chirping outside distracted her as she prepared breakfast. "Those darn birds! Oh Lord, please forgive me again." Wanting the annoying creatures away from her house, she looked around her kitchen to find something to throw out of the window.

Why were the birds chirping anyway?!? Do birds still chirp after the summer has passed? Bertha asked herself. It was autumn, late September to be exact. It was time for them to head south. She moved to the open window, watching as the birds tweeted and sang. One sat perched on the black awning of her white brick house as if he owned it. Another sat on a tree branch. It seemed as if it was staring directly at her while performing its morning melody. "Shoo birds!" she yelled. "Get out of here!" At that moment, she knew her neighbors must have thought that she'd lost her mind. So, she quietly closed the window, pulled the blinds down and retreated toward the bathroom for a bandage. That's when she saw it: The wall calendar read September 26.

Oh, that's why! She thought to herself. She stared at the calendar for a full minute. Today would have been her sixty-second wedding anniversary. She and Dallas would have been married sixty-two years today. For just a moment, Bertha stood frozen in time, memories rushing through her mind. She repeated sixty-two out loud this time. "Sixty-two.

Whew, Dallas can you believe it, sixty-two years?" Resuming her walk to the bathroom, she kept whispering sixty – two.

After grabbing her bandage and alcohol from the creaky old medicine cabinet, she made her way back to the kitchen and sat at the table. While she mended her wound, the birds began chirping again. She could hear their song even with the window closed and the shades pulled. This time Bertha started chuckling. *So that's why the birds are here.* "Hey Dallas, my love. Hey, Martha Baby," she called to the songsters.

Her two angels—her husband, Dallas Sr., and her oldest daughter, Martha—were coming to sing her a beautiful Happy Anniversary melody. She normally didn't believe in signs, but lately she'd seen so many that she believed that God sent tiny glimpse of Heaven to help us make it through this journey on Earth.

Joining the birds, she broke out into song, "Do you know what today is? It's our anniversary." Feeling the moment, she jumped up and started dancing. Ignoring her cracking bones and stiff hips, she danced around her small kitchen island, enjoying every moment.

Life was different over the last ten years. After Martha, her oldest daughter died, the family struggled to lay her to rest. Martha, the oldest of seven sisters, was such an integral part of the Green family.

Finishing her dance, Bertha grabbed her breakfast plate and coffee and made her way to the living room. Every space, every corner, every piece of furniture there was adorned with photos of her family. And each held a memory. "Those Greens, my Seven Wonders." Her eyes caught the photo of a pair of high school sweethearts: She and Dallas graduating from Masters High School together. The two met in Mrs. Holmes' ninth-grade history class and had been inseparable since. Oh, the memories. The biggest fight they'd ever had was on graduation day. She never thought they would mend their relationship after that.

Dallas planned to attend college in Chicago and wanted Bertha to come with him. But she was set on staying put in Masters. The history of Masters was rich and abundant, and she wanted her future children to grow up in a town where they didn't feel discrimination and prejudice. Masters was founded by freed slaves and had an aura that spoke of excellence, entrepreneurship, culture, self-built wealth, and pride. She wanted her future offspring to experience that. She remembered the argument like it was yesterday. Grabbing a picture of her and Dallas, Bertha sat down in the big, oversized recliner that Dallas loved so much. She'd worked up quite a sweat with that burst of energy and all that dancing. Rubbing the dust off the picture, and running her fingertips over the frame, she leaned back into the chair, remembering the night she and Dallas almost let go of their relationship.

It was Friday evening after their high school graduation. They were standing outside her mother's house on Thornbush Road. It was a shotgun house built by her great-great-grandfather, a founding father of Masters. It held a huge family room and three small bedrooms. At 11:30 that night, she'd snuck out the window in her bedroom, praying that it didn't creak, to meet Dallas on the porch. He was dressed in khakis, a black polo-style shirt, and black loafers. He looked confident and cocky; he sounded the same when he said, "Bertha, have your bags packed by Tuesday night!"

"Why, Dallas?"

"We are going to Chicago. I got accepted into Chicago State University to major in education. You already know this, Bertha."

"Dallas, I don't want to go to Chicago," Bertha pouted. "I thought we were going to get married and have a family in Masters. I want to stay here and work at the strawberry plant."

"What kind of life is that, Bertha?" Dallas mocked. "You don't want more for your life than to stay and work at a plant? The world is so big, Masters is so small. I want more for *us*."

Dallas placed his hands firmly, but lovingly, on her shoulders. "We can come back to visit Masters anytime."

Bertha pulled away. "I don't like the tone you are using with me." She sat on the steps, folded her arms, and stared up at Dallas in disbelief. "You're talking to me like I have no dreams. I have dreams. I have goals. I'm going to work my way up in the plant and use those strawberries to make the best cakes in town. One day, I plan to own a bakery."

Dallas looked at Bertha briefly before he walked away but stopped and turned to face her. "Well, you can stay here with your small-town dreams. I'm leaving Wednesday morning to go to Chicago with or without you." And with that Dallas walked to his car and drove away.

She'd been furious with Dallas. They didn't speak for four days. Then on Tuesday night, before he planned to leave, he showed up with roses and a ring. He proposed and said he was going to transfer to Jackson State University after he completed his first year. He was faithful to his promise. After that first year enduring that Chicago winter, she was sure he was excited to head to warmer temperatures. Once he transferred to Jackson State, he came home every weekend until he graduated. After he graduated from Jackson State, he enrolled in Ole Miss School of Law and graduated before coming back to Masters to marry Bertha and settle down.

Everyone in town came to Dallas for legal advice. He was kind and warmhearted. He and Bertha disagreed about all the pro bono cases he took on, but honestly, God always provided, and they had more than enough.

Bertha rose slowly from the recliner, placed the picture of the two of them on the coffee table before turning her attention to the last picture on the coffee table before she rested her breakfast plate and coffee cup. It was taken a few months before Martha died. She smiled. The smile didn't reach her eyes. It stopped at her face. Her hands shook as she held the picture in her wrinkled hands. Her breathing slowed as tears rolled down her face. The Seven Wonders, each dressed in purple, stood in the picture looking like fresh crisp bills. It was the day of Charity's grand opening of her publishing company. So many memories. Even Leona, her wayward youngest daughter, was in the picture. Bertha sighed. She needed to call and check on her baby girl, Leona, the only one who took after her father and became a lawyer.

Each week like clockwork Bertha called her daughters to check on them. Death sure makes you cherish life more. Last week, she laughed with Mabel, her second oldest daughter, until she was in tears. They recounted the events that took place after Martha's death. It seemed like all hell broke loose after Martha passed away. Mabel's husband, Lonnie, tried to set her art studio on fire. Mabel was known as the creator. She could paint, mold, sculpt, and decorate anything. People paid big money for her paintings. Lonnie was trying to destroy her livelihood by setting fire to her studio. But his plans were thwarted, and a divorce was the best thing for them.

That same year, Tammy, Reggie's fling that lasted much too long came to the Masters' annual homecoming service commemorating the founding fathers and mothers of Masters. She showed up to the church's homecoming ceremony and tried to fight Sonya and Reggie. Her two-year affair with Reggie ended abruptly and she was furious. Her well was dry, and she was not having it. She showed up in rare form, hair all over her head and acted a plum fool; the police were called. But in the end, her antics were the very thing that brought Sonya's family back together again.

The year wasn't all bad. Sam Love, Charity and Joi's father, checked himself out of the mental hospital. The story behind that is massive. Constance and Leona finally made amends. Those two used to fight like cats and dogs. It does a mother's heart good to know that her children get along well.

Joi, Martha's baby girl, graduated from Julliard and got married in New York. The groom bought his tuxedo much too late, and the pickings were too slim. She snickered hysterically remembering the faces of the Greens when he walked out in a purple tuxedo. Lilly and Pastor Jeffries started dating and got married a year later. Ryce, Diane's husband, shocked the whole church and family by announcing his call to the ministry. It was quite a shock. Ryce went from living as a head engineer at the strawberry plant to a crackhead, to converting others to Christ. God is simply amazing.

No, the year of Martha's death wasn't all bad. It's amazing how you mark time with certain events: The year before and the year after Martha's death became her way of recalling life. She heaved a sigh as she looked at the last picture on the bookshelf near the door. It was Dallas Green, Jr., the son she never carried, and his family. Although she tried for a boy, every pregnancy produced a beautiful baby girl. Few people knew Dallas Green, Sr., stepped out on their marriage, giving the Greens a baby boy.

She remembered the day she found out. Her heart still dropped into her stomach even to this day. She didn't even know if heartbroken was a suitable word to describe her pain. Crushed. She'd cried for days and locked Dallas Sr. out of the house. He laid outside their bedroom window for two days singing love songs until the neighbors called the police. There was nowhere to go, a house full of girls, no job, and no formal education, so she stayed. Over time though, her love for Dallas, Sr. resurfaced. She learned to forgive again and again and again. Every time she thought about it, she learned to forgive again.

The pain she felt was unbearable. It was as if she was suffocating. Her appetite was gone and yet she stood in front of a stove 3 times a day to feed her family. She felt as though her heart was shattered into a thousand pieces. Dallas was the only love she knew. Her first love. Her only love. She felt betrayed and cast aside. She didn't think she would ever recover from the heartbreak. Going about her regular daily chores and activities, she never told any of her daughters about their new little brother. Martha found out because she was so nosey and was always snooping around, but she kept the secret to her death. But Martha's daughters, Joi and Charity were the ones who revealed the secret to the rest of the family. That whole escapade was heartbreaking yet freeing and refreshing.

The Green legacy could now continue with Dallas Jr., and he was now a part of the family. It took Bertha a few years to totally welcome Dallas Jr. and his family into her family, but she eventually let her heart win out over her ego. And she was so happy that she did. Dallas Jr. was a replica of Dallas, Sr. His mannerisms, his soft voice, his height and especially his loving nature. She'd been so mad when she found out that they'd name his illegitimate son, Dallas. How dare they? But now she could certainly see his father's character spilling out and he was indeed a junior.

After staring at the picture, Bertha finally announced out loud to no one, "*I need to call and check on Dallas, Jr. and his family. Maybe he can bring the kids to see me this weekend.*" Dallas recently moved back to Masters and started working at the Strawberry Plant. He'd followed in his older sister, Martha's, who was an engineer, footsteps and became an engineer as well.

Dallas Jr. loved Martha and Martha loved him. Dallas Sr. would take Martha to visit Dallas Jr., although Bertha would be livid. She later realized that it was the best thing for all three of them. They developed a bond that couldn't be broken. *"Yes, I need to call and check on Dallas Jr."* she stated again, staring at the picture.

Oh, how she missed Dallas Sr., but the memories kept her sane. They'd created enough memories to last a lifetime.

Still reminiscing about the past ten years since Martha's death, Bertha smirked. Charles Dickens wrote it right; it was the best of times and the worst of times. Thinking about those ugly Green suits her daughters wore to Martha's funeral made her wince. How she wished she could have seen Martha's face to behold her sisters that day looking like six jolly green giants. Shaking her head, she thought about her girls. Dallas would be so proud of them now. Their Seven Wonders. She smiled thinking about her girls and her stepson.

"My how one death created a new life. Rebirth. Whew, chile!" she laughed. "Honey, that's biblical." Bertha briefly hummed the tune to "The Old Rugged Cross" before stopping to listen to the birds. She sat quietly, allowing them to serenade her as she drank her morning coffee. When the birds stopped crooning, she made her way back to the kitchen to look out the window just in time to see them fly away. Instantly, she started singing, "I'll fly away, oh glory, I'll fly away. When I die, Hallelujah by and by, I'll fly away."

The ringing phone interrupted her singing. She picked it up quickly.

"Good morning," Bertha spoke in a welcoming Southern-belle drawl.

"Happy Anniversary to you. Happy Anniversary to you. Happy Anniversary dear Grandma, Happy Anniversary to you!" Bertha's smile beamed so bright that even the sun envied her. It didn't matter that Charity delivered the song off-key.

"Hey, my love."

"Hey, Granny."

13

Sternly, Bertha responded. "What did I tell you about calling me, Granny? Call me Grandma or Grandmother."

"Okay, Sis. Green," Charity giggled, using Bertha's church name. She knew that would irritate Bertha even more.

"Charity Love! Don't make me drive to your house this morning. You are not too old for a spanking."

"I would beg to differ. I'm almost forty."

"You are not!" Bertha yelled, then lowered her voice, and whispered, "Are you?"

Not bothering to answer, Charity changed the subject, "I just love you so much, Grandma. What are you doing?"

"I just ate a piece of my famous breakfast casserole and coffee with Dallas Sr. and Martha."

Charity remained silent. Had her grandma lost her mind? She knew her grandmother had been through a lot, in the past few years, but having breakfast with her grandfather and mother was completely out of control.

She asked again, "So what are you doing, Grandma?"

"Girl, I'm not crazy! Two birds were outside of my window just chattering away, and then I realized what today is. I was feeling some type of way this morning and now I know why. It's my anniversary, and I believe those birds were my husband and daughter wishing me well."

"You made me scared for a minute," Charity joked. "That's quite a coincidence."

"Chile, nothing is a coincidence in the Kingdom of God," Bertha remarked. "I believe they were encouraging me to keep pressing on, Miss Charity."

"Indeed, Grandma. Indeed."

Bertha paused to take a sip of coffee. "What are you doing today?"

"I'm up writing. I have a book signing later this afternoon with one of my new authors. And then I'm going to meet Carmen for a late dinner." Carmen was Mabel's oldest daughter and the sister/cousin/best friend of Charity. "I called to see if you wanted to have breakfast with me, but you're already up and at it."

"Yes ma'am. Us old-timers get on up and get the day started."

"You want to tag along to the book signing and then go to dinner with me and Carmen?"

"No, Chile, I'll leave all that fun to the young people. I'm meeting the ladies at church for a missionary meeting and then I want to check on Lilly and Sonya. They are both walking around here just as big as houses. Old and pregnant. I don't know why Lilly waited so late in life to have a baby, and why Sonya keeps having all those kids."

Charity burst into laughter. "Look at the pot calling the kettle, Grandma. You're a mess."

"I know, honey. God ain't through with me yet."

"Me either, and with me He has a lot of work to do," Charity stated truthfully.

"With all of us, my dear," Bertha added.

Bertha paused for a moment before speaking, "Charity you're on the go so much. My wish for you is that you slow down and enjoy this journey called life. It moves so quickly. Before you know it, you're eighty and wondering where the time went. Smell the roses, baby. Embrace the ride. Life is just like a roller coaster; it has its ups and downs. But believe me, the ride is amazing."

Charity silently contemplated her grandmother's words before speaking. "Thank you, Grandma. I will. I'm going to learn to embrace the ride."

"Alright, my love. Be safe out there and give Carmen a hug and a kiss for me. Don't forget to call me when you make it back home safely after all your moving around today."

"I sure will. Love you, Grandma."

"Love you more baby. I'll talk to you later." Bertha Green hung up the phone with her signature words; never goodbye, always "see you later."

Martha Love would be so proud of her babies and her husband, too. Joi, an adjunct music professor at Juilliard, was also singing all over New York City. Sam Love made his way out of hiding in the mental hospital and started using that engineering degree. He was now a manager at the strawberry plant. And Charity was writing and publishing books and managing new authors. She was a go-getter, a nonstop workaholic. She would never say it out loud, but Bertha worried about her all the time. She realized that Charity was "a boss" as the young people would say, but she wanted her to slow down, pace herself, fall in love and truly heal from Martha's death and her recent breakup with her long-time beau, Patrick Kilpatrick.

Bertha walked over to her granite kitchen counter and poured herself another cup of coffee. "Those Greens," she whispered. "I'm so blessed." She never thought she would feel this type of joy again after Martha died. Losing a child creates such a void in your life. Burying a child is a visceral pain that lingers deep into your core. That was a mighty blow, but God comforts. *Weeping may endure for a night, but joy comes in the morning.* Lost in her thoughts, she almost missed the light tapping on her kitchen window. *Busy morning,* she thought to herself. She peeped out and grinned. She'd prayed for the joy that comes in the morning after Dallas Sr. and Martha died. She blushed as she went to open the front door of her home. Her morning arrived, and she was surprised by how joyful she was.

CHAPTER 2
GREEN GOODIES I

If Mabelle, Dallas Sr.'s mother didn't know anything else, she knew loving her family and baking good desserts. When Bertha married Dallas Sr., Mabelle took her under her wings, and they baked together all the time. As a result, baking became a critical part of the Green household. Each Green daughter learned to bake delicious goodies and pastries, but for Lilly it became her passion. She baked with such heartfelt love. When Mabelle suggested they open a bakery, Lilly was always in agreement. As a final gift to Lilly, when Mabelle died, she left her enough money to start the bakery. That was 39 years ago and here Green Goodies still stood as a testament to her love and passion.

"Lilly, when are you going to sit down and get some rest?" one of the Green's Goodies' regular customers exclaimed. "You are always on the move!"

"I know right," another customer added as Lilly sauntered from the kitchen carrying a caramel cake. Placing the cake on the counter near the ladies, she smiled as she twirled and headed back to the kitchen, bringing with her this time a peanut butter cake.

"Ladies, I'm fine. I heard walking is good for you when you're pregnant." Lilly paused waiting for more comments from the Green's Goodies' Amen corner.

Lilly was forty-nine and expecting her first child. If everything went according to plan, she would celebrate her fiftieth birthday with a newborn in her arms. It was an unexpected twist in her life, but one she embraced with warmth and excitement.

"Pregnant?" exclaimed one of the patrons with surprise. "Girl, I thought you just gained some weight."

Another customer chimed in, her tone dripping with disbelief, "You're pregnant?"

Lilly, ever patient, responded with a smile, "Yes, ma'am, Mrs. Lewis. Seven months."

Mrs. Lewis, raising an eyebrow, probed further, "Isn't your sister pregnant, too?"

"Yes, ma'am. Sonya is pregnant, too," Lilly confirmed, her voice steady.

Mrs. Hunt couldn't resist a sarcastic remark, "Wow! When the end of the world comes, there will be a Green pregnant," she said, rolling her eyes and smirking.

"There sure are a lot of y'all Greens," Mrs. Lewis added, looking at Lilly with a scrutinizing gaze.

"Yes, ma'am, there are," Lilly replied, her patience wearing thin with the two older women.

Turning away, Lilly headed back to the kitchen, her hips swaying gently as she balanced the new weight of her baby. She went to fetch the last strawberry pie, her mind swirling with thoughts. She shook her head at the nosy women of Masters, a small, sarcastic smile playing at the corners of her lips.

Lilly had always been the most patient of the Green girls. She had a deep love for her family, friends, and her husband. Before meeting her husband, Pastor Jeffries, she had been on a constant quest to lose weight, never realizing her own beauty. With her strong legs, well-defined figure, and sophisticated style, she was a striking presence. Her smile could light up any room, and she was known for singing off-key tunes and performing self-choreographed dances.

Now, she was the light of Pastor Jeffries' life. As she moved through the kitchen, she couldn't help but roll her eyes at the memory of Mrs. Hunt's sarcasm. Lilly pressed her lips together, not in irritation, but in amusement at the idea that there would always be a Green to carry on, no matter what the world threw their way. She was probably right!

Green's Goodies was a vibrant gem on Main Street, nestled at the bustling corner of Everett and McCain. The building's facade was a unique blend of Southern charm and modern flair, covered in light olive-green brick. Above it, a neon emerald sign gleamed brightly, proudly declaring the shop's name. While some townsfolk viewed the bright sign as a flamboyant display, others saw it as a beacon of warmth and hospitality, welcoming all who passed by.

Lilly moved with a gentle grace as she emerged from the kitchen, her hand resting lightly on the swell of her belly. Her auburn locks, tied back in a loose ponytail, shimmered under the soft lighting, framing her face which bore the gentle glow of pregnancy. Her cheeks, naturally flushed, added a youthful vibrancy to her appearance.

"I'm afraid we're out of strawberry pies," Lilly announced, her voice carrying a hint of her Southern accent," and I won't be heading back into the kitchen today. I'm starting to feel a bit worn."

"Girl, you should sit down!" exclaimed Mrs. Hunt, her voice layered with concern and the hint of an authoritative tone only the elderly could muster.

Mrs. Lewis, never one to shy away from giving advice, chimed in, "Pastor Jeffries needs to make you stay at home."

Lilly, a picture of composure and humor, raised an eyebrow playfully. "Make me?" she retorted, a subtle smirk playing on her lips as she rolled her eyes at the two older women. Her posture, strong and confident, suggested she was not easily swayed by unsolicited advice, yet her tone remained light, showing her good nature.

As Lilly settled into a chair, she exhaled softly, the weariness of the day catching up with her. The lively chatter of Green's Goodies continued around her, a testament to the community spirit she cherished, and to the Green's enduring legacy in the heart of the town.

Mrs. Hunt and Mrs. Lewis could be a part of the Gray Hair Club. They both had gray hair that hung down their backs and beautiful wrinkle free skin. She was sure they were something else in their hay day. Now here they sat gossiping about the goings on in Masters. They were a feisty pair and regulars at Green Goodies and Lilly loved ever minute of their banter and fuss.

"The last time I checked, I was grown and could make my own choices. Besides, I can't stay home," she groaned, rubbing her belly. "I'll go crazy in the house all day. Being here at the bakery makes for a great distraction from being big and pregnant." She gave a smirk to the older ladies as she continued sitting to rest her legs.

Pastor Jeffries, once known as the town's heartthrob, and his first wife moved to Masters to work at the Strawberry plant. His wife was killed in a car accident not long after their arrival. In a blink of an eye, the congregation at Goodwill Baptist church, where he pastored grew by at least fifty percent: all single women. But Pastor Jeffries turned down all advances, allowing his broken heart time to mend. Once he started healing, his eyes landed on Lilly Green and he never saw anyone else. That was ten years ago.

"Just take it easy," Mrs. Hunt inserted. "You want a happy healthy baby. I know because I had nine babies, and all of them were happy and healthy."

The door chimes rang signaling another entrance into the bakery. As if on cue, Pastor Jeffries walked in with a huge smile. He walked directly to Lilly as she sat still talking to Mrs. Hunt and Mrs. Lewis and stooped down and wrapped her in a tight bear hug, leaving her blushing. "Don't do that, Lilly," leaned into him and whispered coyly.

"Of course," Mrs. Hunt inserted, "That's how y'all got into this trouble in the first place."

Rolling her eyes, Lilly laughed, "We're just doing what newlyweds do."

"Ummmphh," Mrs. Hunt offered as she took a sip of her coffee.

"Newlyweds!? After ten years can it still be considered newlywed status?" Mrs. Lewis raised her coffee to her lip and blew on it before taking a sip. Pastor Jeffries turned his full attention back to his wife.

"I just came to check on my beautiful wife," he smiled and continued rubbing Lilly's back in a circular motion.

"I'm good, honey. I'm just bringing out the day's goodies. No more baking today and one of the Green girls should be coming in soon to help me out."

"Just don't overdo it. We want a healthy baby that can keep up with us on our daily walks." His forehead wrinkled into a slight frown as he spoke, "and I want a healthy wife." Pastor Jeffries with his black wire framed glasses and black business suit was always professional. He and Lilly were once heavy set or better yet, overweight, but they started walking each morning together and lost over 75 pounds each. That walk forever bonded them as friends and then as husband and wife.

Lilly, stood leaning into her husband's embrace and rubbed the side of his torso, "I promise to take it easy, honey." She reached up and planted a kiss on his cheek.

"I know you will." turning to the gossiping gray hair committee, he smiled, "Ladies take good care of my good thing."

Grinning sheepishly, they both offered, "Yes's" in unison.

"You're leaving so soon," Lilly pouted, holding on tighter to his waist.

"Yes, I have a meeting with Reggie about his Boys to Men Mentoring Program. I just wanted to see your face before I went to church."

Lilly beamed brightly, smiling a million-watt smile, "You are so good to me!"

"That's because you are good to me." He leaned down and planted a kiss right on her lips.

"Ok baby, I gotta go. I love you. I'll see you at home tonight. Call me if you need me and don't work too hard." He walked out the door giving final instructions.

Lilly stood staring after him for a full 60 seconds. "That man has you in a trance, come on back to earth girl," Mrs. Hunt laughed.

"I'm not in a trance. I just realize how blessed I am to have that man."

"Indeed, you are," Mrs. Lewis agreed.

Twenty minutes later, the door chimes sounded again.

Lilly looked up and instantly felt a sense of warmth and comfort.

"Hey, Charity!"

"Hey, Auntie! How are you doing today?" Charity walked straight to Lilly and gave her a tight hug. "Hey little one," Charity added, rubbing Lilly's belly. "Are y'all still going to wait until the day of the birth to find out the gender?"

"We sure are! We are an older couple, and we are going to just wait to see what God blesses us with."

"Honey, that's how we did it in the old days anyway," Mrs. Lewis remarked. "We didn't have all these boy-girl parties."

"What's a boy-girl party?" Mrs. Hunt asked, confused.

"You know when the parents are trying to figure out if it is a boy or a girl."

"Really, they have parties for that? Why don't they just ask the doctor?" Mrs. Hunt asked.

"Chile, these young people..." Mrs. Lewis responded.

Chuckling, Charity intervened in the conversation. "It's called a gender reveal party. The doctor normally seals the gender results in an envelope and gives it to a family member. They then plan a party to reveal whether it's a boy or girl."

"That's just too much!" Mrs. Hunt said, scooping a piece of her green almond croissant into her mouth. Still chewing she kept talking, mouth full of almond croissant, "We waited, and the doctor told us what we were having."

"Well technology has advanced, and now people want to know in advance." Charity flashed a smile at Mrs. Hunt.

"I think I'm up for the surprise," Lilly replied.

"What do you want, Lilly?" Mrs. Lewis prodded.

"I just want a healthy baby. At my age I'm high risk. So, a healthy baby is our desire, whether it's a boy or girl."

"I think it's a girl," Charity said with a smile.

"Why?" Lilly was surprised by Charity's guess.

"Because I just need a girl to spoil. My niece lives in New York, and I don't see her often enough, so a baby girl in Masters to spoil would be great."

"How is Joi doing, Charity?" Mrs. Hunt probed.

"She's doing well. Teaching and performing all over New York. You know she doesn't let the grass grow under her feet."

"That's good for her. I saw her pictures online the other day. She looks more and more like Martha Love as she gets older. She has her dark coarse hair that hangs down her back, that beautiful shape and definitely her whole face."

Laughing, Mrs. Lewis continued, "and you have Sam Love's whole face."

Charity paused for a moment thinking about the faces of her mother and sister. They were both beautiful chestnut brown-skinned slim ladies with dark heavy hair flowing down to their mid backs. Charity inherited the butt and hips of her grandmother, Bertha and though her hair was thick it was shorter and her curls untamable. "Yes, ma'am, Joi is the spitting image of our mother. They could be twins."

"They say the oldest girl always looks like the dad," Mrs. Hunt added. "You and Sam could be twins. I heard that Sam is over there at the strawberry plant, running that engineering department well."

Charity had Sam's whole face with a head full of hair. She didn't inherit the height of her mother or father, but she had Martha's bright smile and Sam's bright brown eyes and his small button nose. He also had his swagger. When she walked into the room, you knew without a doubt that was Sam Love's oldest girl.

"Dad is doing well. He's been doing much better since he left the mental hospital. We have dinner every third Sunday. Most of the time, Joi flies in to visit. I'm proud of him. I think he misses Mom more than the rest of us. So many wasted years." Charity's voice trailed off. She looked into the distance, a tear threatening to fall down her cheek, wiping it quickly, she rubbed her hands together and wiped them on her coat as if wiping away a piece of the past. Looking around to make sure no one saw her moment of vulnerability, she continued her conversation.

"Who's helping out at the bakery with you today?" Charity asked, turning her attention to Lilly.

"Girl, I have no idea. I have been so busy I didn't look at the calendar in the back. One of those Green girls will come strolling in to help."

"I have a couple of hours to spare; I'll hang around to help out."

"Aww that's so sweet of you, Charity! Thank you." As Charity went to put on her apron and wash her hands, Lilly looked at her with concern. She just hadn't been the same since Martha's death and her break up with Patrick. Still ever the energizer bunny, she just kept going.

Lilly and Charity worked in comfortable silence to process and pack the morning orders. Mrs. Hunt and Mrs. Lewis continued to talk, laugh, and reminisce about their days as young schoolgirls in Masters. After about an hour and a half of working and taking orders, the door chimes of Green's Goodies announced the entrance of Diane.

Wearing a bronze-colored jumpsuit, Diane was the picture of fashion. Her brown ankle boots and matching purse made her look like she'd just walked off a runway. Smiling, she threw her hand up and waved, "Hey, Ladies!"

"Hey, Diane!" Charity and Lilly spoke in unison. The morning crowd thinned out. One college student was in the corner reading a book. The afternoon crowd would arrive soon and start churning with excitement.

Green's Goodies expanded a couple of years ago, adding a coffee bar and daily Danish pastry selections along with cakes and pies. Customers now became regulars and stayed for extended periods creating a home-style coffee shop-like atmosphere. The town gossip was free, and many came just to indulge in the gossip, but once they tasted the goodies, they stayed.

"What's got that big smile on your face, Diane?" Lilly asked.

Diane stood at the corner of the counter, eyes twinkling. Folding and unfolding a napkin, her hands shaking with glee. She flashed another smile and continued, "Well... I think Ryce may be getting a chance to pastor a church in Memphis. I'm so excited!" The excitement was tangible. The sparkle in Diane's eyes was contagious. She looked happier than she'd looked in years.

Diane's announcement took the wind out of Lilly's sails. "What? Are you serious?", Lilly took a seat at the countertop stool and stared at Diane in awe.

"Does this mean that you all will have to relocate?" Charity also sat down on one of the stools and looked at Diane. "Memphis is two hours away."

"I'm not sure of all the particulars yet, but I'm just happy for him. He has been wanting to pastor that church for a while now."

"Well, it's a perfect time. The kids are all in middle and high school so they will be okay with moving away." Lilly stated half-heartedly.

She sat still on the stool in front of the counter, her eyes shimmering with unshed tears as she regarded her sister, Diane with a mixture of pride and sadness. Her heart swelled with emotion, a myriad of feelings swirling around.

"You two can have a fresh start in Memphis," Lilly expressed, her voice soft and bittersweet. Her words were a gentle acknowledgment of the new chapter her sister was about to embark on, a journey that would take them away from the familiar comforts of home. "Although, I'll miss you."

Ryce and Diane met while attending Bethune Cookman College. Though they attended the same high school in Masters, they'd never met. They noticed each other in the hall, but no personal contact was made until college. For their last three years of college, the two grew inseparable. Six months after college graduation, they married and moved back to Masters.

Ryce got a job as a chemist for a major pharmaceutical company that moved to Masters that same year. Diane worked part-time at Green's Goodies helping Lilly in the early days. She gave birth to two sets of stair steps: Sarah and Lisa, and Lionel and Jeremy. Working around their schedule, she'd leave the bakery in time to grab the kids from school or daycare and have dinner waiting for Ryce when he made it home.

When Ryce was promoted, everything changed. He was no longer the attentive husband and doting father that Diane and the kids adored. When promoted to supervisor of his department, that man was replaced by one who was irritable, quick tempered, and heavy-handed. The old Ryce was soft-spoken; his quiet demeanor being the reason so many people loved him. His handsome looks were the reason he was adored by women. Standing six-foot-three, he was slim but muscular. His dark wavy hair was always styled in a low-cut fade, and his skin was dark as chocolate syrup and silky without any blemishes.

Overnight, it seemed, he changed from saint to a sinner, from a loving father to a hateful dictator. Diane thought it was just stress. The kids were put on high alert to be nice and kind and stay out of their father's way. It wasn't until the money in their joint account was missing and their brand-new Ford Explorer was found parked in front of a house in the roughest part of town that Diane was told by the police that it was sold for little or nothing and the money was used to purchase drugs. After robbing and stealing from most of the citizens in Masters, Ryce left Diane and the kids to move on and find other victims.

Years later, Ryce returned sober and preaching, trying his hardest to reconcile with Diane. But she struggled for so long with the kids and rebuilding her life that she fought Ryce tooth and nail before she'd agreed to family and marriage counseling. Now she was finally following her heart. She seemed happier since her family was back together. The kids were now seventeen, sixteen, thirteen and twelve.

Diane interrupted Lilly's thoughts, "I know, but I would sure miss all of my family in Masters."

"Remember, it's only a two-hour drive," Charity chimed in.

"That's true." Diane responded, walking to the counter where Lilly sat and lay her head on her sister's head. "I would sure miss being with you every day, Ms. Lilly." She rubbed her belly, and their heads stayed touching in a tender moment of sisterly love.

The Greens were a close bunch. Moving to different cities and states was historically only for college or jobs that would always lead back to Masters. Bertha instilled in her children that Masters was home, and they took it to heart. Rarely did any Green offspring go anywhere to live besides Masters. It was a family tradition to raise the kids in Masters. Now Joi, Martha's youngest, was a wild card and never moved back to Masters after finishing her education at Julliard.

A few more minutes of silence passed, then Lilly spoke up, rubbed Diane's hand, and slowly got up from the chair. "Okay ladies, let's get finished baking the cakes and cupcakes for Mom's fashion show tomorrow."

They baked. They chatted. They laughed. By the time the bakery closed, one hundred cupcakes and a three-layer Green's Goodies specialty cake were ready for Bertha's annual fashion show.

CHAPTER 3
CHARITY LOVE

Charity lived for a good walk. Saturday mornings, she would leave her house at the break of dawn and walk the streets of Masters waving hello, stopping to engage in conversation, or peeping in the various Mom and Pop shops throughout town. As Charity Love strolled through the park in downtown Masters, the rhythmic pattern of her steps matched her racing thoughts.

Walking had always been her solace, her therapy during the chaos of life. Her walks allowed her mind to wander, to create, to find peace in a clouded world. The crunch of gravel beneath her feet echoed the weight on her heart as she replayed the last few days, weeks, months, and minutes that she spent with her mother and the breakup with Patrick. After years of love and partnership, their relationship had reached an unexpected end, leaving Charity drowning in a sea of emotions.

Despite the ache in her chest, Charity fought hard to keep her intact. As a bestselling writer, she had channeled her strength and vulnerability into words that resonated with readers worldwide. Her pen became her sword, and her stories were a testament to the resilience of the human heart. In this moment of heartbreak, Charity knew that her own story was far from over. It was a plot twist she hadn't anticipated, but she was determined to navigate this new chapter with grace and resilience.

With each step, Charity felt a renewed sense of purpose stirring within her. The breakup with Patrick was not the end but a new beginning. As Charity continued her walk, she made a silent vow to herself - to embrace change, to find healing, and to walk boldly into the unknown.

Charity's biggest faults were that she never asked for help and never would stop walking. She never allowed anyone to see her weaknesses, to visit her pain, to answer the call of her need. She kept it all inside, walking the strong lonely walk, one draped in a mask of confidence and high self-esteem. The people-think-you-have-it-going-on walk. The one that screams *Wealth! Power! Influence!* It accepts awards, mentors students, gives back to the community, nurtures family, and holds friends tight through every crisis. Yet it strolls into a half million-dollar home each night alone. Yep, Charity had that walk.

The ten years that had passed since Charity lost her mom, had been trying and difficult for not only her, but the entire Green clan. Their lives were all altered in various ways. Because she continued to rush to the aid of others, Charity never found the complete peace and healing that she needed. So, she walked. That was her therapy. Always has been, probably always would be.

Today was no different; her calendar was filled. That's how she liked it. The more she planned, wrote, worked, and helped others the easier it was to forget how much she detested her own life. She could meet friends for lunch or dinner at Lin B's, the newest restaurant to plant its roots in Masters. They could talk about their day, laugh at their children's little funnies—all while she could forget that she had dreams and goals that were slipping away with each breath. She could focus on her friends, their new houses, new business ventures, their babies, gossip about exciting dates and love lives. All the while, she'd anxiously wait for her chance to take her walk home. No one knew that she was tired, slowing down, losing momentum; walking on one broken leg with pins and plates and a touch of arthritis. She played the part well.

Patrick had long since left. Maybe it was because of her strength or the absence of it. Maybe it was the workaholic that kept her busy all night long, or the words "lack of emotional support" that he seemed to slip into every conversation. What he failed to realize was that Charity was giving all she had to give. To survive, she'd blocked out so many emotions. There was no crying, no touchy-feely-hugging moments. Charity was that side hug, half-smile, pray-for-you-in-passing, get-your-life-together chick. She was bold, beautiful, and strong. Yet too many times she lacked emotion.

A glimpse could be caught of Charity gazing off into the sky, her eyes glistening, her pain visibly present. She carried it well, like a trophy or a merit award; wore it like an expensive suit tailored to fit every curve of her body. She held onto that pain in order not to forget how deeply it hurt and to never venture there again.

CHAPTER 4
THE BREAKUP

In the months leading up to her relationship demise, Charity noticed that lately something was different about Patrick. He wasn't his usual happy self. She always counted on him for his jokes and light-hearted manner. Lately, there'd only been silence.

They now shared Charity's home. Martha Love was surely turning flips in her grave. When Charity came home most nights, he seemed distant. The jokes stopped, and the bantering was no more—only the occasional grunt here and there. She then tried to become the fun one.

There was dinner in the upstairs theater room, spontaneous trips to their favorite vacation spots, random trips to their favorite stores, and game night with friends and family. But the quietness persisted. She tried to talk it out, but Patrick was cold. It was Patrick's intellect that attracted Charity; the political banter as they would debate about policy and economics. Patrick, somewhere down the emotional line, resolved that he was giving no more.

Racking her brain, she tried to remember their last argument, the last disagreement. But to her knowledge, there hadn't been one. She packed his lunch and stuffed funny little notes inside that would surely make him laugh. Her last-ditch effort was the scavenger hunt she planned for his birthday. Clues were left at his job, in his car, and at the house. On the morning of his birthday, they talked briefly. The excitement in her voice was evident. This scavenger hunt would be the *pièce de resistance*. Patrick was indifferent as Charity hinted at the excitement planned for the day. She'd asked if he was okay, if he was excited about his birthday. He'd replied with his usual grunt.

That evening, the clock struck seven, then eight, then nine. Charity called and called. First his office number and then his cell phone. No answer. She began to worry. Had he been in a car wreck? Was he in the hospital? She called his parents, no answer. She checked his social media account and saw only birthday wishes and pictures of the office birthday party from earlier in the day. Was he okay? Ten o'clock came and went; she walked the expanse of their house at least ten times wearing a hole in the carpet. She called Patrick's phone over and over and walked around the house – up the stairs, down the stairs, to the bedroom, through the kitchen, back to the den and finally she sat at her desk still refusing to shed one tear. Midnight came and still not a word, her calls were now going straight to voicemail. She left over ten voicemails and twelve text messages. Worry was erased by anger then apathy. Emotionally drained, she walked to her bedroom, tumbled into her king-sized bed and fell asleep. That's how the story of Charity and Patrick ended.

Charity continued her walk. She was driven during the day, leading meetings, receiving new book deals, starting a mentoring program, and just keeping life moving. Her walk transitioned to a trot and was definitely headed towards a run.

She recited her mantras daily. *I will not cry. Blessings on Blessings. I will not cry. Just make it to another day. Just make it through this moment.* As the days moved on, she'd call to no avail, hoping for a pickup, an explanation, a reason, any reason—maybe an apology. She'd finally mustered the strength to pack up his things: business suits, desktop computer, paperwork from his job, bills, workout attire. She'd planned a sale but hesitated to go through with it. Maybe he'd call. Maybe he'd explain what happened. Though she pleaded and begged with her heart not to hope, it did so anyway. In the meantime, she walked and trotted and sometimes ran. Life went on.

Nine months had passed since Charity had heard from Patrick. By June of that year with the impending new season, her life was returning to normal. The emotions she couldn't manage were stored away—packed nicely in a box labeled "For Another Day" and stored on the top shelf of her closet. Sitting at her desk sipping her morning coffee, she opened the newspaper. What she saw shifted her emotions into a quiet rage: Patrick and a gorgeous woman standing on the steps of a beautiful church in Marilyn, Mississippi. His parents stood beside the gorgeous couple, smiling, glowing from cheek to cheek. Twisting the knife, the headline read: *The Son of the Prestigious Kilpatrick Family Weds in Lavish Style.*

The dam broke. Her mantras were ineffective. Tears ran down her face. Heartbreak entered the smallest crevices and weaved its way through her chest. She couldn't even muster the strength to walk. She sat for hours. The TV news had long ended. The sun had hidden its face behind the clouds. Darkness overshadowed the earth. Throughout the day, her phone rang and hummed with missed calls and text messages. The computer's screensaver scrolled for hours. Walking was out of the question. Her heart and feet were too heavy. Sitting would have to do. Sitting and crying.

The next day, she dragged herself out of bed, sold what she could of Patrick's belongings to a nearby consignment shop and donated the money to the local children's hospital. What she couldn't or didn't sell, she took to the local thrift store donation center.

That was the final chapter of Charity and Patrick. And just like that, Charity started walking again.

CHAPTER 5
THE FASHION SHOW

The grand ballroom of Masters, Mississippi's most prestigious event venue was a breathtaking sight to behold. Its soaring ceilings and opulent chandeliers cast a warm, golden glow over the elegantly dressed patrons milling about. The air was abuzz with anticipation and excitement, a palpable energy that electrified the space as guests admired the stunning fashion on display.

Bertha Green, the mastermind behind the Annual Night of Fashion, stood at the entrance with a radiant smile. She'd outdid herself again! Her attire was nothing short of spectacular—a shimmering gown of emerald silk that caught the light with every movement she made, accentuating her regal presence. Her eyes sparkled with a mix of pride and satisfaction, reflecting her unwavering commitment to the cause that lay at the heart of the evening's festivities.

Every year since 2003, Bertha hosted the annual fashion show to raise money for the Masters, Mississippi homeless shelter. When Mayor Baley told Bertha there was a problem with homelessness in Masters years ago, she was heartbroken. She'd once known every family in her small town, but the strawberry plant brought people from all over for the lucrative jobs. But when the strawberry plant laid off 30 percent of their workforce in 2002, homelessness began to rear its ugly head.

Bertha worked tirelessly to ensure that she could continue to donate food and clothing to keep the shelter running. Her goal was to one day alleviate the need for it altogether. For the past twenty years, she'd forced or voluntold her daughters to model her efforts. The Seven Wonders brought in people from all over Mississippi to support the shelter. Bertha's fundraising goal was twenty thousand dollars this year, and she planned on making it happen. It was to be the fashion show of the year!

The scent of fresh flowers filled the air, mingling with the subtle notes of expensive perfume and cologne worn by the attendees. A string quartet played softly in the background, their harmonious melodies weaving through the conversations that ebbed and flowed like a gentle tide. Models in exquisite attire glided gracefully across the parquet floors, each outfit a testament to Bertha's impeccable style and eye for detail.

As Charity approached her grandmother, she couldn't help but notice the poised confidence that radiated from Bertha. It was as if the years had only served to enhance her remarkable elegance. Charity's heart swelled with admiration for the woman who had become a pillar of strength and hope in their community.

The fashion show was in full swing, the atmosphere was pulsating with laughter and music when Morgan, one of Bertha's granddaughters, walked in with her two best friends, Shay and Tia looking like Ebony showcase models. Their cheeks were flushed; their laughter was loud.

Morgan was the ringleader of the trio. Her eyes were sparkling as her body swayed with the movement of her sequin royal blue dress. She exuded confidence. Behind Morgan, Shay and Tia, followed arm in arm holding each other up. The soft fabric of their dresses flowed with each step they took entering the ballroom.

The young ladies wobbled slightly as they moved through the crowd, arms still looped with each other. Shay was barely able to keep herself upright. Her walk was unsteady. As though no soft music was playing, Morgan started dancing wildly in the middle of the floor.

"Let's party!" Morgan declared her voice rising above the sound of the string quartet. Her loud declaration was met with whispers and stunned looks from the guests and the fashion show patrons.

"Somebody is drunk," Mrs. Hunt whispered to Mrs. Lewis tilting her head towards the three young ladies that were loud and boisterous in the center of the fashion show floor. "I smelled liquor when one of those girls walked by. I can't believe it. I bet Bertha doesn't know one of her granddaughters is drunk as a skunk."

"Child, just a shame." Mrs. Lewis shook her head in disgust.

Charity, overhearing the conversation, went over to her cousin and her two friends. If the Green women were a sight to behold, so were the Green grand girls. Just as beautiful as their mothers with different shades of brown skin and beautiful thick hair, inherited from their mothers styled in a multitude of ways, they were a sight to behold. As Charity approached the group, she smelled the alcoholic scent on Morgan and pulled her aside.

"Have you been drinking, Morgan?" Charity asked in a hush tone.

Yanking her arm from Charity's grasp, Morgan yelled, "Mind your business!"

Unbothered by Morgan's tone and reaching to grab her hand again, Charity continued speaking in a hushed tone while trying to push Morgan towards the ladies restroom, "You should be ashamed of yourself. I can't believe you would show up to Grandma's fashion show drunk. This is so disrespectful."

"Maybe if you tried drankin' you'd lighten up a bit." Morgan's speech was slurred, and her dance movements continued as she tried to wiggle away from Charity's grip.

"Really!" Charity replied angrily. "Oh, and be more like you? Showing up funky drunk to family events. Fighting with boyfriend's ex-girlfriend? Getting fired from the last three jobs you had because you couldn't handle alcohol. Sounds like you're batting a thousand."

"Git ovah yo-self, Ms. High and Mighty. Everyone ain't holy and all religious like you." Morgan wobbled and slurred her face coming close to Charity as her eyes lowered with fire and anger.

"Religion and respect are two very different things. I could care less what religion you are, but to walk into a community event that your grandmother is hosting, drunk is a lack of respect. Don't confuse the two. Respect is still respect every day. And you are being disrespectful."

"And you are being a sour puss. You jus' mad at the world because Patrick left yo ass." Morgan rolled her eyes, smiled sadistically, and she tossed her head full of sister locs to the side and tried to stand straighter in her stance, as if preparing for battle.

"What!" Charity looked as if she was hit with a sack of bricks. She stepped back as if the force of Morgan's words pushed her. "How did this become about Patrick?"

Morgan leaned forward even more, hot breath from drinking in her face. "Oh, everything that you are and do is about Patrick. You really thought that he was gonna marry you. He was cheatin' on you the entire time you were with him. You never wondered why he was content not having sex with you." Morgan laughed. "It was because he was having it with the beautiful television reporter he married. You were just another notch on his belt, dumb-ass."

"Shut up, Morgan! You are drunk and I'm no longer going to listen to this foolishness!"

"Whatever, Charity, I mean—Miss Goodie Two-Shoes. Get ovah yo-self." Morgan raised her hands and started trying to dance again even though her body was looking like it was going to fall over any moment. Any trace of elegance she exuded was now replaced by a drunkenness that threatened to completely drown Morgan.

Charity turned and walked away from her younger cousin. *Was Morgan, right? Had Patrick been cheating the entire time?* She thought to herself. That would explain some things, but it would also make other things darker. She knew what she had to do. She would schedule a meeting with Patrick to get to the bottom of this fiasco. In the meantime, she had to go to her grandmother and apologize for her behavior. Masters' finest members of society were in the house for the fashion show, and she didn't want a single word to be uttered to her grandmother about her argument with Morgan.

Finding Bertha in the crowd mixing and mingling with guests, Charity greeted her, her voice carrying a hint of apprehension. "Hey, Grandma."

"Hey baby." Bertha replied, her face radiant under the soft lighting. Bertha was glowing. She stood poised near the entrance, welcoming guests with a gracious smile that seemed to light up the room.

Charity took a deep breath, the weight of her earlier confrontation with Morgan still heavy on her shoulders. The vibrant colors of the models' outfits created a vivid backdrop as she continued, "I just want to apologize for the fashion show fiasco. Morgan and I had words and almost got into a screaming match."

"What? Why?" Bertha's expression remained calm, her eyes searching Charity's face for answers.

Charity glanced around nervously, noting the curious gazes of onlookers, and leaned in closer, speaking in a hushed tone. "Grandma, she is filthy drunk," Charity confided, her voice barely a whisper amidst the clinking of glasses and soft hum of conversation. "I told her it was disrespectful to show up to your event drunk like that."

"Drunk? Morgan? Here? Now?" Bertha's barrage of questions began as she lowered her eyes in confusion and her face wrinkled up.

"Yes, ma'am. And some of the socialites of Masters heard us arguing. I'm so sorry." She reached out, clasping Bertha's soft, weathered hands. The contrast between her youthful energy and Bertha's seasoned calm was stark.

Charity's apology hung in the air. Her voice was filled with sincerity, her eyes reflecting the regret she felt over the altercation with Morgan.

Bertha nodded; her demeanor was unflappable. "I will talk to her later. Let me greet the rest of my guests." She released Charity's hands, gave her a quick peck on the cheek, and turned to the approaching guests with her signature smile.

Charity continued to stand near her grandmother, looking on as she greeted and mingled with friends from all over the state of Mississippi. As patrons poured into Bertha's Annual Night of Fashion, Bertha embraced and hugged many of them. Charity observed her grandmother's grace and charm, her sequined gown shimmering as she moved. The bustling atmosphere seemed to fade into the background as Bertha turned back once more, enveloping Charity in a gentle hug. Her voice was a soothing murmur in Charity's ear. "Go on now, Charity, and enjoy yourself. Stop worrying. Families fight and have disagreements. It's nothing new and it doesn't mean that we don't love one another. It will all work out."

Charity looked at Bertha in shock. Something was different. She normally would have had a fit about two of her grandchildren exchanging barbs in public and above all else in mixed company and on top of that, at one of her events. However, this time, she looked so cool and calm that her new demeanor frightened Charity.

Charity pulled back slightly, her eyes wide with surprise. Bertha's composure was definitely different to the chaos Charity had anticipated. The usual fire in Bertha's eyes was replaced with a serene calm that was both comforting and unsettling. Charity couldn't help but wonder what had brought about this change.

As she stepped back into the lively crowd, Charity's mind buzzed with thoughts of the confrontation with Morgan, the accusations Morgan slung out about Patrick, and the unexpected grace of Bertha. The elegant affair continued around her, a backdrop of colors, laughter, and music, while Charity mulled over the deeper currents beneath the evening's surface.

Bertha, however, remained unruffled. Her demeanor was one of serene composure, a reflection of the wisdom and grace she had cultivated over the years. Her response was gentle but firm, a quiet assurance that all would be well. The unexpected calm of her reaction was a shock to Chairty. Bertha was a testament of strength and resilience beneath her polished exterior.

As Bertha moved about the ballroom, her presence was a beacon of warmth and hospitality. Each handshake and smile was met with genuine appreciation, her gratitude for their support was evident in every interaction. The ballroom buzzed with life, the laughter and chatter of the patrons, a melody that underscored the success of the event.

Charity lingered for a moment, watching her grandmother navigate the evening with a grace that seemed almost effortless. Bertha's Annual Night of Fashion was more than just a showcase of style and elegance—it was a celebration of community and compassion.

As the night unfolded Morgan seemed to have calmed down a bit. She and her two friends were sitting at a table all looking sluggish and worn. Their high probably coming down now. *Cheap liquor* Charity thought to herself.

Finally, night meandered to a close, the guests who'd marveled at the stunning array of fashion on display as well as the pieces of art created by Mabel started trickling out of the ballroom. The models, handpicked from across Mississippi, moved with confidence and poise, their attire, a reflection of Bertha's impeccable vision. The event was a triumph, a resounding success that promised to meet and perhaps even exceed the ambitious fundraising goal set by its illustrious host.

As Charity stood watching the Fashion Show end, she carried the quiet reassurance of her grandmother's words as a reminder that, no matter what challenges they faced, the strength of family and community would always prevail.

CHAPTER 6
SUNDAY DINNER

Sunday dinners were once the hallmark of Southern families. After church, families would gather to laugh, talk, and reminisce about days gone by. Soul food was the order of the day. Sitting at the table with someone for a meal creates bonds that last lifetimes. After Martha's death, Sam Love promised his girls that he would meet with them at least one Sunday a month for dinner.

Charity was her father's daughter. She inherited his dark chocolate skin and dark curly hair that hung freely and wildly down her back. But most days, she kept her usual high messy bun. Charity always wanted the least amount of attention on her. She was heavyset and always trying to lose weight.

Martha would always say to her, "God gave the right stuff to the right person. If I had big legs and hips and big breasts, I'd be a force to be reckoned with." Charity also had Sam's seasonal eyes. In the fall, they were deep brown, in the spring, they were hazel, and in the summer, his eyes were almost clear. One could see straight through them and into his soul. She also inherited his business sense, though she used hers legally.

Sam's strong presence was Charity's most powerful possession. Even though they could walk into a room, not say a word, or utter a sound, everyone would feel their aura. Some force field or energy would grab the room, and it was as if their presence held all present captive.

Joi was Sam's correct change. She had his vibrant spirit and his love for music. Sam and Martha met at a jazz club when Martha was Leona's self-proclaimed manager. Leona, the Green's baby girl and the seventh wonder, could sing like a bird. She could croon and scat like the artists of old. Joi was outspoken like Sam and never hesitated to say what was on her mind. She was beautiful, built like a brick house, and carried a voice that could soothe a weary soul.

"Guess who's back in town?" Joi said as she sat on the island of Charity's kitchen watching her cook Sunday dinner.

"Who?" Charity asked as she prepped the vegetables for dinner.

"Patrick." She eyed Charity to gauge her response.

"Who is Patrick?" she said, without looking up. Charity refused to give Joi what she wanted. After her confrontation with Morgan, she vowed to just be quiet. Talking seemed to get her into too much trouble.

"Your ex, Patrick. You know, the guy you were with for six years."

"Oh really? How do you know?" Charity continued chopping vegetables and never looked up as Joi spoke.

"I saw him at the bank yesterday. He asked about you."

"I hope you didn't answer."

"You're a mess. I couldn't be rude."

"Why?" Stopping to stare at Joi, Charity held the knife mid cut. "Why?" she asked again forcefully.

"Because we weren't raised that way." Joi leaned over the counter towards Charity and grabbed a piece of broccoli, laughed and leaned back onto her stool.

"Whatever, Joi! You have been rude and mean plenty of times in your life. This was a good time to be both."

"All he asked was, how is Charity doing?"

"And your response?" Charity questioned with a clenched jaw and a tight-lipped frown.

"I just said that you were doing fine. That you had just finished another best-selling novel."

"Really?"

"Yes, that is all that it was. Just niceties."

"Umm."

"Char, what would you want me to say?"

"Hmm. How about, *not a darn word*!" Charity chunked the knife on the cutting board and stared at Joi in disgust, her eyes squinting and her nose wrinkled up like something smelled bad.

"Wow! You really are still mad. I thought by now that you would be over him." Joi paused for a moment before continuing. That's why what Morgan said made you so mad. You still like him. You're definitely not over him." Charity confided in Joi about the fiasco with Morgan at their grandma, Bertha's fashion show and asked her opinion about what Morgan said. In normal Joi fashion she'd told Charity to let sleeping dogs lie and move on.

Charity studied her little sister briefly before she continued, "Who said I'm not over him? Just because I don't want his name mentioned in my house."

"Yes, the fact that you don't want anyone to say anything about or to him." Joi jumped up from the stool and made her way closer to Charity, grabbing more vegetables. Charity slapped her hand. "Stop it!"

"I just think sleeping dogs need to stay asleep, Joi," Charity answered sarcastically. "Isn't that the advice you gave me as well?"

"I did and I meant it. All I said was that he was home and that he asked about you. I will never mention his name in this house ever again." Joi blew out a deep breath and twirled around on her stool agitating Charity even more.

"Thank you! I truly appreciate that." Charity replied with all the heartfelt sarcasm she could muster up.

At that exact moment, the doorbell rang.

"Get the door, Joi. It's probably Daddy."

Joi moved off the stool with ease and excitedly skipped to the door. It was Sam Love. "Hey, Daddy!" She grabbed Sam Love in a tight hug. "My baby girl!" Sam exclaimed and held his baby girl in his arms. As she released him, he took a moment to stare at his youngest daughter. She favored her mother, Martha so much. He tried to hold his tears at bay.

Walking into the kitchen, Sam walked over to the island counter and hugged Charity.

"Hey, Dad!"

Sam looked between the two. "I'm convinced that I have the most beautiful girls in the world."

Joi beamed. "You sure do, Daddy!"

"Wow! Who knew she was so conceited?" Charity looked at her dad with a smirk as she went back to dicing onions and peppers.

Monthly Sunday dinners were now a ritual with Charity, Joi, and Sam since Martha had died and Sam checked himself out of the mental hospital. It was their ninth year of getting together.

Sam did well as an engineer for the strawberry plant in Masters. Though Joi and her husband, Derrick lived in New York with their two-year-old daughter, Madden, Joi flew to Masters by herself so she could be there for the dinners. It was a tradition they started and vowed to always continue.

"Dad, how are things at the plant?" Charity asked as she continued preparing the food.

"Things are pretty good. I think I'm going to retire soon."

"Dad, you've only been working there four years," Joi huffed.

"Yes, I know, but I want to play my music, and Leona and I have been talking about starting our group again. After five years I will be fully vested in all the stocks, bonds, and the 401k plan. I can retire next year if I decide to do so."

"Well, that sounds good. Maybe you and Leona will allow me to sing on a song on the album," Joi added enthusiastically.

"That sounds like a plan," Sam said, still looking at his girls.

"Well, can I write a song for the album?" Charity asked. "I can't sing like Joi, but I can write lyrics."

"Go for it! You can write a song for Joi to sing. It will be a Love song. Get it? Love—like our last name."

"We get it, Dad." Joi cringed at her dad's corniness. Joi and Sam had a tumultuous relationship when he first checked himself out of the mental hospital. Joi thinking that Sam went away because of her, always resented him and felt like he chose safety over her. Their relationship was much better now after years of open communication and many apologies on both sides.

"What's for dinner, Charity?" Sam walked over to the stive and peeked into the pots and pans as Charity placed stood over them, stirring in seasoning. Charity wasn't known for her cooking. She was a recipe-based cook who knew measurements and amounts. Many a day she and Bertha collided in the kitchen when asking for measurements. Bertha would reply, "Charity I cook and bake with love. I just taste it to see how it makes me feel."

"But I don't know what a smidge or a little sprinkle is, Grandma. I need spoonfuls and cup sizes," was always Charity's reply.

Bertha would just laugh and say, "Just keep using your recipes Charity, I can't help you."

"I made salmon, sweet potatoes, broccoli, and squash. For dessert I made my famous pineapple salad."

"I just want the pineapple salad!" Joi said. "Why are you eating so healthy?"

"Because I have about twenty-five more pounds to lose, and I plan on doing it soon and very soon!"

"So, we all have to suffer for your twenty-five pounds?" Joi pouted and opened the fridge looking for snacks. "Do you have some sodas at least?"

Swatting Joi away from the door of the refrigerator, she said, "no but there is a pot of tea on the stove."

"Yuck! Tea!?"

Exasperated, Charity stared at Joi, "You act just like a two-year-old!" Shaking her head at her little sister, she gave her a crooked smile, "You know you are welcome to cook, Joi. You never volunteer."

"I live in New York, Char." Joi was frustrated.

"Umm, ma'am, you can buy groceries in Masters and cook here."

"Whatever, Charity," Joi grumbled, picking up an apple and crunching on it.

"Whatever back to you, Joi. Do you cook for Derrick?"

"Derrick is an awesome cook, so there is no need for me to be in the kitchen."

"What do you feed Madden?"

"Charity, she is two years old. She eats whatever we eat—just in smaller quantities." Joi stared at Charity in awe. "Two-year-olds eat what adults eat in our household, jut in smaller portions!"

"Poor two-year-old! A mess, Dad! She's a mess." Charity looked at Sam and shook her head.

"Charity, everyone is not like you. I don't want to spend my days in the kitchen."

"Joi, you darn well know that I do not spend my days in the kitchen. I run a company and sit on the board of directors of three companies, so get out of here with that."

"Ladies," Sam interrupted. "What is going on today? This is not like my girls to be arguing over anything, let alone who is the better cook."

"Dad, Charity is mad at me because Patrick is back in town, and I spoke to him. I was only being nice. It's not even like I had a whole conversation with him. He asked how she was, and I told him. And she has had an attitude since the moment I told her."

Refusing to respond, Charity didn't look up from the salad she was preparing. After a brief pause, she said, "Dad, I made a pickle sauce for the salmon. I think you'll like it."

"See, Dad. She won't even talk about it." Joi's tone was demanding but childish.

"Dad, I asked her earlier not to bring his name up in my house, and yet she insists on continuing to do so."

"Charity, maybe you need to go to therapy. I'm not saying that you're crazy or anything like that. But sometimes when we don't deal with issues, they just fester and become more and more of a problem. I should know." Sam looked at his oldest daughter with concern. "I've been going to a therapist through my job. It's been the best decision that I ever made."

"Dad, I'm fine."

"I'm sure you are, Charity. But I want you to be more than fine. I want you to be superfantabulous!" Sam grabbed his oldest daughter in a bear hug. As Charity tried to fight him off, he held her tighter.

Charity relaxed in his arms and couldn't help but grin at the word her dad used to say all the time when she and Joi were children. Until Joi's 10th birthday, Sam had been an outstanding father who lavished his daughters with love and attention. But Sam ever looking for a quick dime, got involved with the wring type of guys. To keep his family out of trouble, he checked into the mental hospital secretly and stayed there until Martha died. He hadn't meant to be there that long, but he was scared that his family would be in danger if he was out. He knew the Green machine as the Greens were fondly known in Masters would not be touched because of Dallas Sr, a well-respected lawyer, so he made the choice to leave his family. It was the biggest mistake of his life, and he still lived that regret every day. He never even got a chance to make amends with Martha or say goodbye. He'd wasted so many years, but he was back, and he wasn't going to let his babies go.

Finally pulling away from her dad and placing a kiss on his chick she headed back to the stove, "Dad, I'm making my way to superfantabulous every day. Let's eat!"

After setting the table and sitting down, Charity looked at her sister. "Joi, you say the prayer since you like talking so much."

"See, Dad. I told you she was mad."

"Joi, just pray." Sam looked at his daughters. Despite the tension in the room, he was so happy that he was here to enjoy this moment. Being locked up in the mental hospital for years while his daughters grew up without him always broke his heart. Learning of Martha's death doubled the pain, but it also made him soar. He wanted to be the best dad that the girls had ever known, so he made it a point to always be there no matter what. Times like these caused his heart to ache for Martha, but he also felt complete. Being back in the good graces of his girls meant life was worth living again. It took some time to get Joi back to speaking to him, but he persisted.

The mental hospital became his way of escape when he was involved in bad dealings with those hustlers. He knew that his girls would be okay because they were members of the Green family and the family was well-respected. But those small-time criminals wouldn't flinch at taking his life.

As the dinner progressed, the mood lightened. The sisters talked and chatted with ease.

Joi shared stories of Madden's mischievous behavior: How Joi folded the laundry and Madden took it all out of the basket and laid on top of it on the floor. Madden would sing along with Joi even if she didn't know the words or the songs. Sam loved hearing about his granddaughter.

"Joi, next time you come home bring Madden and Derrick with you," Sam suggested. "I haven't seen my grandbaby and son-in-law in years now."

"I will see how Derrick's schedule is and let you know."

"Why don't you bring Madden with you anyway, Joi?" Charity asked as they started putting up the dishes from their meal.

"This is my break time from those two. As much as I love them, I need a break here and there. It also gives Derrick's mom a chance to come over and babysit Miss Maddy."

"Well, I want time to bond with her as well," Sam said. "Next time, do your dad a favor and bring her to Masters."

"Okay, Dad. I will see what I can do!"

"Make it happen, Joi Sun!" Sam only called her Joi Sun on two occasions: when she was on stage and when he wanted a big favor. He really wanted to see Madden. It was short for Joi, you are my sun. He made up songs when she was little, and Joi Sun was one he had sung often to Joi.

"I gotcha, Dad."

Sam stood and stretched. "Alright ladies, I'm headed over to Dallas' house. The Sunday afternoon football games have started, and we are going to watch. Reggie should be there too."

"Well enjoy, Dad." Charity leaned in to give him a hug.

"Come on over, Joi." Sam pulled both daughters into a group hug. As he held them, he prayed. "Father, thank you for this time with my babies. Thank you for their health and strength and their continued success. Allow them to always put you first and place a shield of protection around them as they go about their daily activities. In Jesus' name, we pray, Amen."

"Okay, my beautiful girls. Be good to one another. See you later. Joi, when are you leaving?" Sam asked turning to look at his youngest daughter, who was the splitting image of her mother.

"I'll be here until Tuesday morning."

"Maybe we can have lunch tomorrow."

"Sounds good, Dad. I'll walk out with you." Joi turned to Charity. "I'm going to head to Kaya's house for a girls' night. See you later."

"Good night, Dad. Be safe, Joi. See you later." Charity waited for them to get into their cars and then closed the door behind them.

As Joi made her way out to a girls' night, Charity sat in her oversized chaise lounge chair, with her laptop looking off into space. *Maybe I should call a therapist and talk over my issues about Patrick,* she thought to herself. Maybe there was a vestige of something there that she needed to let go of. She goggled five-star therapists.

Dr. Lisa Lesure. Picking up her phone, Charity added the name and number to her contacts. Soon, she would call and make an appointment. *A little talk couldn't hurt,* she hoped.

CHAPTER 7
THE FAVOR

When she was little, Charity loved Thursdays. Even now she had a sweet spot for Thursdays. The hump day was over, and she was headed to the weekend. She always enjoyed quiet time on Thursday nights. She would gather her materials on her favorite oversized chaise lounge chair and read books, edit books from her authors, write and normally doze off to sleep. She loved Thursdays. These were her nights to be productive. Even her rest, she considered productive, because if she fell asleep, she always reasoned that her body needed that moment of respite.

This Thursday as Charity sat in her lounge chair trying to finish editing a workbook for one of her new authors, her phone rang incessantly. Her friends and family knew that Thursday nights were for her, and she was dreading thus interruption. Annoyed, she answered the phone with a frown and a huff in her voice.

"Hello!"

"Hey, Charity! I have a huge favor to ask of you."

"Hey, Sari. How are you?" Charity asked as gently as she could.

"Oh, I'm sorry Char. How rude of me. I'm ok, just stressed beyond measure."

"A huge favor on a Thursday night? What's going on, Sari?" Charity placed the workbook on the edge of the chaise lounge to give Sari her full attention.

"Just promise me that you will listen to the entire request before you say anything. Don't say no, until I say all that I want to say."

Sari Jefferson was the owner of Sports by Sari, a full-service, upscale recruiting, sports reporting, and marketing firm. She was known nationwide for her no-nonsense sports writing and knowledge of every type of game. Players and coaches often called her for public relations assistance, marketing packages, and player interviews.

"Wow! Now that's a request. I will not say no until you tell me all about your dilemma."

"Okay so here is the request. I was supposed to have a sportswriter to cover the Milwaukee Mustangs this weekend. I asked Raleigh Lambert to cover the game. She's a game reporter, but she's come down with the flu. I called her and she sounded terrible. I thought Barry White was on the other end of the phone," Sari inserted while laughing nervously. "I need a sportswriter out there fast." After catching her breath, Sari continued. "And Charity, I know that this is asking a lot at the last minute, but I really need you."

Charity took an audible breath, "Sari, Ummm, you do realize that I'm not a sportswriter?"

"I do realize that. However, you are a writer."

"That I am. And you do realize that I know nothing about football?"

"Charity, I know." Sari's voice raised an octave. "I realize all of that. But you are a dynamic writer, and I thought perhaps, you could get a few tips from Reggie about football."

Charity's uncle Reggie was a former professional football player. He was married to Sonya, and he'd made his retirement home in Masters. They had 4 sets of twins. Sonya was now pregnant with her last set of twins or so they told everyone, but only time would tell.

"You do also realize that it is twenty degrees or colder in Wisconsin now?"

"Yes, I do." Sari's voice now deflated. "But think about it like this. It is a paid-for trip. You are only going to comment on the major parts of the game. Like the W or the L."

"What the heck is the W or the L?" Charity asked jokingly.

"Charity!!! Don't do this to me!" Sari's voice was playful yet concerned.

Charity started laughing. "Girl, you are way too much. You call me on a Thursday night to become a sportswriter by Sunday afternoon?"

"It's a needed vacation for you. Fly out tomorrow morning and stay until Monday. I got you! I will pay for a whole week if you want me to. I have no one else that is credible enough to do this."

"Number one, Sari, a vacation would be someplace like Hawaii, Jamaica, the Bahamas—the freaking South of France. This is merely an assignment. Number two: Is there no one in all your contact lists that can assist you with this?"

Without answering the questions, Sari countered, "Charity, please don't make me beg. I'm in such a tight corner and my husband is already mad at me for triple booking. If you do this for me, then I will only be double-booked, and then I can work on that for the remainder of the evening."

"Ooohhhhh!!!" Charity shrieked! "You better be glad, I love you! I guess I will call Reggie and see if he can go over all things football with me tomorrow morning. I will fly out Saturday morning."

"Why can't you ask, Reggie?" Charity asked sarcastically.

"Reggie is not a writer, Charity."

"But he is a guest commentator all the time. He is literate. I'm almost positive he can write!" Charity added, laughing.

"Writing and commentating *are not* the same thing, Charity." Sari sounded exasperated.

"Well, why don't you call Reggie to commentate, and you can write? I really don't care how you do it Charity, I just need it done."

"Whew. Ok, Sari. I'll do it. But you better know how much I love you for doing this. Sports are nowhere near my comfort zone."

"Thank you, Charity! I love you! I promise you I will name my firstborn child after you, regardless of whether it's a boy or a girl!"

"You are silly! I don't think you should name a boy, Charity. I'm just saying."

"I'll call the boy Char and the girl Charity. Since Charity is another name for love, I could just name my baby Love, whether it's a girl or boy. Thank you. I love you, Charity!"

"Okay, Sari, I guess I love you too to take on such a last-minute assignment!"

"I will send the information over via email in the next hour or so and I'll even send extra money so you can live it up in Wisconsin." Sari fell into a relaxed laugh.

"You are too kind!" Charity giggled.

"Charity, there's just one more thing. I will send you a FedEx package to the hotel on Saturday evening. In it will be your press pass as well as the format for the *Sunday Sensation Write Up*. This week we are featuring Isaiah King. You will have about an hour with him."

Silence. Charity didn't say a word as Sari finished the details of the *Sunday Sensation Write Up*.

"Charity?"

Still no answer. Sari nervously inquired again.

"Charity?!"

"I'm here," Charity finally answered. "I'm just trying to figure out what world you are living in and what made you think it was ok to call me like this with all of these BIG requests."

"Char, you know it must be an emergency for me to call you like this. Please understand and remember at the beginning, I told you to hear the entire request before you said no."

Charity sighed. "Yes, you did. Okay, Sari. I will do it, but you owe me. This is huge. I have to learn football in one day and then interview one of the world's best quarterbacks?" Charity leaned her head back and sighed thinking of her schedule and all that she had to do. Why did she commit to this? Shaking her head she tuned back into the conversation.

"Well, one thing is for sure, Isaiah is such a cool dude that you will be comfortable. He's down to earth, and he is from the South. You two will have something in common. He knows all about that Southern hospitality. And all the questions will be provided for you. You're going to be great, Charity. I have so much faith in you." Relief eased into Sari's voice as she realized that this was one more thing, she could take off her plate.

"A mess. That is what you are, a whole mess!" Charity laughed. "Ok ma'am. Let me call Reggie and see if he can help me with this assignment."

"Ok, I will send you the flight information as soon as I get off the phone. Love you, Char!"

"Love you too, Sari! Enjoy your weekend."

"You too!"

"I'll try." Charity hung up the phone and shook her head at her friend from college. Always moving and grooving, there was never a dull moment with Sari.

CHAPTER 8
ANOTHER FAVOR

The Warren household was always bustling with sound and movement. With 4 sets of twins, there was never a dull moment in their home. The scent of freshly brewed coffee lingered in the air, mingling with the subtle aroma of cookies cooling on the countertop.

Reggie Warren leaned against the kitchen island waiting for the cookies to cool so that he could beat his 8 kids in getting the first one. His face bright with a smile as his kids and wife all stood watching and waiting on the timer to indicate the cooing period was over. He loved being a family man, a present husband, and an involved dad, now that his NFL days had come to an end.

As he waited for the cookies the phone rang. "Hello." Reggie Warren answered the phone with cheerfulness in his voice, keeping a watchful eye on his cookie opponents.

"Hey, Reggie. How are you?"

"I'm better than great! Is this my favorite niece, Charity?" His jovial demeanor radiated with warmth and affection, a testament to the bond he shared with his "favorite" niece.

Charity chuckled softly, her laughter resonating through the phone, "Yes, it is. And I know you say that to all your nieces."

"No just you and Joi and Carmen and Morgan and—"

"Okay you can stop, now Reggie." Charity smiled.

"To what do I owe the pleasure of speaking to Miss. Charity Love, entrepreneur, author, and writer extraordinaire?" Reggie stated in a celebratory tone.

"I need a favor, Reggie. I've been asked to cover a football game for the Milwaukee Mustangs this weekend. Like Sunday, and honestly, I know nothing about football."

"Wow! So, you are headed to cover the number one team in the nation with the number one quarterback and running back in the nation and you know nothing about football."

"Yep! Reggie, that's correct. But I do know the basics. I know what a touchdown is, the rest is umm well, just plain ole Greek."

Amused, Reggie asked the ultimate question. "So, who sent you to do a task this insurmountable?"

"Sari Jefferson."

"Sari? Owner of Sports by Sari? It seems like she would know better."

"Tell me how you really feel, Reggie." Charity huffed into the phone laughing at her uncle's joke.

"Listen Charity, you know you called a football fanatic. I have loved the game since I was seven years old playing right over there in Masters Field. You know good and well I want whoever is reporting the information to do a great job. You are an awesome writer, but are you an awesome sports fan? Heck no!"

"Well luckily, I have you in my life, Oh Great and Favorite Uncle of Mine! I'm calling to ask you a huge favor."
Reggie was a former professional football player and the husband of Charity's aunt, Sonya. Sonya and Reggie had four sets of twins and a fifth set on the way: some fraternal and some identical. Jaylin and Kaylin were eighteen-year-old high school seniors, Mona and Monique were sixteen-year-old prissy teenagers, Leslie and April were twelve-year-old sports fanatics like their dad, and Kera and Keith were ten-year-olds who clung to Sonya like white on rice.

It was a blessing that Reggie was the number one NFL quarterback for several years. He needed every penny to raise all ten children. With his endorsements, special appearances, guest commentator gigs, and other investments, the Warrens did well and didn't want for anything,

"What's the favor, Charity? To teach you everything I know in less than twenty-four hours?"

"No, Charity added with glee, "it's to pack up you and your wife and find a babysitter for your kids and head to Wisconsin with me for the weekend. It will be like a mini vacation." Charity tried to make this trip a vacation when it was anything but. She realized that she was failing miserably when Reggie started laughing uncontrollably.

"You know Milwaukee is not a vacation spot." Reggie laughed again and Charity couldn't contain herself any longer before she started cackling too.

"Reggie, I know it's not a vacation spot. I just had this same conversation with Sari."

"And yet you have the nerve to ask me about taking my wife for a getaway to a spot that, outside of the football game on Sunday, is dead."

"Reggie, I think it will be a lot of fun to go and have this time with Sonya. There's a lot that happens in Wisconsin."

"Charity, you do realize my wife is seven months pregnant and that she is expected to have twins and that traveling by plane will have to be approved by her doctor?"

"What about by train?"

"Charity, you should be a comedian!"

"Ok, so what if Sonya stayed here with the kids and you came with me to the game?"

"Charity, let me check with Sonya and let her check with the doctor to see what he recommends."

"Thanks, Reggie. Even if none of these plans pan out, I'll be at your house at nine o'clock tomorrow morning to go over all things football. I'm so excited that you are going to help me. I hope things work out so that you and Sonya can travel with me to this game. It will be big fun."

"I love your enthusiasm, Charity. It's always a good time when I enter a football stadium again. I'll see you in the morning. Have a good evening."

"You too, Uncle Reggie," Charity offered sweetly.

"You're really laying it on thick, Charity. Good night."

Charity hung up the phone. Her smile was big. What she wouldn't do for her friends. Sari owed her big time. But that was Charity's nature. She loved giving and helping people and she did it with love. Martha Love would always say, "Anything you do, do in the spirit of kindness and love."

In all she did, Charity tried her best to resonate with love. In fact, her name was double love: Charity Love.

CHAPTER 9
THE PREGNANCY

"I'm not lying, Veronica. He is the father of my child."

The floor-pacing was followed by a brief pause. "Are you sure? I just can't see him being the father of your child," Veronica said with trepidation in her voice.

"Well, he is." Tammy's tone was definite – the opposite of her best friend.

"Ok." Veronica offered no further rebuttal. She pulled the phone away from her face and stared at it in shock. Making a face into the receiver, she kept listening to her friend, Tammy, go on this impossible journey of paternity.

"Are you calling me a liar?" Tammy asked with malice building in her voice.

Shaking her head, Veronica exhaled hard, moving the phone away from her ear again. "I'm not calling you anything! But even *you* have to admit it's kind of strange that he is the father. When was the last time you saw him?"

"Three months ago. When he came to visit," Tammy said, rolling her eyes upward. "But before that, seven months ago —*when he got me pregnant*!"

Another pause.

"Listen, Veronica. I only have a couple more minutes left on the phone, but you need to tell Karen and James the good news when you talk to them."

"When are you coming home?" Veronica asked quietly. She knew Tammy was cooking up a plot and she wanted no parts of it.

"Hopefully in the next couple of months. Right in time for the delivery."

"Wow!"

Veronica sat in silence, stunned by Tammy's revelation of her pregnancy. Timidly, she asked her next question, "What did he say when you told him that you were pregnant?"

"I haven't told him yet."

"What!!" Veronica yelled, losing all her decorum. "Have you lost your mind? Why not? What in the world are you trying to pull?"

"Calm down, Veronica. I'm going to tell him when he comes for the next scheduled visit. It should be in like two weeks."

"Girl, you are barking up the wrong tree," Veronica warned.

"No, I think I'm at the right tree *and* with the right man *this time*," Tammy countered sarcastically.

"I don't think you want to mess with the Green Machine. Those people are well connected—as you well know."

"I have never directly messed with the Green Machine, and I don't plan on it now."

Tammy dismissed Veronica's concerns and changed subjects, "On another note, we have to start planning my baby shower. I want it to be pink and green."

"Are you having a girl?"

"Yes, a beautiful baby girl for my man and me," she said in a sing-song voice. "I'm going to name her Anna Rae—Anna after my mom and Rae after my dad."

"Wow! You have already picked a name? Girl, you are doing the absolute most!"

"I also want a Green's Goodies green cake with pink and green icing for my baby shower."

"Really, Tammy?" Veronica placed the phone down on the kitchen table and stared at it in disbelief. She wondered if this conversation was being recorded on Tammy's end. Probably so. *Aren't most jail phone calls recorded?* Veronica asked herself.

"Yes, really!"

"Do you have a death wish? I think you're asking for trouble. As your friend, I would say drop this fiasco." Veronica started to try to talk sense into her childhood friend but thought better of it.

"What fiasco? You're calling my baby a fiasco?"

"Right, *your* baby! It's *not* his baby."

"It *is* his baby. I know that we were together even if you don't believe me. Anyway, I have to go now. Tell everyone I said hello, and I'll be home soon."

"Okay, Tammy. Take care of yourself and please be careful."

"I'll see you soon, my dear." Her voice dripped like warm molasses as the line went dead.

Staring at the phone for the last time, Veronica felt a knot developing in her stomach. She wanted no parts of Tammy's shenanigans.

CHAPTER 10
THE FOOTBALL GAME

The stadium was alive with the sounds, each one a vibrant thread in the level of excitement that enveloped the crowd. The roar of the stadium rose and fell in a symphony as excitement vibrated through the atmosphere. The announcer's voice boomed over the loudspeakers, making announcements and setting the tone for the game.

The scent of beer, peanuts, and popcorn mingled in the crisp air, creating an intoxicating aroma that was quintessentially football. Cotton candy vendors weaved through the throngs of spectators yelling for customers and selling their wares. The anticipation was tangible. The energy of the crowd reverberated throughout the stadium.

Reggie's excitement was just as infectious as the cheers that echoed around them. After the game, they were preparing to conduct an interview with the now world-renowned quarterback, Isaiah King—a man whose name had become synonymous with excellence on the field.

"Football Time!" Reggie exclaimed to Charity and Sonya, his voice brimming with enthusiasm and nostalgia. His eyes shone with a light that spoke of cherished memories and the enduring magic of the sport. "It will always be a season alive with possibilities for me."

Isaiah King, the subject of their latter interview, stood on the football field speaking with a reporter, his presence a commanding force amidst the bustling activity of game day. His athletic frame was clad in the iconic colors of his team. His gaze was steady, yet there was a glimmer of youthful excitement in his eyes.

"I remember the first time I suited up for an NFL game," Reggie began, his voice a blend of reflection and awe as he recalled his first NFL game. The memory was vividly etched into his mind like a cherished photograph. "I was young, just twenty-two. I remember trying to decide whether to be excited or nervous, anxious or worried."

As Reggie spoke, the sounds of the stadium seemed to fade into the background. It was a moment suspended in time, a glimpse into the heart of a man whose journey had been shaped by the roar of the crowd and the thrill of the game.

Sonya and Charity walked side by side as Reggie outpaced them headed to the stadium entrance. Game day excitement was in the air and Reggie was like a child in a toy store. He hadn't stopped smiling, talking, and reminiscing since he made it to the stadium parking lot. Thousands of people gathered for one of the best games this season. Spirit and Excitement permeated the air making for a max amount of energy. Reggie, Sonya, and Charity made their way to the press box. The Milwaukee Mustangs versus the Boston Bobcats. Reggie's smile beamed brighter than the sun, brighter than the weighty diamond rings worn on the fingers of the players' wives.

Sari Jefferson made it all happen, and effortlessly. A mix-up in her schedule afforded Charity the opportunity to write up on the game and to interview the quarterback. Excited, but not knowing anything about football, Charity insisted that Reggie and his wife join her and give her pointers. The trip was seamless. No hiccups—all done in presidential style.

A limo arrived at the airport to pick up the trio, and two suites were reserved at the Conquer Hotel, one of Milwaukee's high-class hotel chains. Press passes were provided for all three as well as a dinner reservation at La' Pete' with Isaiah King.

Reggie coached Charity throughout the game. Telling her the plays, the calls, the ultimate referee decisions, and making fun of her special assignment that was taking its toll on her. Charity took notes and asked questions like a schoolgirl the day before a big exam.

After the game, the limo took all three of them to La' Pete'.

The maître' d' seated the trio and asked for their drink orders. Charity, in regular Charity-form, ordered water with lemon. Sonya did the same. Reggie, though, asked for a gin and tonic.

"When did you start drinking, Reggie?" Charity asked when the maître' d' left with their drink orders.

"I don't drink often, but this is a special occasion. I'm so excited to see one of my guys again. This young cat is the truth. He knows the game; he does a great job at executing plays, and most importantly he's humble and gives back all the time. I can respect someone like that."

Charity smirked. "Isn't this the same guy who was all over the paper a few years ago for being with all kinds of women?"

"People change," Reggie looked at Sonya, "can't they baby?"

"They absolutely can if they want to. I think they have to be motivated to do something different." Sonya grabbed Reggie's hand, giving it a squeeze.

"What made you want to come back home after all the time you spent with Tammy?" Charity asked as she looked at the exchange between the couple. Sonya cringed at the mention of Tammy's name.

Reggie and Sonya were married for seven years when Tammy pulled a two-year interception on their relationship. Reggie left his family to be with her. For Sonya and the kids, there were no phone calls, visits, school plays, or sick days. Once a month, Sonya received a $10,000 check from Reggie's accountant. That was the most contact they had with Reggie for two years. He decided that he was leaving them for good.

Tammy was succeeding in carving her path of destruction until one bounced check changed the course. Her actions exposed her as a thief and Reggie admitted that he'd made a mistake. After months of counseling, Sonya and Reggie began rebuilding the Warren clan.

"Honestly, Charity, it was God," Reggie confessed. "The night after I got that phone call from Sonya looking for me to tell me that my monthly child support check bounced, I couldn't sleep. I shrugged it off as no big deal, but I thought about her and the kids all that night and the next. I decided to come home just to make sure it was over, and I could file for the divorce and move on with my life with Tammy. But when I looked into the faces of my wife and my babies, I couldn't bear to leave them again."

"Wow, what a restoration," Charity responded with tears in her eyes.

At that moment, Isaiah walked up to the table. "Reggie Warren, in the flesh! Great to see you, man!" Reggie stood to greet him.

"King! What's up, baby? Great game today!" The two football giants fist-bumped then grabbed each other in a brotherly hug.

"Thank you, man! You know I learned from the best," Isaiah offered dabbing Reggie up.

"Aww, flattery will get you everywhere!" Reggie joked.

Isaiah turned to Charity and Sonya. "Now who are these beautiful women?"

Pointing to Sonya, Reggie announced, "This is my wife, Sonya Warren, and our last set of twins that she is carrying." He turned to Charity. "And this other beautiful young lady is my niece, Charity Love."

Isaiah turned his attention to Sonya first, "Sonya, a pleasure to meet you." Sonya shifted in her seat to shake Isaiah's hand as he leaned down and hugged her gingerly as his gaze landed on her belly. "The last ones you say," he smirked, turning to look at Reggie.

"Yep, the last of the Warrens," Reggie winked at Sonya who changed positions to get more comfortable in her chair.

He then turned his six-foot four frame toward Charity and emitted enough heat with his presence to warm a small home. Charity held her breath. *This man is beautiful; a demi-god*, she thought. His broad shoulders and trim waist were covered in a black suit and a white-collared shirt. The top three buttons opened to show a few sprinkles of chest hair. He had a dimple in his right cheek, and his caramel-colored skin was flawless. He had an aura that surrounded him that cried out masculinity.

"Charity Love," Isaiah glowed. He grabbed Charity's hand before she could respond. "You have the privilege of interviewing me today."

"Privilege?" She asked as frowned before she could catch herself.

"Yes, privilege."

"Oh ok." Charity bit her tongue and vowed to not mess this interview up for Sari. "Yep, that's me."

As the tension mounted, Charity looked at Reggie, helplessly. She wanted to ask about the point at which Isaiah's humility would arrive. Still, she had to admit the man was gorgeous. Behind that beautiful smile he had an easygoing manner that normally made anyone in his presence feel at ease. Except for today. Except for Charity.

Isaiah took the seat between Charity and Reggie. Charity scooted her chair in the opposite direction of Isaiah and closer to Reggie in a gesture screaming, "Protect me." This man made her nervous, and she had no idea why. All she had to do was ask questions for the interview and move on with life.

Charity zoned back into the conversation.

Isaiah was teasing Sonya. "This was the only guy you could find to marry?" Isaiah motioned to Reggie as his face broke into a wide grin.

"Really, Isaiah?" Reggie smiled.

"Yes, Reggie. How did you find a beautiful woman like this?"

"Finding her wasn't the problem; the challenge has been keeping her and my family intact."

"Hey, let's not get too deep, man. I was just joking."

"I'm just trying to give you a piece of advice, youngster."

"Well, old-timer, I appreciate it."

Isaiah turned his attention to Charity. "So Charity Love, or should I say, Love, Love. How are you?"

"It's Charity Love, and I'm fine, thank you, Mr. King."

"Mr. King is my father. I'm Isaiah." He winked. Her stomach turned a flip when he winked at her. *Control yourself*, Charity thought to herself as tried to get this man out of her system.

"Ok, once we get settled, I have a few questions for you." Charity remarked in her professional manner.

"I have a few questions for you, too." His tone was seductive.

"Well, too bad you don't get to ask the questions this time," Charity sneered sarcastically.

Without hesitation, Isaiah persisted. "Then maybe we can schedule a time for me to ask questions of you and get the answers I need."

Nervously, Charity fidgeted with her napkin. "Mr. King, I don't think that will be necessary."

"Isaiah," He corrected, leaning closer to her.

"Isaiah, I don't think that will be necessary."

"Really, Charity?"

"Really, Isaiah."

He stared at her for a full thirty seconds, wreaking havoc on her nerves.

"Really!" She was poised to say more, but the waitress arrived to take their food orders.

Isaiah looked at Reggie for any kind of assistance. Reggie looked off at another table but not before he caught Sonya's eye and flashed a smile. *This interaction is better than all the plays on the field tonight*, Reggie thought to himself.

"She plays hardball I see," Isaiah mentioned to no one in particular.

"You misunderstand," Charity said. "I don't *play* at all."

CHAPTER 11
REGGIE AND SONYA WARREN

A week had passed since the dinner fiasco in Milwaukee. Sonya called Charity over to help her create a baby book for the new twins. Each set of twins was gifted with a baby book created by Charity.

Reggie had taken the kids out for ice cream to give Sonya and Charity a little private girl-time. As they sat at the table planning the details of the book, Sonya brought up Isaiah.

"So, Charity, I think Isaiah likes you." Smiling Sonya poured a bag of lays into a bowl for Charity. Wearing a colorful pink and purple flower covered jumpsuit with a white t-shirt, Sonya wore pregnancy well.

Recently, dying her hair honey blonde and getting it shaped to fit her face, she didn't look like the mother of 8 kids. Sonya's naturally curly hair swirled around her face making her look like a cabbage patch kid. Much of her pregnancy weight was in her face. She waddled over to the kitchen table after grabbing some apple juice from the fridge and sat beside Charity.

"I think Isaiah is a jerk." Wincing at the thought of Isaiah, Charity opened the small bottle of apple juice, shook her head at Sonya, and added, "a complete jerk!" before taking a sip. Charity's green swing dress brought out the color of her light brown eyes as the sun hit the kitchen window brightening her eyes and hopefully her mood about Isaiah.

"No, Charity, don't say that. I thought he was a lot of fun."

"He is too young for me anyway, Sonya."

"Girl, age is merely a number. Who cares about anyone's age in this day and time?"

"I care. But more importantly, he is so arrogant."

"See, I didn't get that impression from him." Sonya leaned into the table and wiped a chip crumb off Charity's cheek; Sonya was always in mother mode. "I think his demeanor goes along with him as a football player. He has to be strong and direct and yet still maintain his fun personality. I thought he was great."

"Well, you can date him!"

Literally howling, Sonya looked at Charity, threw her head back and slapped her thigh. "You have jokes. I already have a big strong football player in my life who I absolutely love. He drives me crazy, but he is the one that my heart still leaps for, even after fights, infidelity, and a breakup, counseling, eight kids and a new set of twins on the way."

"I'm proud of you two for going the distance, Sonya. I don't know that I could have recovered after two years of seeing the man that I loved and married walk around with another woman."

"Charity, it was the hardest thing I have ever done." Sonya's eyes spoke volumes. She covered her face with her hands. "I was so embarrassed. I don't think I have cried so much in my life. But I always knew that I still loved Reggie. No matter how much I wanted to stop loving him, I couldn't." Uncovering her face, she stared at the kitchen table before looking thoughtfully at Charity. "Jesus and therapy are the only reasons I am here today."

"Wow! I guess I can understand a little. That's some enduring love."

"Yes, it is. Believe me, prayer and therapy really help."

"I'm sure it does."

"Have you thought about it, Charity?"

"Thought about what?" Sonya reached out to grab, Char's hand as she looked her in the eyes.

"Therapy."

"Therapy? Me? I'm a strong woman. I can handle things. I just need a long vacation." Dismissing Sonya's notion of therapy, Charity continued sipping her apple juice and snacking on her chips.

"Really? A long vacation with unresolved problems and pain is not a vacation." Sonya stared at her for a long time.

"What makes you think I have unresolved problems, Sonya?" Charity huffed.

Ignoring the hostility in Charity's voice, Sonya continued to press. She felt that Charity deserved happiness and joy and was going to see to it that she received both.

"Charity, really? We all have unresolved issues. I'm only saying something because I care. Your mom died, and right after that Patrick left without a word and got married to someone else. If it were me, I would've been devastated."

"Well, it's not you and I'm fine, Sonya." Charity stood with her empty apple juice glass in hand, headed towards the trash can. Charity, always looking for a reason to walk away. Sonya stood up and followed Charity, grabbing her arm as she walked. Charity turned around to face her aunt, her expression clouded with pain.

"Charity, I know that you are a strong woman, and that you have been through quite a bit in a short amount of time. You deserve a fresh start."

Sonya pulled Charity over to the counter of the island, sat her down on one of the stools and gave her a big hug. Sonya was more like a sister to Charity than an auntie. Martha's younger sisters were closer in age to Charity. From birth they'd loved her as if she was their own. When Martha passed away, they continued to love those Love girls. Joi and Charity now had six sister/auntie/moms to look after them. Charity leaned in and held Sonya tightly.

"Listen Charity, I just want you to experience happiness and love that doesn't come with struggle. For the first time in a long time, my and Reggie's love is easy. Don't get me wrong, we still have so much work to do, but we are managing so much better with the help of our therapist."

Charity pulled away from Sonya, turned and looked out of the kitchen window. Gathering her thoughts while trying to hold back tears, she recited her mantras in her head: *I will not cry. Blessings on Blessings. Just get through this moment.*

"I don't doubt any of that, Sonya," Charity admitted after collecting herself. "I just don't know that I'm ready to discuss Patrick or Mom. Both are gone and they were both an important part of my life. I just feel like I'm spiraling out of control and trying to hang on by a thread while maintaining my business and help these new authors." She placed her head in her hands and emitted a sob as her shoulders trembled.

"That's why I said a vacation may not be the best thing, but maybe some therapy to see what you need to do to bring your world back into balance." Sonya embraced Charity again and held her longer. All her baby weight resting on Charity's arm.

Charity tensed up and stood abruptly. "I have to go. I have a deadline to meet, and I need to get started soon. Next week, I'll send the finished proofs for the baby books." Charity hugged Sonya as she headed toward the door.

"Be safe, my love."

"Thank you, Auntie. I'll see myself out."

"I'll call you later, love you!" Sonya called as Charity walked out. And with that goodbye, Charity walked again. That strong lonely walk.

CHAPTER 12
RYCE AND DIANE SMOTHERS

Ryce was packing his bags when Diane walked in with her off-key singing. "I will bless thee Oh Lord—" Dressed in a flower dress and high-heeled combat boots, Diane was an absolute anomaly. She was always making up her own style of fashion.

"Hey, Baby," Ryce called out as she entered the house.

"Hey, Love." I'm upstairs in our bedroom.

Diane ambled slowly up the steps still singing her off key song. Arriving in their bedroom, she gasped. "What are you doing?"

"I'm packing, Diane." Ryce answered bluntly. Ryce had their brown leather luggage opened with shirts and boxers strewn on the couch beside his Sunday suits. He looked relaxed in a pair of worn jeans, a t-shirt, and running shoes. He consistently wore khakis and button-down shirts unless he was presenting or preaching. This new look made him look more approachable and friendly.

"Packing for what?"

"I got the call I've been waiting for—the church in Memphis. They want me, so I'm headed there now."

"So, did you forget you have four children and a wife, *and* that we are trying to rebuild our family? Were you even going to tell me?" Diane questioned, staring at Ryce like he'd grown an extra head. Her hands pressed against her tiny waist and her face contorted in a frown, she stood waiting on an explanation.

"Yes, I was going to tell you. I just don't like goodbyes."

"So, you'd rather just leave and not say anything?"

Continuing to pack his things into the suitcases strewn across the bedroom couch Ryce said, "I was going to call you once I got settled and checked out the lay of the land. I need to make sure that I secure us a place to live and then I'm going to come back and get you and the kids."

"Why don't I believe that?" Diane asked. She walked towards Ryce rolling her eyes and neck, clenching her fingers. The veins in her neck looked as if they would pop out. Her face was flushed with pure hot anger.

Without looking up, Ryce replied, "Because you have trust issues?" He kept his eyes on the clothes as he put them in the suitcase, refusing to look at Diane's face. His hands shook a bit from nervous energy. He held his breath as he waited for Diane's response. He knew it was coming.

"Oh really, who gave me trust issues?" Diane yelled!

Ryce finally stopped packing to look at Diane. "So, all your trust issues come from me?"

"You're the only man that I have been with my entire life. Every trust issue, every ounce of insecurity and every bit of confidence that I lack is directly attributed to you."

"That's absolutely insane, Diane! You give me way too much credit." He slammed the suitcase shut and lowered his eyebrows.

"You know, I really thought you changed. Are you back on drugs? What are you running from?"

Ryce opened the small carryon bag and resumed packing in silence. Diane, however, refused to let the conversation go. "Maybe the better question is who are you running to?" she said.

"So now I'm back on drugs and running to someone else?" Shaking his head, Ryce laughed. "If I didn't know any better, I would think that you were the one on drugs."

"That was hurtful!"

Ryce blew out a breath and adjusted his Clark-Kent like wire-framed glasses. "And you don't think your words are hurtful, Diane?"

Breathing heavy, Diane stared at Ryce. "I'm done talking to you for the night. You are so selfish. So once again you leave me here with these kids, your kids. Do you plan on paying child support or sending money to help us out at all this time around?"

"Diane, I have explained to you that I'm going to Memphis to pastor a church!" He threw a pair of slacks into the suitcase. Sweating, he ran an open hand over his wavy brown hair.

"Does this so-called church know you have a family? They didn't make provisions for all of us to come with you?"

Unassuming, meek, and pretty mild, he rarely became aggressive or mean unless he was under the influence of drugs and alcohol. Tonight, he was doing his best to remain calm as Diane grew more and more upset.

Ryce worked hard over the last ten years to turn his life around. Yet again, he feared losing his wife. "Diane," he whispered, trying to maintain his calm, "I'm going to look for a place to stay and to see what Memphis has to offer. I'm going to look for schools and everything else. While I'm doing that, you can wrap up things here in Masters, making sure that we can sell this house, getting the kids' report cards and shot records together. We all can't go at the same time without preparation."

Agitated, Diane shook her head. Falling back on the couch and wrapping her arms around herself, she rocked back and forth and cried. *Maybe I'm having a panic or anxiety attack*, she thought to herself. Ryce came and sat by her; comforted her.

Diane and Ryce's love had a storied history. They married soon after a whirlwind college romance. But at some point, drugs came between them, destroying their dreams. They were a family in conflict; totally broken.

Embracing Diane, he whispered, "Diane, I promise you that I'm not on drugs. This offer is legit. The current pastor is transitioning to a new city by the end of the week, and they need me to come and meet with him and get acquainted with the ministerial and church staff."

"Ryce, this decision should have been made as a couple, as a husband and a wife." She laid her head on his chest and cried. Wringing her hands together nervously. "We are not at a place where you can sneak surprises on me like this. I am still struggling with trust." Her dark black curls fell forward covering her face. Ryce moved them to the side and laid a kiss on her cheek. Leaning back on the couch, Ryce pulled Diane beside him and held her tightly allowing her tears to flow.

Rubbing her back, Ryce tried to comfort her, "Diane, I told you about the possibility months ago. You seemed so excited then. I'm trying to improve our lives. Why are you making this so difficult?"

"You just don't get it, Ryce. I *am* excited. But you haven't said much about it in the last few months. I thought the offer was off the table and you were moving on to something else. Now, I walk in and you're packing. It just reminded me of you leaving us last time."

Diane took a deep breath trying to calm her nerves. "Do you know what it felt like to be here with the kids struggling to put food on the table, to buy clothes, and keep all of us emotionally sane? You took everything from us and left us with the scraps. We did our best to build from the broken pieces. But to do it again? I'm not sure any of us will survive it."

Ryce's eyes glistened with tears. The hurt and pain were evident on Diane's face, in the sag of her shoulders, in her countenance. He felt rotten. "I'm not doing that again. I'm going to secure a great opportunity to elevate us, to take all of us to the next level. I promise I'm not abandoning you, Diane. I promise. I made a vow to God that if He allowed me to get clean again, I would serve him no matter what. I promised him that I would honor and love the wife he blessed me with and children he gave me. I can't break my promise to God, so you're safe."

Ryce shifted his body and wiped tears from Diane's face before holding her again, tighter. "I know you see me working hard, Diane. I haven't missed a support meeting. I've tried to be present for the kids even though they are teenagers and hate to see me coming." He chuckled at the thought of his kids' faces when he visited their schools or even their bedrooms.

"I'm so sorry I hurt you so much so that you can't see the glory of our story. I'm going to pastor this church, get acquainted with my leadership team, meet the members, and then come back and get my wife and kids. God is promoting us. You have to believe me."

Ryce leaned in and kissed Diane, who continued to cry. "Please believe me. Please trust me. I know that I'm asking a lot, but I'm coming back, I promise I am. Can you trust me, baby?"

Tears soiled Diane's face. She began to inhale deep breaths. She was scared out of her mind. "Ok. Ryce," she conceded. Her heartbeat began to steady. "We shall see what happens. I love you and I'm trying to regain trust. This move is just so soon after getting our rhythm back."

"I know, Diane, but I promise it's for the best."

Ryce stood up and pulled Diane up from the couch and wrapped his arms around her. They stood locked together for what seemed like minutes. Taking her hand gently in his, he led her to their bed on the other side of the room, where he slowly undressed Diane and then he undressed. "Let's go to bed, baby. We'll have a big breakfast in the morning catered by Chef Ryce and discuss things with the kids before I leave for Memphis."

Moving their clothes that were scattered all over the bed, he pulled the comforter back, Ryce lifted Diane and placed her onto the bed.

"I love you so much. You are my princess, Diane. I never want to hurt you again. I'm so sorry for upsetting you and leaving our kids. Please forgive me. As soon as we all get to Memphis, we need to resume our family counseling."

"We do," Diane agreed. "I love you too, Chef Ryce." She snuggled next to Ryce letting her heartbeat sync with his. She prayed silently that this would work out. She prayed for her husband's wisdom and for her strength. "God, do it again," she whispered.

"Good night, my love!" Ryce tightened his grip on her and buried his face in her hair.

"Good night."

Going from wounded to whole takes work. Love is an action word, but communication seals the deal.

CHAPTER 13
THE THERAPY SESSION

On a brisk November morning, Charity was walking to her car when the pace of her breathing changed. It became more labored and heavier; her inability to inhale felt torturous. Once the episode subsided, she let it go; chalked it up to stress. Three days later, another episode hit her even harder and much longer. She knew it, felt it. It was time to go to the doctor and figure out what was going on with her health.

A week later, she made the decision to go to her primary care physician. After the examination, her PCP sent Charity to a local clinic for a mental health evaluation. There she received a diagnosis of anxiety and severe depression and was prescribed rest and therapy sessions for six weeks at least three times a week with a board approved psychiatrist. She changed her schedule to only work half days for the next two months.

It wasn't until December when Charity decided to attend that first therapy session. After making her first appointment she found herself afraid. The night before, she tossed and turned, begging sleep to overtake her and grant her rest. Sleep came but only in spurts. There was never a complete hour of peaceful rest.

Entering the office of Dr. Lisa Lesure, Charity signed in and then sat in the reception area twiddling her fingers nervously. The waiting room was a haven of warmth and peace, with soft lighting that cast a gentle glow over the waiting room.

When her name was called, she entered the office and settled into the love seat, its cushions plush and faced the doctor. Studying the walls of the office, adorned with serene artwork, their colors a soothing balm to the chaos within, Charity asked, "What do I say?"

Dr. Lesure, seated across from her in a sleek black chair, exuded an aura of wisdom and calm. Her red and black wire-framed glasses perched on the bridge of her nose, framing eyes that held a depth of understanding. Her hair, a cascade of mingled gray, fell past her shoulders in soft waves.

Dr. Lesure looked over her red and black wire framed glasses at Charity. "Whatever you want to say.", She pushed back mingled gray hair that hung past her shoulders.

"Are you going to start off talking, asking me questions?" Charity asked.

"I can." Dr. Lesure's face held no expression.

"Ok." Charity felt relieved.

"What brings you in?" Dr. Lesure asked in a calm and steady voice.

"Well, that's a loaded question." For the first time in months, Charity hadn't pulled her hair in a messy bun. She let her curls hang down and frame her face. She wore a red sweater that complemented her caramel skin and made eyes glisten ever so slightly. She rubbed her hands on her pant leg wiping the never-ending flow of sweat before responding to Dr Lesure's loaded question. However, before she could respond, Dr. Lesure continued.

"Is it, Charity? Something or someone had to bring you in."

"My dad, aunt, and sister recommended that I come to therapy a few months ago. I have also had a series of panic attacks. I didn't know what they were at the time, but since then I have also been diagnosed with severe depression and anxiety." Charity paused and sighed deeply, "There is just so much that brings me in. My mother died a few years ago. She was my best friend. A piece of me left that day and I don't think it has healed. I don't think it will ever heal." Charity's hands were restless, her fingers entwining and untwining as she gathered her thoughts. Charity's voice trailed off.

"Did your dad, sister, and aunt recommend therapy because you took your mother's death hard?" Dr. Lesure raised her eyebrows slightly, listening intently, nodding occasionally, her presence a silent assurance that Charity's vulnerability was safe here.

"No, not specifically."

"So why did they recommend therapy?"

"My sister actually recommended it because she saw my ex and *I* didn't want to talk about it or him." Charity laughed nervously. "Not at all. And yet *she* continued to talk about it."

"You were upset with her for mentioning your ex?"

"I guess so," Charity shrugged.

"A yes or no answer will suffice," Dr. Lesure stated without hesitation.

"Yes," Charity answered in a hushed tone.

Dr. Lesure studied her for a moment. "Was he abusive, mentally, physically, and/or emotionally?"

The mention of her ex-boyfriend brought with it a fresh wave of hurt and confusion. Charity's hands were clenched into fists, her knuckles white. "No, he is an upstanding guy; well, educated, financially well off, handsome—all the qualities that you would want in a man. He checks all the boxes."

"Then what happened?"

Charity looked at the black-and-white portrait on the wall: a picture of a sunset. Interesting that a sunset in all its beauty would be captured in black-and-white, she thought.

"Charity?"

"Sorry." She rubbed her hands together, coming back to the moment.

"What happened?" Dr. Lesure waited patiently for an answer.

"Nothing really. We lived together or as the old folks would say, we shacked. I guess we just drifted apart. A year ago on his birthday, he left for work and never returned. A few months later there was a news story about his wedding to a beautiful woman."

"How did that make you feel?"

"Sad, of course. I was happy that he apparently found happiness, but I was totally sad. He left without a goodbye." Charity felt as if a weight had been lifted. Somehow by just getting out her feelings, she felt a pressure start to release in her body. *Maybe she was wound up too tight,* she thought to herself.

"Is that important? Would things have changed or been different if he would have left and said goodbye." Dr. Lesure typed a note down as she awaited Charity's response.

"I'm not sure. The heartbreak would still be there, I guess, but maybe if I'd known why he left, I could have some closure."

"The 'why' would have made you feel better, you think?" Dr. Lesure typed notes on her laptop, paused and looked at Charity again. "Or maybe not."

"Maybe not," Charity conceded.

Charity looked around the small office, studying the awards, the books on the shelves, the flooring, anything that would help her calm down to get her mind out of this moment, to stop these tears from falling. Once she felt the tears were held tightly in and that her throat was no longer clogged with emotion, she added pensively, "So, here I am."

"Tell me what you would have said if he told you that he was going to leave."

Charity studied the intricate design on the Persian rug. Looking at the beautiful colors, she whispered, "This is hard."

"Healing isn't easy," Dr. Lesure said. "If it were, everyone would be in therapy. But it's difficult and people run away from it all the time."

Dr. Lesure leaned back and crossed her legs. "I will pretend that I'm him. Ok?"

"Ok," Charity answered uncertainly and a bit despondently.

"Hey, Charity. Can we talk?"

"Sure."

"Remember I am playing like I'm your ex. Are you ready?" Charity nodded hesitantly as Dr. Lesure continued. "I know that you know that things have been very different lately."

"Yes, they have been."

"I just don't think things are going to work out between us."

"Why?"

"Charity, I just really can't see a future with you."

"Really? Why?" Anguish clouded Charity's face like a blanket settling on a bed.

Dr. Lesure paused her questioning to look closely at Charity. Dr. Lesure switched courses, "What I'm gathering from your questions is that you just wanted a reason."

"Yes. I wanted to know what I did wrong. Did I gain too much weight or was I too loud or too ambitious or too religious? I just need to know why." Her voice reached its peak, almost a slight scream. She crossed her arms while her legs shook with anxious energy.

"Why is that so important?"

"Because I can self-reflect, and I can try to do things differently and learn from my mistakes. Dr. Lesure's gentle probing helped Charity confront the unresolved questions that had haunted her, and as she spoke, the tension in her shoulders began to ease ever so slightly. It was as if speaking the words aloud had given them form and substance, transforming them from nebulous fears into something tangible, something that could be faced and, ultimately, understood.

Dr. Lesure reached out to Charity and grabbed her shaking hand. "Can I share something with you?"

"Of course!"

"For the right person none of that will matter. For the wrong person those are the only things that will matter. Do you understand that you are enough with the help of Jesus Christ? Do you understand that you are wonderfully and fearfully made?"

"I guess so."

"Here's your homework for the next session. You are to write a letter to your ex. The letter can contain no questions. Don't ask why. It has to simply express how you feel. Write it as honestly as you can."

"Are we going to send it?" Charity looked with dread at Dr. Lesure.

"Do you want to send it?"

"I don't know." Truthfully answering the question, she looked at Dr. Lesure with quiet consternation.

Dr. Lesure studied Charity once again. She realized she was such a complex young lady. There was so much hurt, and pain wrapped up in this successful young lady with so much talent, style, and grace. She knew she had her work cut out for her. "Let's just take one step at a time. Write it first. Then we will decide what we will do with it."

"That's fair," Charity looked up at Dr. Lesure her heartbeat studying. The fear of sending the letter to Patrick made Charity's heartbeat with anxiety.

"I can reassure you that I will be here with you every step of the way."

Closing her laptop and taking out her agenda book, Dr. Lesure scribbled notes on the page and turned her attention back to Charity.

"That's all for today. Charity. This will be a long arduous process but, hang tough, you can do it."

"Yes, ma'am."

"On your way out, stop by the receptionist desk and schedule an appointment for next week."

Charity slowly gathered her belongings and walked toward the door before looking back as Dr. Lesure typed more notes into laptop.

"Thank you, Dr. Lesure."

"Thank you, Charity," Dr. Lesure, who had moved back to her desk and was typing, glanced up from her laptop, "for trusting me with your pain. We will get through this together with the help of God."

"We sure will. Have a great day, Doc." *Charity realized the journey would be long and filled with challenges, but she also knew she was not alone.*

"You too!"

With that, Charity turned and walked out: A strong, lonely walk that was filled with a new ray of hope.

CHAPTER 14
LEONA GREEN (MONROE)

Leona paced the living room, her mind a whirlwind of emotions—anger, fear, and a lingering doubt that gnawed at her heart.

Her pink silk robe trailed behind her like a shadow, a stark contrast to the turmoil within. The room was dimly lit, the soft glow of a single lamp casting long shadows on the walls, mirroring the uncertainty she felt.

"Where have you been all night?" Leona walked behind Monroe as he meandered into their home. Her long pink silk robe and matching nightgown moved with the sway of her hips as she approached Monroe. Her narrow eyes studied him. She looked him up and down from head to toe, noticing each feature. After studying him from head to toe, twice, Leona's brown eyes smoldered by anger looked dark and scary.

Monroe looked up from his phone.

"I was out with the fellas." Monroe's tone was dismissive as he turned to face Leona. "I told you that I was going to hang out with them."

"Monroe!" Leona yelled, "You're lying! I can tell when you're lying!"

Monroe looked up and stared at Leona for a full minute, then shook his head.

Monroe and Leona's relationship was rocky from the very start with a few smooth patches but mostly rough terrain. Monroe could barely keep a job, and they fought all the time in the early years of their relationship. Leona was the youngest Green and the only sister that had followed in their father's footsteps and became a lawyer. Early in the relationship she was better known throughout the small town of Masters Mississippi for the domestic violence reports filed against Monroe than her law skills.

After much work and therapy and a renewed sense of love, the two had reached smooth sailing. Monroe was now supervising several sanitation departments throughout the city of Masters, and they were engaged to be married.

"Lee!" Monroe raised his voice, using her nickname. "I'm marrying you. I'm not seeing another woman. We have been over this time and time again. You can look through my phone if you want." He extended his hand, offering his phone. Leona reached for it calmly but pulled her hand back as if it were poison.

Monroe offered a sinister snicker. "Really, Lee?"

"Yes, really!"

Monroe stared at her again. "So, you don't trust me?"

"Not at this moment. Not when you have been out all night and haven't answered a call from me! WHERE HAVE YOU BEEN!?!" Leona screamed hysterically. She ran both of her hands through her hair and held them there as she clenched her hair. Her face flushed; she glared at Monroe.

"Lee," Monroe countered calmly, "I told you that I was with the boys and have been with the boys all night. I don't know why you can't get that through your mind. I'm not and have not cheated on you in the last four years."

"Monroe, hand me the freaking phone." Leona's tone was now deadly.

"You can have the damn phone, Lee! I'm not cheating on you!" Monroe stood, tossed the phone at Leona, and walked upstairs to the second-floor landing of their home.

Leona sat on the sofa looking at the phone that fell on the side of the sofa when Monroe tossed it. It was face down. *Should I turn it over*, she pondered. After a moment, she did. It was unlocked. She could go through it, checking phone logs and messages, and seal her fate. Or she could just go with her gut. Either way she was miserable.

Lately, Monroe was secretive. He'd been staying out late and coming home at the crack of dawn, mostly on weekends. He always blamed it on his friends. But was he really with them? Was he really hanging with boys? Lee was tired. She needed answers. If she couldn't trust him now, why bother to get married?

Leona tossed the phone back on the sofa and looked around their home. Her beautiful baby mansion that sat in the heart of one of Masters, Mississippi most premiere neighborhoods. She sat and stared out the large window and watched the sun as it poured its rays through her beige curtains.

Though the earlier years were hard, she could honestly admit that Monroe was doing great in his new job. He had received another promotion and was now managing over a hundred employees. Most of the time Monroe came straight home or went to the gym to work out after his shift. As of late though, from Friday night to Saturday morning, he was always MIA. Because of the past, Lee couldn't help but think that maybe Monroe had eased back into his old ways. Determined to get to the bottom of this, she walked upstairs. The phone remained face down on the sofa.

"Monroe!" Lee called as she made her way to their bedroom. "Monroe!"

No answer.

"Monroe!" She called for the third time before she realized the shower was running. She sat on the side of the bed and waited patiently for him to come out of the bathroom.

When Monroe walked out and saw her sitting on the bed, he sat down beside her, dripping wet, towel slung around his waist. He rubbed his wet hands down the side of the silk gown.

"Lee, I promise you I'm not cheating on you. I promise you that. We have had so many problems in the last ten years, honestly, you know we have not had any issues since Sarah Knight—and that was eight years ago."

Sarah Knight and Monroe had a brief fling that ended up in all the papers in Masters. It was a short-lived affair, but the effects were long lasting. After counseling and much prayer, they'd mended their relationship, but now here they sat.

"Monroe, I understand everything that you are saying. However, I need to know the truth. You can't expect me to believe that you leave here on Friday nights and stay out until Saturday mornings and you are not dealing with a woman."

Monroe breathed deeply. "Please know that I'm not dealing with a woman. I do have some other issues, but a woman is not one of them."

Lee leaned her head on Monroe's shoulder. "You asked me if I trusted you earlier, but if you trust me then you would share your world with me. You would allow me the opportunity to help you even if you think it will break us up. How are we supposed to go into a marriage with secrets and not trusting one another?"

"I'm not sure, Lee. But I need to work through some things first and then we can sit down and talk it through."

"Really, Mon? I can't believe you!"

"Lee, I promise you, it's not what you think. Please believe me when I tell you that there is not a woman involved." He stood to return to the bathroom to finish dressing.

"Ok," Lee whispered. She walked to the other side of the room and changed her clothes to head to work. "I'm headed to the office for a few hours. I'll be back later."

Lee resolved that she would have to just wait and see what happened. She stood at the entrance to the bathroom door wearing black slacks and a baby blue button-down shirt. Her black kitten heels pulled the look together.

"Monroe, we are getting married in less than a month. If you can't trust me with whatever it is that you have going on, then I'm not sure that we are meant to be together."

Monroe looked down at his hands and sighed again. "I know, Lee. Can you give me a few days to try to gather my thoughts and then I promise you, I will tell you everything that I have going on?"

Lee didn't look back at Monroe as she slipped on her leather jacket and walked out of the bedroom. "See you later, Monroe. Sweet dreams," she said sarcastically.

CHAPTER 15
THE SOFT SPOT

"Hello." Constance leaned over to answer the phone. She thought it was just ringing in her sleep until Princeton nudged her. "Hello," she said again, this time looking at the clock on the nightstand to get her bearings: 3:42 a.m. *Who would be calling at this hour?* she thought.

"Mom!" She heard the caller saying. "Mom, can you hear me?"

"Markus! What's wrong? Where are you?" Markus' voice snatched her completely out of her sleep. She sat straight up in the bed and frantically reached for the clock again. What time was it? Her sleepy eyes tried to register the time. Frantically she asked, "are you ok Markus? Where are you son?" Her heart raced waiting on his answer. She knew no good news came any time after 3:00 am.

"I'm at The Soft Spot. The police are here. Can you meet me at the police station?"

"What!" Constance yelled, sitting all the way up and putting her feet on the floor on the side of the bed. Princeton jumped up when she yelled. Until then, he remained laying down.

"What's wrong, Constance?" Princeton leaned over and grasped her arm as she held the phone.

"Mom, just meet me at the police station, please. They are taking me to the station on South Sticks Street."

"Markus, what in the world?!" Constance started taking her hair rollers out of her hair as she felt around with her feet for her slippers that were somewhere on the side of the bed.

"Mom! Are you going to meet me or not?"

"I'm on my way. Let me get dressed." With that, Constance threw the phone down and ran to her closet to find clothes.

Princeton was on her tail, hurriedly changing even though Constance had yet to tell him what was going on.

"Constance, where are we going?"

"Princeton, that was your son, Markus, on the phone. He is being taken to the police station. He was at the Soft Spot. I don't know what happened. But we need to meet him at the police station." Three rollers hanging on by a thread, Constance raced in the bathroom to wash her face and brush her teeth. Throwing on a pink jogging suit, her thoughts wandered as she raced from the bathroom to the closet looking for shoes and socks. Princeton was on her heels, zigzagging through their room to find his clothes as well.

The Soft Spot was a quaint little jazz club in the seedy side of town. The owner hosted the best local and national acts. It was packed to capacity nightly by townspeople and visitors alike. Most came to sample the best hot wings that the world had ever known. The wing sauce was made fresh daily by Janet Curry. The recipe was passed down from the first Curry slave that arrived in Masters. Rumor, was she kept the recipe for the secret sauce in a vault, and only one other person in the family had the combination.

After they finally got dressed and made it to the car, Princeton let out a low, "What? The! Hell!!!" as he backed out of their garage.

"I know. Come on, let's go and see what this boy has done now." Constance sat in the passenger seat fidgeting with the straps on her shoulder bag. Her nerves were shot.

Markus had been a hothead since childhood. He was never a bad kid, but he'd never back down from a fight. He was the thin and nerdy type; the guy who kept to himself but was always surrounded by people because he had the energy and pizzazz people loved. By day, Markus was the senior accountant at Masters Financial Group. By night, he played the saxophone with a group of three guys who were all mellow. They called themselves the Mellow Mosaic! Recently they had a special guest appearance by Sam Love and Leona Green. The Soft Spot was on fire that night and Leona scatted for hours.

Constance and Princeton drove out of their subdivision like forty going north to the police station.

When they arrived, Nicholas, the oldest son of Princeton and Constance, was sitting in the corner on his phone.

"Nicholas, what happened with your brother?" Constance demanded.

Nicholas ended his call. "Mom, I'm not quite sure. He just told me to meet him here. He said something about a fight."

"A fight?" Constance shook her head from left to right in a fast motion. She sat down, then stood up and walked the expanse of the waiting room. "A fight?" she questioned again, holding the straps of her shoulder bag for dear life.

"What in the hell!" Princeton quipped again.

"A fight! He's too damn old to be out here fighting folks!" Princeton shook his head. Nicholas stood and patted his dad on the back. Clean shaven dressed in all black, he looked like he was wide awake at 4 in the morning.

Princeton and his two sons looked like triplets. All caramel mocha skin with low cut haircuts. Markus was the tallest of the three. All were lean and often worked out together at Masters most popular gym, Beyond Fitness. Nicholas and Princeton stood side by side looking like twin brothers instead of father and son.

"I'm so sick of that boy and his quick temper." Constance shook her head as well and she ended her walk and sat down on the bench that Nicholas had occupied just moments before.

"Mellow Mosaic my butt! There is nothing mellow about him! Doesn't he know he has a corporate job that is at risk?" Princeton paced back and forth now taking Constance's place.

"Mom, Dad, calm down," Nicholas said. His phone beeped. "I may have to go to the airport. I'm on call tonight." Nicholas received his medical degree and was a surgeon—until a few years ago. After the COVID pandemic, he wanted to fulfill his lifelong dream, he changed careers and became a pilot for Sky Airlines. Constance was livid when

Nicholas made that decision. But Nicolas was young and tired of losing patients. At 30 years old, he got his pilot's license and now at 34 he was happier. "We need to hear the whole story before we jump to any conclusions."

"What?" Constance turned with fire in her eyes. "There is not a story that I need to hear. Markus is always losing his temper. I'm positive that he did it again." Constance sat in the chair with her leg shaking uncontrollably.

Leona walked into the police station looking like it was 10 a.m. instead of 4 a.m. She had on her black pumps, business suit, and hair pulled back in a bun. Her black and pink eyeglass frames matched her outfit.

"Hey, family," she whispered as she made her way to Constance, Princeton, and Nicholas, hugging each one. "Have you all seen Markus yet?"

"No," Princeton answered. "Are you planning on taking this case?"

"Yes, I guess. You want to take it? He called me and told me to meet him here, so here I am."

Constance and Princeton started a law firm together nine years ago. They each maintained their own specialties, but recently with the increase in crime in the county, especially in Masters, Leona recommended that they also delve into criminal law.

Princeton was hesitant with all the cases of police brutality; he'd been wary of opening that can of worms. But after the loss of yet another innocent life at the hands of police the year before, Princeton enrolled in a few classes to update himself on criminal law. However, he still specialized in real estate and corporate law.

Lee focused a great deal of her efforts on divorce. Together, they were a force in criminal law. Almost overnight they were known in Masters for helping younger adults receive fair trials. They even recruited Reggie to start the Boys-to-Men Mentoring Program for men and boys either in the system or headed that way. Reggie's organization was doing a great job and making big gains. He even started bringing in current and former NFL players to assist him in reaching the boys.

They were now charged with helping Markus in whatever trouble he found himself in this week.

"Did he give any details about what happened, Leona?" Constance asked as she stood to pace the floor again.

"No, he was at the club and told me to meet him there, but by the time I got to the club, they had already taken him away. I tried to get info from the people who were still there, but the police were heavily saturated and moving and pushing people out of there."

"This is working my nerves. This boy and his temper are going to be the death of me," Constance ranted.

"Constance, we don't know what happened yet, just calm down. Sit down and relax," Princeton advised as he directed Lee to the other corner of the room.

Princeton turned to Lee. "So, what are your thoughts?"

"I think they charged him with robbery."

"Robbery!" Princeton looked stunned. "What the hell!" Princeton yelled for the third time. "Who the hell was he robbing?"

"I have no idea." Leona looked at Princeton with her eyebrows raised.

"Well, I know for sure that he doesn't need any money. He makes great money as an accountant and his group makes a pretty penny with all their bookings and performances. They are booked every single weekend."

A moment later, the police captain, David Bryant, walked into the room.

"Good evening, family. How are you all doing? I hate that we must meet under these circumstances."

"What happened?" Constance asked, skipping the formalities and walking over to Captain Bryant.

"We are booking Markus with robbery."

"Who did he rob?" Nicholas asked, chiming in and standing to his feet.

"According to reports, he robbed the owner of The Soft Spot."

"Why in the hell?" Princeton once again asked, trying to find the right words to say. He placed both hands on the top of his bald head and let out a loud sigh. Pacing to the other side of the room and back, he now stood with his gaze fixed on the detective unable to find the words.

"Why would he rob the owner of the club?" Leona asked. "He has played the guitar and saxophone there for the past six years. Why would he rob the guy now?"

"I'm not quite sure, ma'am," Captain Bryant replied. "I have a few of my officers and a detective on the case, but we will continue to investigate."

He looked around the room, before continuing, "I realize that you all are upstanding citizens of Masters; I'm trying to get to the heart of the matter as soon as possible."

"How much is the bail?" Lee asked.

"Bail will be set tomorrow when he is arraigned, but normally the bail for robbery is set at $20,000."

"Twenty thousand? Come on Princeton, let's go." Constance started gathering her things.

"Let's go? Are you serious?" Princeton looked at her in disbelief, his eyes wide as saucers.

"Yes, I am! Let's go!" She retorted.

"Mom, you're going to leave Markus down here?" Nicholas asked walking over to stand near his parents.

"Yes, I sure am!" Constance yelled. "He did the crime; he can do the time. Or he can pay with his own dime!"

"We have the money, Mom! We can get him out." Nicholas was frustrated. Constance always was the dictator, the no nonsense parent. She said what she meant and meant what she said and never ever backed down from teaching her kids a life lesson in integrity or character.

"It's not about the money; it's the principle." Constance put on her mink coat. "Princeton let's go. I'm tired."

Constance turned around and grabbed Nicholas' hand. "Markus knows better. He can stay the night here and clear his head. Maybe this will teach him a lesson about taking what doesn't belong to him."

"I can't believe you are going to leave him down here," Leona said as Constance walked out the door.

As Constance opened the door, she looked back at Lee and said, "You and Princeton can spend your time and money getting him out, but I'm not going to do that."

"Come on, Princeton!" Constance yelled.

"Lee, call me tomorrow and let's go over the details of the case," Princeton said to Leona as he walked reluctantly behind Constance who hastily made an exit to the door.

"Okay, they should arraign him by tomorrow afternoon."

Leona and Nicholas watched in silence as Constance and Princeton walked out of the precinct and drove away.

"You know I love my sister, but she knows she gets on my nerves with that foolishness," Leona said.

Nicholas nodded in concurrence. "I honestly don't have any words. I have to get back to the airport. I'll see you all tomorrow."

"Love you, baby."

"Love you too, Auntie."

CHAPTER 16
THE MENTORING CALL

"Hey, man!" Reggie answered his cell phone looking at his caller ID. Isaiah King was on the line. "Thanks for reaching out."

"It was good seeing you at the game." Isaiah reminisced about the game that Reggie, Soya and Charity attended a few weeks ago.

"Man, I miss the adrenaline rush that comes with getting ready for the game, playing the game, and even sitting on the sidelines. I miss it all." Reggie spoke excitedly remembering his days of playing in the NFL. Reggie was a mentor now to many of the young players in the NFL. Isaiah being one of his favorites. He was more like a little brother to Reggie. Their paths crossed at a training camp that Reggie spoke at one year and they had kept in touch since that time.

"I understand, you know it's the greatest feeling in the entire world. How do you retire from this and go on to live a normal life?"

"Please let me tell you how *abnormal* my life is. I have eight kids and two more on the way," Reggie offered a hearty laugh before continuing. "My life is anything but normal."

"Yes, I noticed, but to be honest, I was checking for your girl, Charity that night at the restaurant."

"Aww, I see, I see!"

"So, she's your niece, right?" Isaiah questioned Reggie.

"Right. My wife, Sonya, is her aunt, her mother's sister."

"So, is she married, engaged, dating? I didn't see a ring on her finger."

"No, she's single as far as I know."

"That's good to know. She's a three-piece." Isaiah burst out laughing.

"What's a three-piece, or should I even ask? You young cats are too much for me."

"She's working, smart, and beautiful!"

Reggie roared with laughter. "I hope you don't use that as a pickup line."

"I don't have any pickup lines. I just appear and the women come running."

"Well, sir, I don't think Charity is that girl. But let me know how that works out for you."

Isaiah started working on his plan out loud, "When I come down there for the mentoring program, you can set us up on a blind date."

"Are you confirming that you are coming for the mentoring program?" Reggie asked in a serious tone.

"I will be there, no worries."

"Wow! Thank you! You do realize that you are the number one player in the league. This will be huge. The boys are going to have a ball!" Enthusiastic, Reggie continued. "I figure you can have a talk with them, we can play a little ball and then maybe we can end with a cookout. Man! This will be great for the kids. I'm too excited." Isaiah could hear the excitement in Reggie's voice as his pitch went up to meet his energy.

"Yeah, I see, you're so excited that you didn't answer my question," Isaiah pointed out.

"Which was?" Reggie asked slowly.

"Are you going to hook me up with Charity when I get there?"

"Oh, that question." Reggie leaned back his office chair and twirled the ink pen he was holding around a few times and pondered Isaiah's question. He'd always heard when it comes to matters of the heart proceed with caution. He heard a pastor in Memphis, Pastor Edwin Brown, say those words and they always stuck with him. He knew how difficult love was and he wanted no parts of the love lives of others. He was still trying to make sure that he never made a misstep again in his own relationship.

"Listen, let me tell you, I love Charity. Her mother was a great lady and took good care of this family until she died. She was the Green glue. I don't want anything to happen to Charity. She has been through a lot. The question is: *Does she even like you?*"

"You got jokes man! If you hook us up, I can find out if she has a man and if she's interested."

"I'm not into hooking people up," Reggie answered honestly. "How about this—I will invite her to everything that weekend and I will see if Sonya will host a dinner at the house and make sure Charity is invited. Now from there, you will have to do the rest."

"That sounds great! I can hook myself up!"

"Okay, bro man. We will be in touch as the time gets closer. I will send you the agenda and the itinerary for the weekend. Be safe on the field."

"Gotcha! Take care, I will chat with you soon. And thanks for hooking me up with Charity."

Reggie gave a long sigh, "Isaiah, I am merely putting you in the same space with her. I am NOT," Reggie emphasized, "hooking you up."

"I'll take that. I can hook myself up! I'll catch you later man."

Reggie hung up, smiled as he shook his head and stood to stretch and thought to himself: *That young brother has a lot to learn.* He laughed out loud, and *Charity is a good teacher.*

CHAPTER 17
JAIL

Lilly, Diane, Sonya, and Mabel showed up at 7:30 a.m. on the first Wednesday in December, on Constance's porch where matching his-and-hers black and white chairs sat perfectly positioned, "To what do I owe a visit from the infamous Green girls?" Constance asked, swinging the door open after the first ring.

Mabel made her way through the door and spoke first. "We've decided to go to the jailhouse and visit Markus."

"I have a headache," Constance lied. She winced theatrically as she glanced towards the window where rays of golden sunlight flooded into the room. "The sun is shining so bright; it will only make my head hurt more. I think it's a migraine. I called Nicholas so he could come over and give me something for the pain."

Leona, ever the skeptic, raised an eyebrow. "So, are you never going to see Markus, Constance?" Leona asked, her tone a mixture of curiosity and concern.

"I will see him when he gets out of jail." Constance replied curtly, her words clipped as though the very thought was a burden she couldn't bear to carry.

Diane, standing with her arms crossed, looked at Constance in disbelief. Her eyes were wide, reflecting both shock and disappointment.

"Wow, you are really something else."

Lilly, the peacemaker of the group, decided to chime in, her voice gentle but firm. "He is still your son, even if he made a mistake," she reminded, her gaze softening as she spoke.

"Yes ma'am," Diane interrupted, her voice rising with an edge of exasperation. "My children make me mad every day, but there is nothing that I wouldn't do for them."

Constance rolled her eyes, a gesture that spoke volumes about her disbelief in their words. She moved with deliberate grace, sitting down on her plush, velvet chaise lounge, its deep emerald color, bringing out the color in Constance's lounge wear.

"Diane, has your child ever robbed someone before? Better yet please explain how you make a mistake and rob someone?" She leaned back on her chaise lounge. "You all are welcome to have a seat," she said, waving her hand dismissively at her sisters, "but know that this—" she gestured broadly, "was unnecessary. He had my name all over the newspapers because he wanted to take something that belonged to someone else."

"Constance, you don't know what happened. You are just jumping to conclusions." Leona said, trying to inject reason into the heated conversation.

"I know that he robbed *someone*." Constance repositioned herself on the chaise lounge with the elegance of a queen adjusting her throne. She turned to her other sisters, who remained standing, their expressions a mixture of pleading and persistence. "Please have a seat; looking up at you is making me dizzy," she sighed dramatically, then leaned back, cradling her head in her hand as if the weight of the world—or at least her troubles—was too much to bear.

The room was silent, except for the distant chirping of birds outside, an ironic reminder of the peace and harmony that seemed so far out of reach inside the house. The sisters exchanged glances, each pondering the next move in this delicate dance of family loyalty and personal pride.

"But you don't know why, and you are not even willing to listen to him." Leona looked at Constance, puzzled by her reaction. "And I don't want to sit down!"

Rolling her eyes again, Constance grunted. "You can listen to him, Lee. That's why they pay you the big bucks."

"Okay, Constance. Just remember that your son will remember this day, the day that you decided *not* to support him."

Constance stood, walked to the door and opened it, indicating that her sisters should leave her house. "Bye, ladies. Have a great day."

With a huff, Diane walked to the door. "You don't have to be so mean, Constance." She narrowed her eyes and shook her head.

"Listen, Diane, when your children break your heart then let me know how it feels."

"You know a mother's love is unconditional," Leona said as she walked towards the door.

"How would you know, Lee? What child have you had?"

"Wow, Constance. That was a low blow." Lilly's face scrunched into a frown. "How can you talk to your sister like that?"

"I have a mother, so I do know what a mother's love feels like. And I'm the one helping your child because *you're* being foolish?"

"No, my child was foolish, and I'm not wasting my time bargaining with him and the police to get him out of something that he knew darn well was wrong."

"You don't even know the complete story," Sonya refuted.

"And I don't want to know. Again, ladies please leave." Constance opened the door wider, indicating the need for their exit.

"Bye, Constance," Mabel said. "As a mother, you should always choose your children first."

Constance continued to hold the door open for her sisters. "Once again, bye ladies."

As the sisters walked to Lilly's car which was parked closest to the driveway, Leona quipped, "Oh that girl gets on my nerves. She is so doggone stubborn."

"She's been that way her whole life." Sonya reasoned as she waddled to the car big with baby as the old folks would say.

"I can't believe she is not going to come see her son," Diane complained.

"It's fine. We will go and see about our own nephew." Leona turned back and glared at the front door of Constance's house, hoping she was still looking out.

"I hope he's not too upset that his mother is not coming," Lilly ranted.

Constance was always a hothead, stubborn to a fault. She was more concerned about her reputation than what drove Markus to rob the owner of The Soft Spot. Once she had a thought in her head, it stayed there forever. Princeton was the only man patient enough to deal with her and the only man she listened to other than Dallas Green, Sr.

"He knows his mother quite well. I'm sure that he'll understand," Mabel inserted. Who's driving? Leona asked.

"I can," Sonya offered without hesitation, she had the biggest vehicle to haul all her kids. The Green sisters all hopped in Sonya's extended Escalade and started their drive.

"You think Constance will be mad that we left our cars parked in front of her house," Lilly asked with a hint of concern as they pulled off.

Laughing Leona, answered, "We will find out when we get back."

Sonya interjected, "or she will call in the next thirty minutes fussing about it." They all laughed as they continued their journey to the jailhouse.

∞ ∞ ∞ ∞ ∞ ∞ ∞ ∞ ∞ ∞ ∞

The atmosphere in the jailhouse was stark, with cold, gray walls that seemed to absorb any warmth or comfort. Fluorescent lights buzzed overhead, casting an artificial glow that heightened the sterile feel of the room. The air was tinged with a faint smell of disinfectant, mixed with a subtle hint of anxiety that seemed to radiate from the visitors.

"People, remove all items from your pockets and lay your bags on the conveyor belt," the guard said as visitors entered the east side of the jailhouse. His delivery was without emotion. "As soon as you place your bags down, walk through the metal detector."

Lilly, determined yet visibly tense, was the first to step forward. Her heart pounded in her chest, echoing the clatter of her heels on the hard linoleum floor. As she walked through the metal detector, a piercing beep filled the air, causing her to flinch.

"Ma'am, did you remove all items from your pockets?"

Lilly jumped; her cheeks flushed with embarrassment as she fumbled in her pocket

. "Oh, shoot, I have my jump drive in my pocket."

Annoyed, the guard raised his voice. "Ma'am you need to remove *everything* from your pockets."

Her hands were shaking. "I'm so sorry, sir. I'm a little nervous."

"No need to be nervous. Go place your things in your bag and walk back through." She stepped forward confidently, her demeanor a blend of reassurance and resolve. Her eyes briefly met Lilly's, offering a silent smile.

Sonya went through next.

"Ma'am you beeped, step to the side and the next guard will pat you down."

"I'm pregnant. I don't need anyone patting me down."

"Ma'am it is our procedure. You cannot enter the jail without a security check."

"Ok," Sonya said, halfheartedly.

The female guard patted Sonya down and let her go ahead.

"I guess it was just the underwire in my bra." She offered.

"I guess," the guard said nonchalantly, then placed the wand back on the desk at the security station. Mabel and Diane went through without incident.

The second guard came into the middle of the waiting room. "All quiet," he announced. The room smelled like old bologna and cheese. The walls were bluish gray with dirt marks from the top to the bottom. The chairs were stained from years of wear and tear and the lights were dimmed to almost dark. The guard continued with his emotionless instructions.

"Only two people can go back. You have a total of twenty minutes. If you have more than two people in your party, you can split the time. But twenty minutes is the maximum time currently allowed per inmate for visitation. The next visitation time is the next hour. Any questions?" He paused to wait for questions.

"If there are no questions, when you hear the inmate's name called, come to the window by the door and you will be buzzed in. Make sure that you leave your things in the lockers as you walk through the door. On your way out the door, you can go back to your locker and get your things. Once again, do you have any questions?" No one in the waiting area spoke up.

There were mostly women present, young and old - all shapes and sizes; their faces: mostly black and brown. All looked troubled.

A new guard emerged from behind the green-colored door that led to the inmates. "Alright, we're about to start calling names now. Jodie Stephens, Michael Benson, Carter Gillespie, Burton Smith, Markus Johnson."

"Who is going first?" Lilly asked.

Leona looked at her sisters. "I am. Mabel, you can come with me and then the rest of you rotate out so that I can get the details and talk to Markus."

"Ok," Mabel said nervously, looking at her sisters. "I'm just going to say hello and come back out."

"Ok!" Diane, Sonya, and Lilly said in unison, and quickly fell quiet. They each looked as if they were afraid to speak.

Mabel and Leona went to the back, where Markus was sitting on a bench by the door. He was dressed in a pair of khaki pants and a matching shirt.

"Hey, baby," Mabel said as Markus stood to greet his aunts.

"Hey, aunties." Markus radiated with joy as his face broke into a wide smile when two of the Green sisters walked in the room.

"How are you?" Mabel asked, rubbing the side of his face and his hair. "You need some good moisturizing lotion. Are they treating you, okay?"

"I'm ok. I won't complain."

"So, tell me what happened?" Leona jumped into lawyer mode asking a handful of questions as they sat down on the bench.

"Whew," Markus blew out his breath slowly. "Calvin Jordan, the owner of the Soft Spot, asked us to commit to performing two days per week. It would be $700 on the weekdays and $1500 on the weekends, plus 10 percent of the door."

"Ok," Leona nodded, taking notes mentally.

"So, we agreed, and the next week we started performing at the club."

"Do you have a written contract?" Lee interrupted as she continued taking mental notes and assessing the situation from a legal perspective.

"I don't." Markus shook his head. "We didn't sign anything. It was a gentleman's agreement. Like granddad used to say, your word is your bond."

"Ok, what happened?" Leona continued.

"Two weeks ago, we performed for two days and never got paid. You know we all have good jobs, so we weren't that worried about the money. So, this week, we performed again. The first day, we got no money. The second day, before we went on stage, I went to Calvin's office and asked him if he had our money."

"What did he say, baby?" Mabel leaned closer, getting into the story.

Leona looked sternly at Mabel. "It's probably time for you to switch with one of your other sisters."

"Ok, Markus, I love you. Please call me if you need anything," Mabel planted a red-lipped kiss on his forehead.

"I will, Auntie, I love you too."

Mabel walked to the lobby. "Who's next?" she asked the remaining Green sisters.

"I'll go." Diane jumped up and quickly made her way to the door. She saw Markus and Leona and shuffled quickly to sit at the bench with them.

"Hey, nephew."

"Hey, Auntie."

Markus continued the story. "Calvin said that he would have the money by the end of the set. When he didn't come out after the set, I went back to his office again. He started talking about how he didn't know if he would have the money to pay us and there was a wad of money sitting on his desk, so I took it and walked out."

"Markus!" Diane screamed.

"I know, Auntie. I shouldn't have done it. But I was sick of the runaround."

"Whew, Chile," Leona muttered under her breath.

"And you don't have a contract?" Leona asked again.

"I don't."

"So, then what happened?" Diane asked.

Lee looked at her. "It's probably time to let one of the others back, Diane."

"Ok," Diane whispered.

"Aunt Lee, you don't play." Markus stated jokingly as Leona sent the Green sisters out as quickly as they got involved in the conversation.

"We only have twenty minutes and ten are already gone." Her voice was nonchalant.

"Ok, Markus, be good." Diane kissed his cheek. "See you later. Love you."

"Love you too, Auntie."

After Diane left, Sonya waddled her way back to the bench and sat down. "Whew, I'm tired."

Markus laughed again. "Auntie, how many months are you now?"

"Eight and a half; I'm ready to drop at any moment."

"Twins again?" Markus asked.

"Yep, this is the last set, too. We are done. I don't care what Reggie says."

Everyone laughed.

"Alight," Leona said. "Let's get back to business."

"So, what happened next?"

"I started splitting the money with the other members of the band and Calvin came from behind and hit me. We started scraping, and someone called the cops. That's all she wrote." He looked down at his hands trying to avoid eye contact with his aunts.

"Did anyone see you go to the office and take the money?" Leona questioned trying to sure up Markus' case and find witnesses.

"I don't think so, but I'm sure he has cameras."

"Shoot," Sonya said. "You should have beaten him down."

"Really Sonya," Leona said, flabbergasted by her sister's response. "We have seven minutes left; you may want to let Lilly come back before our time expires."

"Okay. Bye Markus, we will see you in court. I will be there."

Laughing Markus said, "Thank you, TT Sonya."

"Alright see you in a minute, Lee."

Sonya waddled back out to the waiting room.

"Alright, so did the other members of the group know about the oral contract?"

"Yes, they all knew. We sat down as a group and talked about it, the days we would work, and how much the pay would be."

"Ok, good. During your next call home, give me their names and numbers so that I can start calling them. No one else got into a fight with the club owner?"

"Nope, just me." Markus looked disappointed.

"Hey, Markus."

"Hey, Lilly, how many months are you?" Markus eyes grew larger as he saw Lilly waddle to the table.

"Eight."

"You and Sonya are having babies at the same! Two pregnant aunts at the same time, Markus smiled. "I know granddaddy would be so happy to see all of his offspring."

"Yep. I am sure he would. You'll have some cousins to look after when you get out."

"Cool, I can start a band with them as well."

"Right. Ok Markus, you can think about what else you can tell me. Let me know. We need you out of here fast."

Lilly struggled to sit down on the bench without bumping her protruding belly. "Do you want us to pay the bond money?"

"No, ma'am, the court date is in a few days and Nicholas is supposed to bring the money by Monday morning to get me out of here."

"It's not that bad, is it?" Lilly asked.

"You know everyone is pretty cool and nice. Small-town jail; small-town mentality."

"I believe I have all the information I need. If I think of anything else, call me and I'll be back without your aunties next time."

"Hopefully, you will be home in the next couple of days."

"Hopefully so." Markus looked deflated.

"Well, call me Markus. I think we have a good chance of getting you out of this trouble but stay out of the way," Leona advised.

"You talk to my mom?" Markus asked.

Leona looked at Markus with a sad smile. "I have."

"She's mad?"

"She is. You know she doesn't want to be the talk of the town, and you had her name in all the papers."

"That's all she's worried about? Her name being in the paper?" He paused thinking about his mom, "That seems to be right. She's worried about other people's opinions instead of her son."

Lilly shrugged. "Yep. You know how Constance is. She's a whole mess."

"Ladies, it's time to go!" the guard called from the front of the visiting room.

"Alright son," Leona said standing to her feet and reaching to help Lilly up from the bench. "We love you. Call us if you need anything."

"I appreciate you for coming to check on me. Give my mom a hug for me," he murmured shyly. "Tell her I still love her, even though I know she's mad at me."

"I sure will."

"I won't," Lilly whispered.

Markus looked at his aunt in shock. "I know you won't, Aunt Lilly. The Green sisters are a mess." He laughed at his aunts as they prepared to leave.

"That's right." Lee leaned over and kissed Markus on the cheek.

"Bye, baby," Lilly said.

"Take care, Aunt Lilly. You and Sonya sit down somewhere before y'all drop those loads."

CHAPTER 18
PASTOR KEN AND LILLY JEFFRIES

The living room was usually a sanctuary of warmth and love for Pastor Ken Jeffries and his wife, Lilly, a place where laughter echoed, and their shared history and so many cherished memories. Tonight, however, something felt amiss. The room, adorned with their family photographs, wedding pictures and soft, inviting furniture, seemed overshadowed by an unspoken tension.

When Pastor Jeffries walked in, his presence typically heralded a cascade of affection from Lilly. Her usual ritual was to dash toward him with an exuberance and shower him with kisses and enveloping him in a warm embrace. Their love story was one of fate—a chance evening stroll that blossomed into a lifetime of companionship. Together, they had walked down the aisle, hand in hand, ready to embrace whatever life had to offer.

But tonight, the atmosphere was different. "Hey, my love!" he greeted, his voice exhibiting his usual cheerfulness.

"Hey," Lilly replied, but her eyes remained glued to the stove, her tone distant and distracted.

"Hey? That's all I get?" Pastor Jeffries teased gently, hoping to coax a smile from her.

He took a moment to observe her closely, noticing the subtle stiffness in her shoulders and the way her fingers twisted nervously at the hem of her sweater. Concern etched into his features as he tried to decipher the cause of her unusual demeanor.

Lilly finally looked up, her eyes meeting his with a storm of emotions swirling within them. The usual sparkle that danced in her gaze was dimmed, replaced by a flicker of fear, anger, and worry. Her quick movement as she turned to face him spoke volumes.

Pastor Jeffries stepped closer, his hands reaching out to gently cradle her face, his touch tender and reassuring. "What's going on, sweetheart?" he asked softly, his voice soothing.

She turned away from his touch back to the stove. Then after a long moment, she whirled around quickly to look at him. "How could you?"

The venom and anger in Lilly's eyes and voice startled him. "How could I *what*? What are you talking about?"

"How could you get another woman pregnant?" Pastor Jeffries stepped back almost losing his footing. *Get a woman pregnant?* He thought to himself.

"Lilly, what are you talking about? I have one woman pregnant, and that's you."

Lilly's voice shook as she forced back tears. "Then why did I get a letter from someone named Veronica telling me that her friend was pregnant by you and that she was having the baby early and you need to come and see her?"

The living room, usually a haven of tranquility, seemed to pulse with an undercurrent of tension as Pastor Ken Jeffries extended his open hands toward his wife. His voice was gentle, yet firm, infused with the patience of a man who had guided many through storms of their own making. "Hand me the letter, Lilly."

Lilly handed him the letter, tears rolling down her face. He began to read it.

Dear First Lady:
I just wanted you to know that my best friend in the whole
world is pregnant. Your husband, Mr. Jeffries is the dad. He
needs to come and see about her. She is delivering her baby
soon. I hope you get this letter in time. The doctors have been
trying to stop the baby from coming so early, but I'm not sure
it's going to work.
Please call me at 662-778-3546.
~Veronica

As he finished reading, the paper crumpled in his fist, its edges
biting into his palm. He looked up at Lilly, his expression, a mix of
disbelief and hurt, totally opposite to the loving warmth that usually
defined his gaze. "So, you get a letter in the mail, and you jump to
conclusions?" he asked, his voice edged with a trace of disappointment.

Lilly's shoulders slumped, her head bowing under the weight of
her emotions. "What am I supposed to believe?" she whispered, her voice
fraught with a blend of confusion and vulnerability.

"You are supposed to believe your husband! Have I given you
any reason to doubt me?"

Lilly shook her head slowly, her voice a soft murmur, "No, no
reason at all."

Pastor Jeffries tried to blink back the tears that were forming in
his eyes, his voice heavy with emotion. "Then don't doubt me, Lilly and
don't work yourself up about foolishness. I need you and our baby to be
healthy. You are already going through a high-risk pregnancy. We can't
let anything else get in the way of a healthy baby."

"If you say so," Lilly whispered, wringing her hands.

"I say so. Now, I'm going upstairs to change clothes."
Pastor Jeffries walked toward the stairs and looked back at his wife, his
bride, his beloved, his everything. He never thought he would love again
after his first wife, Melia, died. But then he met Lilly, and he knew that
God had sent him a precious gift. Turning to walk up the steps, his heart
dropped. *How could she not believe him?* he asked himself. She was his first
thought in the morning and the last one he had at night.

He took his tie and shirt off and looked out the window of their bedroom. There was a lake in the back of their small home. It gave him peace to fish in it on Saturday mornings. He needed that peace today.

Pastor Jeffries nodded and whispered a prayer. "Father, give me the words and wisdom for this moment. Give me peace that surpasses all understanding. Help me keep my marriage together." He then walked down the steps and greeted Lilly again.

"It smells good down here. What's for dinner?"

"I made beef stew." Lilly's tone was soft yet guarded.

"Awesome, I'll set the table." Pastor Jeffries set the table and while Lilly fixed their plates. Dinner was quiet.

Lilly tried to wrap her head around who could have sent the letter and still believe that her husband had nothing to do with another woman being pregnant. Ten minutes into dinner, she had to ask: "So, do you know anyone named Veronica?"

"I have no idea who Veronica is; I promise you Lilly, I have no idea who her friend is and who wrote that letter. Did it have a return address?"

"No."

Pastor Jeffries shrugged. "So, I'm going to have to get the silent treatment because of a letter that came in the mail."

"Do you know how many people—women you see daily? Weekly? Monthly? Are you *sure* you don't know a Veronica?"

"Listen, Lilly, if I did know a Veronica, I would know if I had sex with her friend. I don't know anyone named Veronica except for a girl I went to elementary school with over forty years ago. That was when my family lived in New York for a year. I'm so confused on how you could just jump to conclusions about something like this now."

"Can you look at it from my point of view?" Lilly asked, her voice barely above a whisper, laced with desperation.

"Not really. I have never even looked at another woman since I started walking with you ten years ago. I am crazy about you and you only. I cannot believe that you would ever accuse me of this. How strong is our marriage if when the first wind blows, I become convicted without judge, jury, or trial?"

Lilly looked down and shook her head. Her heart was heavy with regret as she shook her head

"I apologize. I've never been married, and I don't need someone coming in to disrupt our marriage."

Pastor Jeffries sighed deeply, the sound echoing with the weight of his emotions. "Let's just finish dinner. I have to prepare my sermon for Sunday."

The first family finished dinner in silence, each lost in their own thoughts. The clinking of silverware against plates was the only sound that pierced the quiet, each tap echoing the unspoken words and unresolved feelings between them. Veronica's letter had done what it was created to do: cause division in their home.

CHAPTER 19
GREEN GOODIES II

The sun made its final round of the day, sending a warm spark through the windows of Green's Goodies where the Green sisters gathered for their weekly business meeting. The room was a charming blend of old-world elegance and modern comfort, with plush armchairs arranged around a large mahogany conference table. The scent of vanilla and cinnamon lingered in the air, remnants from the cakes baked from earlier in the day.

"Hey ladies!" Constance walked in smiling as she entered the conference room at the back of Green's Goodies, her presence brightening the space like a ray of sunshine

"Hey, Constance!" Lilly responded warmly, her voice carrying a note of welcome that cut through the slight tension in the room. Lilly, the family peacemaker, was seated in a deep, comfortable armchair across from the conference room, her posture relaxed as she sipped from a steaming cup of herbal tea.

The rest of the sisters, gathered around the conference table, were absorbed in reviewing notes and discussing plans awaiting the start of the meeting. Constance's arrival signaled the official beginning of the gathering, as tradition dictated that all sisters be present before any decisions could be made.

Bertha, their mother and MaBelle, their grandmother who Mabel was named after, started Green's Goodies in the kitchen of the home house years ago. One day they made the perfect cake and shared the recipe with the Green girls. Lilly had been the first of the sisters to take up the mantle, her passion for baking ignited by countless afternoons spent in the kitchen with MaBelle. Under the watchful eye of Bertha, who served as a silent partner, Lilly perfected the green icing and cake batter through many trials and errors. Lilly turned her love for baking into a flourishing business. Gradually, each sister joined the venture, bringing their unique talents and perspectives to the table, transforming Green's Goodies into a formidable thriving family business.

As the sisters settled into their seats, Diane's eyes narrowed, her gaze cutting through the air like a blade as she fixed Constance with a stern look. "You know you are about thirty minutes late," she stated, her voice tinged with frustration.

Constance, unfazed by Diane's icy glare, met her sister's eyes calm and collected. "I guess your phone doesn't work," Sonya chimed in, her words laced with sarcasm, as she crossed her arms over her chest, a gesture that underscored her discontent.

"My phone works," Constance replied, her voice steady, yet with an edge of defensiveness bubbling up. "I was outside talking to Pastor Jeffries about opening Mom's and Mabel's silent auction fundraiser with prayer."

"I knew that" Lilly answered leaning further into her seat.

"Well, why didn't you tell the rest of us, Lilly?" Leona questioned.

"You didn't ask," Lilly answered nonchalantly.

"Wow! You all are terrible!" Constance raised her voice and leaned forward in her seat opening her notebook indicating that the meeting was about to commence.

"Let's get this meeting started," Diane offered noticing Constance preparing her notebook and writing utensil.

"Are we calling it a meeting? I thought this was going to be fun," Sonya chimed in, forever the optimist.

Constance looked at Sonya with concern her eyebrows furrowed. "Who told you it would be fun?"

"I thought when we stopped having the work meetings during the day and switched them to the afternoon, we would make them fun."

"*We can* make it fun, but we need to go over the logistics for Mabel's Masterpiece opening and fundraiser and silent auction," Diane commented.

"We want to raise at least fifty thousand dollars from both events for the Children's Orphanage in memory of Martha and pick one nonprofit to give ten thousand to help them achieve their mission," Lilly noted.

"I think that's a feasible amount of money," Mabel interjected.

"How much did we raise last year?" Diane posed taking notes on her laptop computer as she waited for an answer.

"Last year it was $27,000," Lilly pointed out.

"So, you want to double the amount from last year?" Mabel clarified.

"Yep, that's the plan." Lilly interjected.

"Ok, so let's go over everything." Mabel pulled out her notebook and started writing feverishly.

"I need all the kids to be present," Diane noted.

"Sonya, will Kaylin and Jaylin be available to serve the Hors d'oeuvres?" Lilly asked.

"They should be. On Sunday afternoons they never really have much going on."

"The other kids can serve as hostesses and greeters."

"Jeremy has an audition for the Masters band that day, but as soon as it's over we will be there." Diane let out a long exhale. "My kids have so much going on. They just tire me out."

"Lilly, do you think you'll be available to make a green cake or green cupcakes for that day?"

"Honestly, I'm not sure, Mabel. I haven't been feeling well lately. I could really use some help at the shop."

"Diane, would you consider coming back for a while just to help Lilly out?" Mabel asked.

"I'm not sure, Mabel. You know Constance and I don't get along and I don't need any drama this time around. Last time, she really hurt my feelings. It took some time to recover from that. Plus, I have enough going on with managing the house and kids without Ryce."

There was heaviness in Diane's voice as she finished speaking and glanced at Constance.

Constance sat silently before she replied as she looked at Diane in awe. "Really, Diane!" Constance. "I really thought you had forgiven me for that last debacle."

"I have forgiven you, but it's so hard to forget." She answered in an even honest tone, her voice free of malice and resentment. "I don't mind helping for a few weeks," Diane added. "The kids and I can pack at night."

"Constance, why can't you help a little more?" Sonya asked, leaning back in the chair and stretching before she stood to walk around the room carrying the weight of two babies.

"I have to see about Markus and go to court for all the trouble that he got into a few weeks back."

"Excuses, excuses! When did you start going to visit Markus at court? Last time, it was your dear sisters who went to visit your son." Mabel shifted in her seat and pointed toward Leona. "That is what you have *her* for. She and Princeton can handle things with Markus, and you can help with the shop. It's all-hands-on-deck time now."

Constance looked shocked but what Mabel said was true. She hadn't spoken to Markus since his debacle at the Soft Spot. With quiet determination, she agreed to help at the shop, remaining cool even though she wanted to say something sarcastic, which was her normal style. But Mabel was now the oldest living sister, and she would show her respect.

Diane, trying to steer the conversation back to the fundraiser, "Let's focus on what's important." Her tone was firm yet held a hint of vulnerability. Organizing the event was critical, and she wanted to ensure its success without letting personal issues interfere.

Constance, feeling the weight of Diane's words, shifted uncomfortably into her seat. "I am willing to help," she offered, her voice carrying a mix of sincerity and defensiveness. "I know I have been absent, but I'm here now."

Lilly, interjected softly, "We're all here for the same reason—to honor Mom and Mabel and to support the homeless shelter and another nonprofit in the community. Let's not lose sight of that."

The room fell quiet for a moment, each sister reflecting on Lilly's words. Sonya broke the silence, her voice gentle yet firm. "We've all had our differences, but we're family. We need to support one another, especially now."

Leona nodded in agreement, her earlier irritation giving way to a sense of unity. "We've been through a lot more together. Let's use this as an opportunity to strengthen our bond."

Mabel, the matriarchal presence in the room, smiled warmly. "I know this isn't easy, but I believe we can make this event a success if we work together, not just for Mabel's Marvels but for a nonprofit organization in the community."

As the meeting progressed, the sisters began to focus more on the logistics of the fundraiser, their shared commitment gradually overshadowing the earlier tension.

They detailed the timeline for the event, ensuring every aspect was covered, from the opening prayer to the closing remarks. Each sister took on specific tasks, aligning their strengths with the needs of the event. Mabel would oversee the auction items, while Sonya ensured the Green grandchildren were prepared for their roles.

Lilly and Diane brainstormed ideas for the green-themed desserts, while Constance agreed to handle the decorations, promising to bring a touch of elegance.

Despite the lingering undercurrents of past grievances, the sisters found a renewed sense of purpose. As the meeting ended.

Diane turned to Constance, her expression softer. "Let's try to put the past behind us, for the sake of the family."

Constance nodded, a small smile playing on her lips. "Thank you, Diane." Constance grabbed her hand and rubbed it lightly. "My mouth gets me into trouble all the time. Even when we were kids, I was a hothead. But I promise to do better."

The Green sisters moved forward, determined to make the upcoming event a success, and in doing so, strengthen the bonds that tied them together. The ladies talked about a few other items before gathering their belongings and leaving for the day.

As they walked to their cars, Mabel pulled Lilly to the side. "Are you okay? You've been awfully quiet and not your normal jovial self."

Lilly mustered up a fake smile and laid her head on her big sister's head for a brief tender moment. Lifting her head, she stated quietly, "I'm just old and pregnant. It's a heck of a combination."

"I know it is, but please don't overdo it. I can see if Carmen and Morgan can stop by and help as well. Take it slow, Ms. Lilly." Grabbing, Lilly's hand, Mabel looked at her with a soft expression, "I love you little sis. Don't overdo it," Mabel repeated.

Lilly smiled, her lips curving into a gentle expression that finally reached her eyes. This time, it was genuine—a smile that spoke of hope and determination, even amidst the chaos swirling within her heart. "I will," she promised,

She then turned and walked to her car. She opened the door and settled into the driver's seat, the familiar scent of leather and lavender air freshener wrapping around her like a comforting embrace. For a brief moment, she allowed herself to savor the solitude, the gentle hum of the engine providing a soothing solace to her frayed nerves.

Though the letter from Veronica was heavy on her heart and mind, she wasn't prepared to share it with her family. The letter sat in her purse like a heavy weight, its presence a constant reminder of the storm brewing in her heart. She wasn't ready to share its contents with her family—not yet. The words were etched into her memory, each line a heavy albatross around her neck.

Part of her longed to confide in her sisters, to draw strength from their unyielding love and support. Yet, another part of her hesitated, fearful of the ripples such revelations might cause in the already turbulent waters of their family life. She needed to find her own answers before she could share this burden with them.

She drove to her subdivision in total silence and lost in thought. As she pulled into her driveway, the familiar sight of her home brought a sense of comfort poured over her like warm molasses. It was her sanctuary, her place of refuge. Though she realized all good things come to an end. Lilly wasn't ready for that 'end' to be her marriage to the man she had waited for all her life.

With a heavy deep breath, she gathered her belongings and exhaled deeply before wobbling her way into the house.

CHAPTER 20
THE COURT DATE

The morning sun filtered through the large bay windows of Constance and Princeton's elegant living room, casting a soft glow over the meticulously arranged furniture. The room exuded a sense of understated luxury—plush cushions adorned a grand sofa and a chaise lounge, as well as a collection of artful vases lined the mantelpiece, each carefully curated to reflect Constance's impeccable taste.

After Princeton lost his job and they had to downsize to a smaller home, Constance was devastated. The one promise Princeton made and kept to Constance was that she could decorate their home as beautifully and lavishly as possible. She'd done an amazing job of adding luxury even during their downsizing.

Leona stood near the entrance, her posture straight and purposeful as she slipped a stack of papers into her black leather briefcase. Her tailored suit, a deep shade of navy, accentuated her commanding presence—a testament to her successful career as a lawyer. Her sharp eyes, framed by stylish glasses, flicked upward to meet Constance's gaze, a hint of concern softening their usual intensity.

"Constance, are you going to court today?" Leona inquired, her voice steady yet carrying an undertone of urgency. She paused in her task, her fingers lingering on the clasp of her briefcase, as she awaited her sister's response.

She'd stopped by Constance and Princeton's home on her way to court to discuss some last-minute details with Princeton about Markus' case.

"No, ma'am, I am not." Constance punctuated every word.

"Are you serious?"

Constance looked at Lee with a stoic expression. "Yes, ma'am, I am."

"Princeton, what are you going to do with your wife?" Princeton walked in the room as Lee was speaking to Constance.

"Just keep on loving her. That's all I know to do after thirty-five years of marriage." Princeton chided as he put on his suit coat and reached for his briefcase.

"Come on, Lee. Let's go keep my boy out of jail for a long time."

"Alright, Constance. You sure you don't want to go?" Princeton planted a kiss on his wife's lips before heading to the front door.

"I'm positive," she said in a sing-song voice.

"Have you even spoken to Markus since he has gone to jail?" Leona questioned Constance like she was a witness on the stand.

"No, I have not. I have talked to Nicholas every day."

"Well, Nicholas has not been to jail." Princeton laughed, grabbing the doorknob and opening the front door of their home.

Constance didn't break a smile. "I know, and that's why I'm talking to *him*."

"You know people make mistakes all the time, Constance," Leona said, still standing by the kitchen table. "Why don't you extend grace?"

The tension between them was palpable. In the quiet that followed, the gentle ticking of an ornate grandfather clock punctuated the silence.

"Lee, you are wasting your breath. Let's go." With the front door still perched open, Princeton walked back over to the table and leaned down and kissed Constance again, rubbing her back for comfort. "See you when I get back. Love you."

"Love you, too. See you later. I'm cooking roast this evening so come straight home."

"Umm, sounds good. I'll be back for dinner, too," Leona said.

"That's fine, Leona." Constance replied sternly to the youngest Green girl.

Constance stood up from the table and walked behind Princeton and Leona. Princeton had started losing his hair, so he finally shaved it all off. Now he only had a mingle gray beard. His black suit, white shirt and gray tie made him look like a silver fox today she thought, "See y'all later." Constance closed the door behind the pair and headed to her office to journal.

The written word was her new pastime. She thought about asking Charity to help her write her first book, but she was not sure that she would make a good author. She had to admit though, putting words on paper and getting them out of her heart and mind were working wonders for her mood.

Constance stopped by the kitchen and fixed her morning coffee, walked into her office that she'd decorated in brown and cream accents and started reading the journal entry from the day before. Her phone rang, interrupting the silence of the morning. After looking at the caller ID, she answered. "Hello, Mom."

"Hey baby," Bertha said in a chipper tone. "Are you headed to the courthouse?"

"No, I'm not."

"Why not?"

Pursing her lips, Constance held the phone away from her ear and looked at it. "Mom," she said, pulling it back, "I have been over this with you and all your children. I'm not going down there to see Markus. He is fine. His aunts, his dad, and his brother are there."

Bertha held the phone tightly and slowly counted to ten. Constance had always been her stubborn child. The one who would turn the game over if she was losing and cry when it was time to get her spanking.

She breathed heavily into the phone with another exasperated sigh, "You're not going to see your own child? I just really can't believe you. You know your dad would be so disappointed in you if he were alive. He believed in supporting the family."

"I believe in supporting family as well, but I'm not going to continue to support stupidity. Everyone makes excuses for Markus' foolish behavior."

Bertha exhaled hard as she lifted herself from the couch. One hand rested on her hip. "Constance Leann Green Johnson, if you don't get up right now and get to that courthouse, I'm going to come over there myself and get you and drag you out of that house and into that courtroom. A mother stands by her children. He has not even been convicted, yet you are his judge and jury. It's sad. Straighten up right now. I'll see you in about an hour."

"Yes ma'am." Constance was reduced to silence and obedience. She reluctantly got up and made her way to her bedroom to get dressed.

∞ ∞ ∞ ∞ ∞ ∞ ∞ ∞ ∞ ∞ ∞

The county court bailiff stood up and spoke: "All rise. Court is now in session. The Honorable Judge Justin Jennings presiding."

The clerk stood. "The first case on the docket is Susan Parson. Bring her in, bailiff."

Escorted in was a shackled Susan Parson.

Two more prisoners were called before Constance eased into the back of the courthouse. She sat in the last row. The bailiff asked her to remove her shades. With an attitude and a roll of her eyes, she complied.

At exactly 11:19 a.m., Markus Johnson's name was called. When Constance witnessed him being escorted in with chains around his wrists and ankles, she jumped up and screamed, "Take my baby out of those chains. Oh Lord, Markus!" She got up from her seat and started making her way to the door from which Markus came. The bailiff grabbed her by the arm and took her back to her seat. She snatched away from his grip.

"Don't you touch me!" she yelled. "And take my baby out of those handcuffs!"

"Princeton, please get her before we are all held in contempt," Leona whispered to Princeton who was seated at the table beside her.

Princeton stood. "Please excuse me, your Honor. I'm going to get my wife."

"Thank you, Mr. Johnson." The judge sternly stared at Constance.

"Let's continue. Ms. Green, are you ready?"

"Yes sir," Leona said standing up from her seat at the table. "We would like to call the first witness to the stand, Harold Mackens. He is a band member of the Mellow Mosaic band."

Harold, sweating and wringing his hands, approached the witness stand.

Leona began to question the witness. "Mr. Mackens. How are you?"

"I'm well, thank you."

"You were at the club on the night Mr. Johnson was arrested, correct?"

"Yes, ma'am."

"Can you explain to me in detail what happened?"

Harold shifted in his seat then sat up straight. "We were ending our set when Markus said he was going to get our pay for the night and the previous night."

Leona moved closer to the witness stand. "Do you know the terms of your payment arrangement with the club owner, Mr. Jordan?"

"We made a deal for two days a week: one weekday and one weekend day. Weekdays were $700 for the group and weekends were $1500. Each day was 10 percent of the door."

"So how much money did Mr. Jordan give you?"

"We never received anything. That's why Markus went to talk to him after our set was over."

"Do you know what happened in the back?"

"No, all I know is that Markus came out and started handing us money. Then Jordan came out and hit him in the back; they started fighting. Someone called the police. And that was about the end of it."

"Thank you, Mr. Mackens."

Judge Jennings looked at Harold. "Mr. Mackens, did you have a contract? A written contract with Mr. Jordan?"

"No sir, we didn't. It was a verbal contract only. We didn't sign anything."

"How many nights did you all play at the club?"

"We played for two weeks, and we still haven't gotten paid."

"Thank you. You may step down."

"Any other witnesses, Ms. Green?"

"I would like to call Mr. Jordan, the club's owner, to the stand."

"Mr. Jordan, please come forward."

There was no movement in the courtroom.

"Mr. Jordan?" the judge asked again. "Please come forward."

"Ms. Green, if Mr. Jordan is not here, we are forced to dismiss the case. Did he have an attorney?"

"Mr. Jordan contacted me the day after the incident to tell me that he was securing an attorney and that I would hear from the attorney soon, but I have never talked to anyone."

"Case dismissed." The judge stated matter of factly. The courtroom fell silent except for the echo of the banging gavel. "Bailiff, take Mr. Johnson to the back and process him for dismissal. Next case up, please."

And with that, Markus was released from prison. Leona turned to look out at the courtroom, and it was like the sun was shining. The Greens were beaming with joy.

Leona motioned for them to leave the courtroom. Nicholas, Bertha, Carmen, Morgan, Dallas, Jr., Diane, Lilly, Sonya, and Mabel all went out to meet Princeton and Constance in the lobby.

"Whew, Praise God!" Bertha yelled as soon as she exited the courtroom. Her blue gray hair glistening in the light of the courthouse. The smile that covered her face reached each Green that stood around her embracing one another. "God ain't nothing but good! Who wouldn't serve a God like this? I've been praying all week about this court case."

Bertha beamed with pride. "Leona, you did a good job. I'm so proud of you."

Mabel reached out to hug Lee. "Yep, little sis, you handled your business. Dad would be proud of you."

"I didn't do anything." Lee said shyly. Mr. Jordan didn't even show up. That's crazy, isn't it?"

"It's a blessing." Bertha beamed, lifting her eyes toward the ceiling of the building and offering a silent Thank You to God.

"What happened?" Princeton asked as he and Constance walked up, joining the group back from getting some coffee in the cafeteria downstairs.

"Mr. Jordan didn't show up, the judge dismissed the case, so Markus is being processed out right now."

"It will still probably be a couple of hours before he is released." Leona stated to the rest of the Green family.

"Are you going to wait for him, Nicholas?" Constance asked.

"No ma'am. I have a flight to catch this evening."

"Aren't you tired of running around with Sky Airlines?" Constance asked, looking at her oldest son. She was so disappointed that he gave up practicing medicine to become a pilot. She hated that he experienced so pain during the pandemic that he walked away from his calling.

"No ma'am, that's how I make my living and pay my bills," he answered matter of factly. He knew her disdain of his new career, but he was excited and filled with adrenaline each time he was in the cockpit.

"I have an appointment this afternoon, Constance. I have to go, but I will be home for dinner." Princeton hugged and kissed her as he started for the parking garage across the street from the courthouse.

"Me too," Leona added, hugging her older sister.

"Come on, y'all, let's go to the house and prepare a feast for Markus," Bertha said excitedly. "Thank you, Lord. I'm going to make all his favorite dishes."

"Well, I guess I'll wait," Constance said half-heartedly.

"It's the least you can do, since you haven't done anything else," Mabel said.

"Don't start with me, Mabel." Constance announced with clenched fists and a set jaw.

Dismissing Constance, Mabel waved her hands in a beckoning motion at the family. "Let's go, y'all." The Greens walked out of the courthouse leaving their sister to face her son on her own.

Constance got in her car and drove to the other side of the jail where the inmates were released. She found a parking space right in front so Markus would see her. Sitting in the car for an hour and a half gave

Constance time to assess her behavior. She was unkind to her son. She needed to apologize. Her overbearing nature often caused rifts, but she was controlling because she loved her family so much and wanted to make sure they were well taken care of and safe.

Markus walked out of the jailhouse and exhaled deeply. The warmth of the sun found him, and he stood for a moment basking in its power. His movements slow and tired, weakened by days of sitting without his normal gym activities and work life. He looked disheveled and unkempt and a little forlorn. His hair had grown out and he looked like he was wearing a football helmet, it was so big. His beard appeared massive on his face. His skin didn't have its usual natural glow. Perhaps a long hot shower would restore some parts of his glow. He looked around for a moment before he saw his mom's car. With a sigh, he walked over. To his chagrin, she had her eyes closed.

He tapped on the window. "Ma?"

She sprang into action, rolling down the window. "Hey, Markus!"

"Hey, Ma. What are you doing?"

"I was praying for forgiveness. I'm so sorry Markus. Constance kept talking before he could place his bags in the car. "I was not kind to you at all. I was so worried about what the town would say that I didn't think about your feelings."

"It's okay, Ma. Nicholas took good care of me. Dad came to see me and of course your sisters came."

Constance leaned out of the car window and reached for Marcus' hand. "I know, but I should've come. I apologize. I love you son. Next time just call the police instead of taking matters into your own hands."

"I was just mad. You know I have a quick temper."

She squeezed his hand. "Yes honey, I know."

"I was enrolled in anger management classes two times per week."

"Really?"

"Yes ma'am."

"Praise God."

Laughing, Markus opened the back door and threw his bag inside. "Ok, Mom!"

"I love you son. Let's get you home so you can take a shower and clean up. Your grandmother is preparing a feast for you at her house."

"Sounds good." Markus circled the car, climbed in next to Constance, and gave her a hug. In a short time, they arrived at Markus' townhouse. He looked down at his hands and away from his mom. He blinked back tears as they sat in front of his home. "I owe you an apology too, mom. I know better than to take matters into my hands. Dad is an attorney, so I know better, but Jordan was wrong, and I was tired of his mess. I felt like I got the guys into this situation, and I need to be the one to get them out of it." He breathed a deep sigh and stared into space; "I messed up big time. I apologize to you and dad for all this mess."

"It's okay son, I probably would have snatched the money too, " Constance laughed, reaching over to rub the back of Markus' head. He was wrong and in the heat of the moment, I may have done the exact same thing. You have always been a warrior for justice. But learn this lesson and work on that temper."

"Yes ma'am, I love you mom. Markus bent his head and laid it on Constance's shoulder. She laid her head on his and silence engulfed the car. Kissing the top of his head, she pulled away. "I'll see you in about an hour." Tears lingered in both of their eyes; the breach that was broken was being repaired.

"Ok. See you at Grandma's."

"Love you, baby."

"Love you too, Ma."

Constance drove away, tears flowing now. Markus wasn't the only one with anger issues. She needed some help as well. Maybe after seeing Markus' progress, she'd take the first step to secure her healing as well.

CHAPTER 21
REGGIE AND SONYA WARREN

The soft, golden light of early Saturday morning filtered through the lace curtains of the Warren house, casting gentle patterns across the master bedroom. Outside, the world was just beginning to stir, but within the cozy confines of their home, a peaceful silence prevailed, broken only by the rhythmic ticking of a clock on the bedside table.

Reggie lay beside Sonya, the warmth of their shared bed enveloping them. The room held a cozy feel that spoke of unhurried mornings and lingering embraces.

Sonya's skin was soft beneath Reggie's touch as he leaned in, his lips trailing a path of tender kisses across her body.

Despite the warmth of his touch, Sonya couldn't help but laugh softly, a melodious sound that danced in the stillness. "That's how we got into this trouble in the first place," she teased, her voice a playful admonishment as she snuggled deeper into the covers. "We are about to have ten kids running around here, Reggie. Stop it!" Sonya whispered.

Reggie kept tickling her, "I can afford ten more."

"The question is: *Who's going to have them with you?*" Sonya leaned into the pillow and blinked repeatedly at her big strong husband.

"Baby, you wouldn't have them with me?"

"No sir, you're going to have to get a young girl for all that."

"Well, I guess I'll just have to settle for ten instead of twenty."

"You're silly," Sonya laughed.

Reggie grabbed her from behind as she lay on the opposite side of their king-sized bed and kissed her neck.

"Stop for real! You know I can't say no."

"Mom and Dad, what are y'all doing?" Kaylin yelled from outside the door of the master bedroom door.

"We are loving each other," Reggie replied to Kaylin, their oldest daughter while drenching Sonya with kisses.

"Ugh," Kaylin added.

"You guys are #TeamTooMuch!" Kaylin crossed her arms and rolled her eyes as she continued to stand outside the door.

"We are not!" Reggie yelled. "What do you want?"

"This is love, Kaylin," Sonya yelled.

"Can you come make some breakfast for your children?"

Sonya sat up halfway. "I cannot! You can make breakfast for your sisters and brothers and leave us alone."

"Yes, Kaylin, leave us alone." Reggie echoed. "We're trying to fall back in love all over again."

"Y'all get on my nerves." Kaylin sucked her teeth and hit the door before walking away and finding her siblings.

"We love you too, baby." Reggie snuggled closer to Sonya as she lay back down. Out of nowhere, tears rolled down her face.

"I never thought I would have these moments with you," she confessed. "Oh, I was so heartbroken for so long."

Reggie turned Sonya around to face him.

"I'm so sorry, baby. If I could take away those foolish years, I would do it in a heartbeat. I hate that I was so selfish. I love you for fighting for us and taking me back. I need you, Sonya. I was miserable without my family."

"And we were miserable without you."

The pair snuggled a little longer. Listening to each other breathe.

"I want Charity to experience this, Reggie." Sonya cuddled closer and said out of nowhere.

"Experience what?"

"This kind of love; this level of love. Not our struggle, but the good part. The part that makes our hearts sing and our kids happy. I want her to have that. I really thought she was going to get that with Patrick."

Reggie fell silent. *I don't want to get involved with matters of the heart*; he thought, remembering his rule. Sonya and Isaiah were both hopeful romantics, but he wanted no parts of this fiasco. He was determined to have a singular focus on his love life only.

Sonya squeezed Reggie's hand. "Hello."

"I don't want to get involved, Sonya."

"Why?"

"Why get involved with something that may still not be beneficial to Charity, and it could possibly make matters worse. I'm not willing to have her hurt anymore. Charity is good people, and I'd rather not get involved."

"Whatever, Reggie." Sonya moved to get out of bed.

Reggie held her tighter. "You know what the therapist said. 'Whatever is not an acceptable response.' You can't get mad at me and walk away."

Sonya huffed. Reggie kissed her.

"Stop. Reggie"

"Nope." As Reggie planted kisses on her head, he pried, "So you are mad because I don't want to interfere in Charity's love life? You're so cute!"

"You could hook her up with Isaiah." Sonya pouted.

"You and Isaiah are going to have me beat up!" Reggie said, falling back on the bed.

"What do you mean me and Isaiah?"

"He called me and asked me to set him up on a date with Charity when he comes to town for the mentoring camp. He wants you to host a dinner and invite Charity."

"Yes!!!" Sonya yelled. She moved out of Reggie's arms and eased out the bed carrying 8 months of belly with her. Sonya's vibrant joy filled the room.

"I'll start working on it now. It's the third week in March, right?"

Reggie stretched lazily, his muscles protesting the idea of leaving the warmth of the bed and turned over in the bed. "You are just too much."

"Get up, Reggie. We need to clean up the house and make everything nice. Let's plan the menu."

Reggie pulled the comforter and pillow over his head as Sonya kept talking about the dinner party. "Leave me be, woman and keep me out of Isaiah and Charity's affairs."

Ignoring him, Sonya walked out the room still preparing her plans for the big hook up.

Shortly, she came back into the room pulling the comforter off Reggie.

With a resigned chuckle, Reggie finally rolled out of bed, his movements leisurely. I agree with Kaylin, "Team Too Much," he teased, his voice a mixture of admiration and playful exasperation.

Together, they walked out of their bedroom to begin the day. The house seemed to come alive around them as the Warren kids started calling their names. Each new moment was a testament of their resilience and commitment to one another. The past was the past and they were moving forward.

CHAPTER 22
ISAIAH'S ARRIVAL

The bustling atmosphere of the airport came into the view as Reggie pulled into the airport parking lot. The vehicle's interior was spacious and inviting, providing a comfortable refuge from the flurry of activity outside. The faint scent of the car's newness mingled with the crisp air conditioning, creating a refreshing calm quite different from the bustling chaos of the airport terminal.

Reggie, with his strategic driving, navigated the Tahoe smoothly through the crowded airport, the powerful engine purring beneath them.

"Man, it's good to see you again!" Reggie said as he finally maneuvered the truck to the baggage claim area to pick up Isaiah.

Reggie stepped out and greeted Isaiah with a warm brotherly hug.

"How have you been?" Isaiah stepped off the curb bringing his bags to the rear of the car.

"What's up, bro," Reggie replied, a broad grin lighting up his face as he helped Isaiah stow his bags in the back. The Tahoe's trunk closed with a satisfying thud, a signal that their journey was truly underway

"So, man how are things going?" Reggie asked, adjusting his seat belt on and checking the side-view mirror.

"Things are going well. I won't complain. But man, if we could have made it to the playoffs that would have been great!" Isaiah answered with a shake of his head.

"That would have been nice. Those Miami Migrants put on a hell of a show out there." His head shake was a mixture of regret and determination, a reflection of his passion for the game.

Isaiah chuckled, a rueful smile playing on his lips. "Yeah, we played okay. But when we watched the film, I saw a few errors that we need to work on."

Reggie looked at his friend and smiled. "Well, this weekend you are not working on any of that. You are going to take a load off and enjoy yourself."

Their conversation flowed easily, punctuated by shared laughter and the occasional silence filled with understanding.

"I'm looking forward to it!"

"You're going to love these kids. Some of them have hard lives and have developed protective shells, but when you break through that, they turn into different people."

"I know and understand, man. I grew up in the streets with a lot of cats that just couldn't get it together."

"We are blessed, man."

"Man, what! But only for the grace of God, there go I!" Reggie and Isaiah said in unison. They both laughed at their statement that church folks of old still used frequently.

"So how is the family?" Isaiah asked.

"They are good. Sonya is ready to deliver any day now. I think she is mad at me. I know for a fact; she doesn't want another child after this."

"Man, I know there is a Guinness Book of World Records for the largest number of twins that a woman can have."

"I'm sure there is something," Reggie laughed. After a brief pause, he admitted, "But let me be honest. This last set was make-up sex. I was gone for two years. I had to work so hard to get my wife back, that I just couldn't let all this love go to waste!"

"Crazy!" Isaiah said, shaking his head as Reggie pulled onto the freeway.

"Yes, I heard about that fiasco with Tammy and her stealing money." Isaiah rested his head against the seat and let out a deep sigh. "Crazy man."

"That was crazy indeed. Let me give you a word of advice. *Ain't* and I said *ain't* nothing out there. Whenever you find that woman who loves you unconditionally, marry her; make her life as easy as possible financially, emotionally, socially—in every way. When you do right by a good woman, she will do right by you."

"It was a miracle that she took you back." Isaiah stated pensively.

"Only by God's grace. Now it was hard to get her to even look me in the face for a while, but we made it through. Communication is the most important part of a relationship."

"Wow! Really? Not love or trust."

"If you love and trust someone but you never say it, how will they know? You must communicate in every circumstance, no matter what."

Isaiah nodded. "I gotcha."

"Are you seeing anyone?" Before Isaiah could answer, Reggie said, "I saw you with Aimee Fitzgerald on the cover of some magazine."

"Yeah, she wanted to attend the Opera performance with me. I thought it was no big deal until I got home and noticed our pictures everywhere and she was excited and trying to move in."

"You're kidding, man!" Reggie shook his head. "She wanted to move in?"

Isaiah nodded. "After the first date."

"Whew."

"I know, right? The moment I destroy my player card, this happens."

"God will send you someone, and she will be great for you. I can promise you that if you wait on him, *He* is going to send the right girl." The two fist bumped as Reggie changed lanes to exit the highway. "We are running by the house first to drop off your things before we head to the sports complex. Last year, I added a mother-in-law suite to the house. It also serves as my man cave."

Isaiah nodded. "Cool."

Reggie continued, a hint of pride in his voice. "You can stay there, or I have a connection at Reynolds Hotel Chain. You make the choice. I did want my kids to get to meet you and talk to you."

Isaiah considered the options, his decision coming easily. "The guest house is fine," he said with a warm smile. "I'm honored that you would allow me to stay the night."

As they pulled into the driveway, the house seemed to welcome them with open arms, its charm and warmth a reflection of the family that called it home. Reggie's offer was more than just a place to stay, it was an invitation to be part of the familial structure of the Warren household. For Isaiah, it was a gesture that spoke volumes of the enduring bond between friends who had weathered many of life's ups and downs together.

∞ ∞ ∞ ∞ ∞ ∞ ∞ ∞ ∞ ∞ ∞

The familiar hum of the garage door opening was a signal that sent waves of excitement rushing through the Warren household. As Reggie maneuvered the Tahoe into the garage, the air was suddenly filled with the joyous cries of his children, their voices a chorus of welcome love.

"Daddy's home!" April's voice rang out, as she dashed to the door enthusiastically only a child could muster. Her declaration was quickly followed by a chorus of her siblings, Keith and Jaylin calling out, "Hey, Dad!"

"Hey, Dad!" the Warren kids yelled in unison as Reggie walked through the door. "Hey babies!" His heart swelled at the voices of his children. He knew he was blessed. He loved the cheerful chaos that was his life.

The children's attention quickly shifted to Isaiah, their excitement palpable as they recognized the famous guest. "It's Isaiah King!" Jaylin exclaimed, his eyes wide with awe, as he bounded over to greet the visitor. Keith was hot on his heels, his own enthusiasm evident as he echoed his brother's sentiments. "Whoa. Hey, Mr. King!" he added, his voice reverberating with admiration.

Isaiah chuckled, his smile warm and genuine as he gently corrected them, "Just Isaiah is fine. Mr. King is my dad."

"Hey, Isaiah." Sonya waddled into the room and grabbed Isaiah's arm and patted it. "I would give you a hug, but this belly is much too big for that. How are you?"

"I'm good." He leaned forward, hugging as much of her as he could. "Reggie said that I can stay in the guest house this weekend. I really appreciate it."

Rubbing her belly and smiling, Sonya was beaming with joy. She was excited to start plotting the hook up with Isaiah and Charity. Coming back to the present conversation, she continued, "I wouldn't have it any other way. You're *practically* family." Sonya's eyes twinkled with a mischievous glint as she responded to Isaiah.

Reggie placed the bags on the floor. "We are just dropping his bags off before we head down to the sports complex to see the kids." He explained, his voice filled with anticipation for the day ahead. The room buzzed with a sense of belonging and camaraderie, the Warren home once again proving to be a sanctuary of love and laughter.

"Okay that's fine. When you get back, we'll have dinner waiting. Are you taking the younger kids with you?"

"I can, that's fine. You, ok?" Reggie asked. He walked over and began to rub Sonya's back.

"I'm good, just a little tired." Sonya yawned.

"Don't overdo it, Sonya. Just order take-out."

"No, Reggie," Sonya leaned on the counter and protested Reggie's demands. "I want Isaiah to have a home-cooked meal."

"He's a big boy. He can cook for himself."

"I'm cooking and that's that on that. Y'all leave me alone so I can get started."

Shaking his head, Reggie leaned down and kissed her. "I love you gal. Take it easy." He turned to Isaiah. "Come on King. Kids, if you are rolling with me, get ready to get in the car. Once we put King's bags in the guest house, we're headed out."

Feet started moving as Reggie and Isaiah made their way outside.

∞ ∞ ∞ ∞ ∞ ∞ ∞ ∞ ∞ ∞ ∞

As they walked towards the guest house, Isaiah spoke, his voice tinged with a hint of envy. "Is it okay to say I'm jealous?"

"Of what? Why?" Reggie raised an eyebrow, glancing at Isaiah with curiosity.

"Man, this life and this love. That's exactly what I want."

"You see how that woman loves you?" Isaiah continued, gesturing towards the house where Sonya busied herself in the kitchen.

"I know." Reggie grinned like a Cheshire cat.

"How did you ever mess that up?"

"Being foolish."

"I'm truly glad you got her back!"

"Man, me too!"

Upon reaching the guest house, Reggie opened the door with a flourish. "This is where you will be staying for the weekend."

Isaiah gawked as he stepped inside the man cave, his eyes widening in appreciation. A large flat-screen TV dominated one wall, hanging above an aquarium teeming with colorful fish. A vast leather sectional couch sat invitingly in the corner, capable of seating several adults comfortably. The suite boasted a full-size, fully stocked refrigerator and, next to it, a wine holder. A microwave was neatly built into the cabinet over the stove.

Isaiah smiled, his eyes taking in the luxurious surroundings. "This is nice!"

"Yeah man, I love this place. With eight kids, every once in a while, I have to duck out."

"I bet."

Reggie patted Isaiah on the shoulder. "Let's head out, man. We're going to be late."

"Yeah, let's roll!"

CHAPTER 23
THE UNOFFICIAL DATE

Sonya's fingers danced over her phone, her demeanor a mix of determination and playfulness. The room was quiet, except for the rhythmic ticking of a clock that seemed to harmonize with her racing heartbeat. The Warren household was normally not quiet, but the kids were at school, and this was her favorite time of day to think and plan. She didn't know why, but she was a bit anxious to call Charity. She glanced at the clock, noting the time: 9:00 a.m. *It's not too early*, she decided, picked up the phone, and pressed it to her ear, a hopeful smile lifting her lips. It was time to put her plan in place.

"Hey, Charity," Sonya greeted, her voice warm and inviting. "I'm hosting a dinner for Isaiah and I'm calling to invite you."

The other end of the line was momentarily silent, and Sonya could almost picture Charity's expression, as she considered the invitation. Charity, always one to value her time and commitments, responded with a gentle shake of her head, though Sonya couldn't see it. "I'm busy," she replied, her voice carrying a hint of reluctance.

Sonya's eyebrows arched in amusement, her tone taking on a teasing edge. "Really? That's funny," she remarked, a playful challenge in her words. "I didn't tell you the date or the time."

Charity's response was firm, "Whenever it is, I'm busy."

Sonya leaned into her plea, her voice taking on a playful, persuasive tone. "Charity," she whined gently, stretching her name in a persistent manner, "please come."

"Why? "Charity asked her voice, void of emotion.

"Because I like Isaiah, and I want you to experience this feeling that I have with Reggie with someone. And I think Isaiah would be a good option."

"Really? Why?" Charity repeated her question and waited patiently for Sonya's response.

"He's funny, kind, adorable, and he's definitely fine. He's also God-fearing and down to earth."

"Oh really? I would love to meet this Isaiah, because the one I met with was just a jerk."

"Please, Charity. Please!"

Sonya turned the tables on Charity. "You owe us a favor anyway. Remember we went to Milwaukee with you."

"How can you hold that over me? You and Reggie had a good time."

"Please, Charity!" Sonya continued begging.

"Oh, ok! What time is dinner, Sonya?"

Sonya smiled and did a slight bounce making sure not to move too quickly with the twins in her belly. "It's today at 5:30 p.m. sharp."

"Ok Sonya, see you then," Charity offered half-heartedly.

∞ ∞ ∞ ∞ ∞ ∞ ∞ ∞ ∞ ∞ ∞

Sonya outdid herself. The dining room table was weighed down with an array of delectable delights: juicy hot dogs in freshly baked buns, sizzling hamburgers with an assortment of toppings, and a taco station with a colorful spread of tacos brimming with seasoned meat and fresh vegetables. Sonya also had a refreshing salad station with spiced salmon, grilled to perfection. The atmosphere was set for an exciting and memorable meal.

As Reggie and Isaiah returned from the Boys to Men Mentoring Program training camp, Sonya's face lit up with pride. Her eyes sparkled as she surveyed the culinary spread, she had lovingly prepared, with Kaylin's assistance throughout the day.

Reggie's gaze swept over the impressive display, and his face broke into a wide grin. "Wow, baby, you've outdone yourself!" he exclaimed, his voice full of admiration.

"We're doing dinner buffet style tonight," Sonya announced, her voice bright with enthusiasm. "So, everyone, just dig in and enjoy!"

Isaiah, eager and curious, looked around expectantly. "Where's Charity?" he inquired without missing a beat. "Is she still coming?"

"She should be on her way," Sonya replied, her tone reassuring. "She had a few errands to run first." As if on cue, the doorbell chimed, and Charity stepped into the Warren home, bypassing the need to knock—leaning on the open-door policy that the Green family cherished, where everyone was welcome.

"Hey, family!" Charity greeted everyone as she entered, her voice sounding like a melodious song.

The kids yelled as they ran to hug her, their faces bright with happiness. "Hey Charity!"

"Come on in." Sonya rubbed her belly and smiled even brighter. "Let's gather and say grace." She turned and grabbed and squeezed Reggie's hand. "Honey, say grace, please."

Reggie could tell his wife was excited about the evening and said a silent prayer that this wouldn't be a fiasco. "God, bless the food and the hands that prepared it. Let it be very delicious and oh so nutritious. In Jesus' name, Amen."

"Everybody dig in!" Sonya, who was just like her mom, Bertha Green, was beaming. She wanted everyone to eat her food and enjoy it. She truly enjoyed preparing food and watching people eat and enjoy it!

∞ ∞ ∞ ∞ ∞ ∞ ∞ ∞ ∞ ∞ ∞

The dinner table buzzed with lively conversation and laughter. Everyone recounted the highlights of their day, from the mentoring program's triumphs to the playful antics that had unfolded in the Warren house.

As the evening progressed, Sonya and Charity moved into the kitchen, rolled up their sleeves as they tackled the aftermath of the feast that Sonya had prepared. The clinking of plates and the gentle swish of water filled the space, as they partook in light conversation.

Isaiah sauntered into the kitchen. He leaned casually against the counter where Charity was stacking clean plates. "Charity, let's go get some ice cream or something," he proposed, his voice carrying a note of hopeful anticipation.

Charity, focused on her task, didn't immediately meet his gaze. "Why? There's dessert right here," she replied, her tone teasing as she gestured toward the leftover treats.

Isaiah smiled, undeterred by her initial reluctance. "I'd like to spend some time alone with you. I promise I won't bite," he assured, a playful glint in his eyes.

Charity chuckled, unable to resist his charm. "I've seen your footage, that's a lie," she quipped, her laughter ringing out like a sweet melody.

"You're funny; have you ever thought about being a comedian?" Isaiah asked, his admiration evident.

"No, I have never thought about being a comedian. I'm content with being a writer," Charity replied, her voice filled with quiet pride as she continued to wash and dry the dishes.

Charity tried to maintain her composure, but a playful eye roll and a soft sigh betrayed her growing interest in Isaiah's invitation. With a dramatic flourish, she set the dish towel down and turned to face him, her gaze appraising. "Come on, Isaiah," she relented, a hint of mischief in her smile. "I guess I'm driving."

"I guess, or I could call a car service." He joked as he followed closely behind Charity.

"Whatever. I said ok. Come on let's go," Charity grumbled.

The pair stepped into the cool night air, the gentle rustling of leaves accompanying their silent journey to Charity's Honda civic. Charity maneuvered the car out of the driveway, her gaze fixed on the road ahead, while Isaiah turned his attention to the passing scenery.

For ten minutes, the car hummed steadily, the only sound in the car was their shared silence. The quiet was comfortable, yet filled with anticipation, until Charity's voice finally pierced the stillness. "You're awfully quiet. What's going on?" she inquired, gently.

Isaiah shifted slightly in his seat, his eyes still trained on the window. "Nothing," he replied, his voice soft and nonchalant.

Charity chuckled, a melodic sound that danced in the air between them. "Nothing, really? A one-liner. You're funny," she teased, her eyes glancing briefly in his direction.

"Why do you say that?"

"Because you made such a huge oration about having this date with me and then we get here, and you say nothing. What is this all about?"

"Can I be honest?" Isaiah asked as he stared at her through the darkness of the car.

"Would you be dishonest?" Charity looked over at Isaiah.

"You know you are something else." Isaiah said of Charity's candidness.

"Really?"

"Yep."

Isaiah rubbed his open palms together. "The honest truth is that I'm totally overwhelmed and a little nervous."

Charity raised an eyebrow. "I really don't think that's true."

With disbelief in his eyes, he turned to face Charity. "Why don't you believe me?"

Offering a measured smile, her tone laced with gentle skepticism, Charity continued. "You're a renowned football player who has been linked with some of the most stunning women on the planet. I can't imagine you're intimidated by someone like me."

"You know something?" he began, his voice a mixture of reflection and sincerity. "I've dated some of the world's most beautiful women, but beauty is the simplest quality to possess. Try being kind, committed, loyal, funny, smart, and intelligent. You might find beauty, but the other qualities are far more elusive."

Charity shrugged lightly, a playful glint in her eyes. "I suppose."

"Charity," he continued, his tone earnest and deliberate, "I just don't want to misstep or say something wrong. I want you to like me, just as much as I like you."

With a teasing inflection in her voice, Charity asked, "And just how much do you like me?"

"I like you more than two football fields put together." Isaiah widened his large muscular arms that extended from one arm to the other.

"Now who's the comedian? How can you like me? You don't even know me."

"That's why we are here. I am trying to get to know you, but you know you're very guarded."

Charity searched for a response. She thought to herself, *no response is a response* and remained quiet.

Isaiah tapped on the dashboard. "Hello?"

"Hello," Charity smiled, coming back to reality.

"You have a lot of walls up."

"I don't think so."

Isaiah threw his head back and groaned. "Really? Girl, you got more walls than No. 45 had when he was trying to build the border at Mexico."

"Whatever, Isaiah!"

Charity pulled the car up to Mr. Randy's Ice Cream Shop. She and Joi came here with Martha Love all the time. She felt melancholy as she slowly got out of the car and thought about her mom. Strawberry banana fudge nut was her favorite mixed flavor.

"You, ok?" Isaiah asked Charity.

"Yes, I'm fine. This place just brings back so many memories of my mom. Happy memories."

They strolled into the ice cream parlor, where a wave of nostalgia washed over Charity, enveloping her in memories of simpler times. The shop was a charming blend of retro decor and the sweet aroma of freshly made desserts. After selecting their favorite flavors, they settled into a cozy booth that offered a panoramic view of Main

Street. Mr. Randy's was a quaint mom-and-pop shop mixed with the newness of a growing business with much more to explore and offer.

Isaiah reached across the table and grabbed her hand. "I want to help you knock them down."

"Knock what down?"

"Charity, stop playing. All the walls that that you have built up around your heart!"

"Hmm really?"

"Yep, I'm strong." He flexed a muscle.

"You're silly."

"Will you let me knock the walls down?" Isaiah's expression was serious.

"I think that is something I need to do on my own."
"So, you're putting more walls up?" Isaiah's voice was gentle, yet probing, as he tried to navigate the terrain of her emotions. His gaze was steady, filled with genuine concern.

Charity's response was silence, a quiet that seemed to stretch between them, thick with unvoiced thoughts and feelings. Her fingers traced the rim of her bowl absently. She appeared lost in contemplation, her eyes cast downward, avoiding Isaiah's earnest gaze.

Redirecting the conversation, Isaiah meddled further into Charity's life. "So, how'd you get into writing?"

"Grief. My granddad died and I was crazy about him. It was the first time that I experienced an up close and in person death of anyone and I was so sad." Her body relaxed but only slightly. "I didn't know what to do with all the pain and sadness, so I wrote a poem about him and the rest is history."

The door opened and a group of lively high school students ran inside talking loudly. "I just started writing and I have never stopped. When I was happy, I would write. When I was sad, I would write. Any occasion is an occasion for writing."

"Do you only write fiction books?"

"No, I write all kinds of books. Self-care, self-help, education, business, finance, instructional nonfiction, and fiction. I just released a blog as well. Writing is cathartic for me."

"Wow! You're brilliant!" Isaiah beamed with pride.

"Not really, I've just found a way to express myself. Some would say I am a Jill of all trades, mastering none."

"Walls!" Laughing, he tossed both hands up.

"What?" Charity stared at Isaiah with wide eyes and a look of confusion.

"The right answer was, thank you!"

Charity exhaled hard. "Thank you." She then turned the spotlight on Isaiah. "How did you become a professional football player?"

"My dad was a high school football coach, and the last thing I wanted to do was play the game."

"Why? Didn't you want to be on your dad's team?" Charity questioned. Scooping up the last part of her ice cream cone with her tongue.

"I thought he was mean; that he worked those guys too hard."

"I bet he did. But he was a good coach, I'm sure."

"He was, but I didn't want to have to deal with him at home and at school, so I played basketball, ran track, and had a brief run-in with soccer." Isaiah leaned back in his chair reminiscing about his former athletic days in high school.

"A brief *run-in?*" Charity chuckled.

"Yes. My soccer coach didn't know anything about soccer. He was an economics teacher, and his job was about to be cut. The principal told him he could keep it if he coached. He literally had a book on the sidelines and was reading as we played."

"No way!" Charity giggled.

"Yes, way. I played half the season and walked away. My dad said that it was time, and I started out with football under his tutelage. He was strict and firm but believed in winning. So, we won the state championship that year and the rest is history."

"Wow!" Engaged in the conversation, her writer's mind and imagination at work, Charity wanted more of the story, "Is your dad still coaching?"

"No, he retired two years ago and now he and my mom just travel and badger me and my sister about grandkids."

"That's funny." Isaiah sat up in his seat and laughed. "Not really, but I just shake my head at them."

"You want kids?" Charity held her breath waiting for an answer. She never thought she would start to like him, but she felt her heart softening to him. She could see why so many liked him now that she'd had some time to hang out with him.

"Of course! A whole house full, like Reggie."

Charity doubled over laughing before she could catch herself. "You better find a strong willing woman to do that."

"I have. I've found one already."

"Really? What does she do? Does she know? Have you told her? What's her name?"

"Charity Love."

"Charity Love," she repeated. "You're so funny. You really should be a comedian."

After wiping his hands with a napkin, Isaiah stood up and extended his hand to Charity. "Let's go, Mrs. King."

Charity looked around.

"Who are you looking for?"

"Who? I'm looking for Mrs. King."

"You're funny."

"Am I?"

"Yes."

"You know I don't want the babies without a wife first."

"Oh, ok."

"Is that your favorite phrase?"

"Indeed, it is."

Isaiah pulled Charity out of her seat like she was as light as a feather and grabbed her close with their faces just an inch away from one another, almost kissing her. "Let's go. I have an early flight tomorrow."

Charity gasped for air. "You play too much!"

"It's my job to play. I get paid to play." Holding her hand in his, he pushed her chair to the table.

"Then play with somebody who likes to play."

"You don't like to play, Charity?" He looked at her inquisitively. "Tell me you like to play, please!"

Without saying a word, Charity released his grip and walked out of the ice cream shop right to the driver side of her car and unlocked the doors. "Get in."

"So bossy!" Isaiah teased.

Charity felt relaxed as she eased into the car with Isaiah. She had to admit he was funny and easy to talk to, and as much as she didn't want to admit it, she was enjoying his company.

"Seriously, I enjoyed spending time with you," he leaned closer to Charity once they were in the car. "What about you? Tell the truth."

"I enjoyed it. I did enjoy it." She said it as if convincing herself. "I had a good time."

Isaiah leaned back into the passenger seat. "I want to do it again, very soon. I'm going to my parents' home for a few weeks. You should meet me there; have dinner with me one night. They live in Nashville."

Charity gave it some thought. "I may come. I'm not sure. But I'll let you know if I get that way. I think it's a bit much that you want me to meet your parents so early."

"Why? I'm trying to court you," Reggie blurted out without thinking. He knew he wanted to spend as much time with Charity as possible.

"I don't know that this is going to work, Isaiah. I'm older than you and every time I see you in the paper or on TV, you're with a new woman. I've had a man to leave me for a beautiful woman. I can't do that again. I just don't think we're compatible."

"Wait? Why? How do you know?" You're basing your decision on what some other guy did. You have got to be kidding me!" He leaned back in the seat and took a deep breath.

"The dating process reveals compatibility. You get to meet new people and find out what you like and don't like. When we start courting, we'll find out if we're compatible or not."

"We shall see, Isaiah."

"I'll text you my parents' address."

"How? You don't have my number!" Do you have my number?"

Isaiah let out a sinister laugh. "Whoops sorry. You didn't give me your number? I wasn't supposed to tell you. You were supposed to just give it to me while we were out on our date tonight but you're so stubborn."

Charity couldn't help but to laugh.

As they pulled up to Sonya and Reggie's house, Isaiah rubbed Charity's hand. "Are you coming in?"

"No, it's late. I'm going to head home." Before she could protest even more, he leaned over and merged her lips with his and eased his tongue into her mouth for a long kiss.

Once they separated, Charity shook her head. "You don't play fair."

Isaiah looked at Charity and grabbed a piece of her curly hair. "I don't think that's the nature of the game."

He opened the door and said, "Goodnight, Love, Love, be careful I'll text you in about thirty minutes to make sure you made it home safely."

"Ok." Charity drove home wondering what was to come of this thing with Isaiah.

CHAPTER 24
THE DINNER

Charity pulled into the driveway of Isaiah's parents' home that stretched out like a winding ribbon, bordered by lush greenery and vibrant flowers. The house itself was a charming blend of traditional architecture and modern elegance.

Isaiah moved with an easy grace as he jogged down the expanse of the driveway, his steps light and purposeful. His presence was magnetic, exuding a confidence that was both natural and inviting. The crisp white of his shirt contrasted sharply with his caramel skin. His black chinos added a touch of sophistication to his casual demeanor. His broad smile, bright and genuine, lit up the features on his face and made him even more handsome.

Charity, stepping out of her car, was mesmerized by the beauty of the surroundings. The journey from Memphis had been long and taxing, the highway stretching endlessly before her. The drive was stressful. With each mile, her emotions and thoughts ran recklessly around her mind, exhausting her before she even made it to the house.

Questions and thoughts swirled around her mind. *Why am I coming to see this man? What if this is all a joke to just use me up and spit me out?* she asked herself. Charity repeatedly contemplated the day that lay ahead. It wasn't like her to be vulnerable and open especially when whatever was happening with Isaiah wasn't clear. By the time she pulled up to Isaiah's parents' home, she was mentally exhausted.

Yet, as she beheld Isaiah's welcoming figure, her apprehensions began to melt away, replaced by a tentative sense of anticipation. His arms, outstretched in a gesture of open affection greeted her.

Isaiah enveloped Charity in a warm embrace, providing comfort that momentarily made the journey less exhausting. Despite her initial instinct to pull back, the sincerity of his gesture coaxed her into relaxing, if only for a moment. His voice, rich and soothing, carried his familiar cadence. "How was the drive?" he asked, his tone infused with genuine interest and concern.

Charity smiled, her initial hesitation and doubt giving way to a sense of ease. "It was pretty decent," she admitted, her voice tinged with nostalgia. "You know I'm used to driving to Nashville. I made the drive all the time when my cousins went to Tennessee State University. Nashville is like a second home to me."

After a book signing in Memphis, she drove the three hours to meet his parents. As Isaiah grabbed her from the car in a warm embrace, she let herself relax for just a moment and leaned into the musky smell of his cologne. He looked like he'd stepped off *the cover of* GQ, Charity thought to herself.

Isaiah smiled. "Glad to know you're familiar with Nashville since your in-laws live here in Nashville. They are excited to meet you, and I'm excited to show you off to them and the world. I've told them all about you."

Charity stiffened, pulled back and looked at Isaiah. "What did you tell them about me?"

"Nothing really, just that you are a beautiful talented writer who owns her own publishing company and puts up walls for a living."

"You did not!" Charity playfully hit Isaiah on the arm.

"I'm just kidding, my love." Grabbing her hand, they started walking toward the front door, Isaiah turned Charity around in an embrace. "Give me a kiss before we walk in."

"No!"

"No? Why?" Isaiah looked at Charity in shock and awe. Rarely did women tell him no. Honestly, rarely did anyone tell him no. He was a celebrity in his own right and not used to people not catering to him.

"Because your parents are probably peeping out the window right now." Charity stated with a glimmer in her eye.

"Who cares?" Isaiah asked holding her hand in his and rubbing her inner palm.

"I care!" Charity announced louder than she meant to. "And stop rubbing my hand like that. You know what you're doing!"

"Walls!" Isaiah stopped rubbing her inner palm but laid a quick kiss on her cheek.

Shocked, Charity shook her head and said, "Whatever, Isaiah."

"I don't like that word."

"What word?"

"Whatever. And I don't care about your walls either." He spun Charity around until she was face-to-face with him. They were so close she could feel his breath on her neck. "I'm tearing those walls down one by one."

"Are you?" Charity wrapped her arms around Isaiah and leaned in for a deep hug.

"Are you still spending the night at your cousin Misty's house?"

"Yes, I've already called her to let her know that I'm coming."

"You know I could get you a hotel room or better yet, my parents offered to let you stay here as well."

"Maybe next time. I think it will be fun to spend the night with Misty. We haven't seen each other for years. It will be like old times."

"Ok, cool. I just wanted to make the offer."

"And I appreciate it."

As they walked slowly to the front door, Charity paused.

"Are you ok?" Isaiah asked.

Charity nodded. Her nerves started rumbling around and dancing to an exotic beat in her stomach. She hadn't met a significant others' parents in years. Not since she formally met the Fitzpatrick's when she was still in high school. Now here she was again, learning a new set of parents. "I'm good. Let's do this."

As Isaiah opened the door, a wave of warm, home-cooked goodness hit her nose. The house was cozy, and the walls adorned with photographs capturing cherished memories and moments. "Mom and

Dad, this is Charity," Isaiah announced, his voice carrying the pride of introducing someone special to his family.

Isaiah's parents, Emma and Isaiah Sr., moved forward with open arms. Emma, a woman whose presence exuded kindness, enveloped Charity in a hug. Her eyes sparkled with warmth, the corners crinkling in delight as she took in Charity's presence. Isaiah Sr., a man with a gentle strength about him, followed suit. "Charity, you're such a pretty girl. Isaiah has told us so much about you. You're a writer and own your own publishing company? That's so wonderful," her voice full of admiration and pride.

Charity blushed slightly, her cheeks tinged with a soft pink as she nodded, her heart swelling with appreciation for such a warm welcome. "Thank you, Mrs. King," she replied, her voice filled with gratitude.

Isaiah Sr.,'s deep voice resonating with curiosity, chimed in, "What do they call that, Emma?"

"Black Girl Magic, Isaiah," Emma responded with a playful shake of her head, her eyes dancing with amusement. "He's too much," she added, casting a loving glance at her husband.

Mrs. Emma had set an elegant table set with her best china. The room was filled with the aroma of the meal. And Charity was hungry and ready to eat. The centerpiece, a vibrant bouquet of fresh flowers, added a splash of color to the table, echoing the warmth and hospitality that filled the room.

"Come on in, baby, and take a seat at the table. I have prepared roast, cabbage, corn on the cob, and for dessert, strawberry cake with vanilla ice cream," Emma invited with such warmth and kindness.

"That sounds amazing!" Charity exclaimed, her eyes widening with delight as she took a seat, waiting to taste the food prepared by Mrs. Emma.

Isaiah Jr. stood at the head of the table and bowed his head. His voice, rich and sincere, filled the room as he prayed, "Lord, thank you for this food. Thank you for my mother who prepared it with love and thank you for another opportunity to fellowship with family and friends. We pray this prayer in Jesus' name. Amen."

Isaiah looked around the table. "Let's eat!"

"We don't meet strangers, Charity. You just dig in and fix your plate. Anything you don't see, just ask for it and I will get it for you." Mrs. King started fixing her husband's plate.

"The food looks delicious, Mrs. King." Feeling relaxed with the King family, Charity made her plate making sure to get a little of everything on the table before sitting down next to Isaiah.

"Thank you. I love to cook." Isaiah's mother beamed as the compliments came in from Charity and nods from her husband and son.

"I can tell."

Charity, a nosey busy body, immediately started asking questions as the feast was beginning. Intrigued by this warm and loving family, she wanted to find out more. "How was Isaiah as a child?"

"He hasn't changed much," his father answered, wiping his mouth and leaning back in this chair. "He was always playing sports. He was interested in all sports for a while and then he finally realized that football was where it was. He was a quiet child most of the time. But his baby sister was so talkative that he didn't need to talk. Have you met our daughter, Rachel?" You could feel the visceral love of Isaiah, Sr. as he spoke about his children. His eyes sparkled with pride and joy.

"I haven't. I have heard so much about her, though."

"She's a whirlwind. And Jr. has spoiled her more than we have."

"I have not!" Isaiah Jr. disagreed.

"If we said no to anything that she wanted, she would call her big brother in a heartbeat."

"And what would he do?" Charity glanced at Isaiah with a smug smile.

"Buy her whatever she wanted."

The doorbell rang as dinner continued. "Sr., get the door please." Mrs. King nodded to him as she continued eating.

Mr. King stood up and put his napkin in his chair. "Are you expecting someone, Emma?"

"Not a soul other than my baby boy and Charity."

"Jr. you have a visitor," Sr. called out.

Isaiah got up to go to the front door and ran smack dab into his friend, Kimberly Troy. He frowned. "What are you doing here?"

"I heard you were in town, and I wanted to see you," Kim grabbed Isaiah in a tight embrace. Five seven and size zero, Kim was all legs. She could easily be a supermodel. Her unbridled curly auburn hair was her trademark.

"I have company. Can you come back later?"

"No, I'm here now, Isaiah," Kim purred like a kitten.

Kim walked past Isaiah into the dining room where Charity sat with Isaiah's parents. "Hey, everyone." She looked directly at Charity. "Hey, I'm Kim."

"Hey Kim," Charity responded politely.

Isaiah looked at Charity with hooded eyes.

Mrs. King invited Kim into the kitchen to fix her plate. Isaiah's dad went to join his mom in the kitchen.

Isaiah sat down at the table with Charity.

Silence followed.

Finally, Charity took a deep breath and asked, "Who's that girl? Is she staying for dinner?"

"She's an old friend, and yes," Isaiah answered curtly. His eyes remained on his dinner plate and more silence ensued before Charity spoke again.

"Oh ok, well I'll go." Her voice was low and muffled and almost a whisper.

"Ok," Isaiah answered.

"Ok? Really?" Charity's voice grew louder as she struggled to maintain her composure.

"Really what?" Isaiah put his head down on the table for a brief second before he looked up at Charity.

"So, you don't care if I go?" Charity pushed her plate aside and looked Isaiah in the eyes. Her normally pleasant personality was gone now and the gentle nature that she was known for was replaced with a stare of confusion.

"I do care, but I don't want a scene."

"Oh ok, WOW! Well, I'll be sure not to make a scene on my way out." Charity picked up her purse and stared at Isaiah for a moment. Just then, Mr. and Mrs. King were walking back into the dining room.

"It was nice meeting you Mr. and Mrs. King," Charity stated as she got up from the dinner table, gave each a hug and started towards the front door. Mr. and Mrs. King looked perplexed and confused and looked from Charity to Isaiah. Finally standing near the front door, Charity thanked the Kings for dinner again.

Mr. King, Isaiah's dad, followed her, "You leaving so soon Charity?"

Yes sir, I have a long drive back home tomorrow and I should get my rest. It was such a pleasure meeting you and your wife. You're such sweet people. Thank you for your hospitality."

Mr. King opened the front door of their home for Charity and stepped on the porch with her. Before she could turn to walk away, Mr. King grabbed her hand. "Kim's mom and my wife are best friends. She's always welcome, but I can understand your position."

Mr. King continued before Charity could respond, "My son should have said something, but he is not one for drama or conflict unless it's on a football field. I apologize for any confusion." His kind eyes held Charity's for a moment. He looked so sincere.

Holding back tears, Charity simply nodded her head at Mr. King. She turned, head held high and walked down the steps of their front porch. that strong lonely walk. She walked that strong lonely walk back to her car and drove away.

∞ ∞ ∞ ∞ ∞ ∞ ∞ ∞ ∞ ∞ ∞

As Charity drove away, Isaiah met his father on the porch watching the car become distant in the horizon. Walking back into the house and heading straight to the dining room, Isaiah stared blankly at the half-finished plate in front of him. Regret running his thoughts. His parents were quiet as they joined him at the table.

Isaiah's parents were seated at the table, their usual lively conversation replaced by a quietness that seemed to settle over the room with an unexpected weight.

Kim sat savoring her meal with a contented smile. Her eyes sparkled with genuine appreciation as she complimented Mrs. Emma, her words a heartfelt acknowledgment of the love and care that went into every dish. "Mrs. Emma, you've outdone yourself again. I have loved your cooking since I was a little girl."

Mrs. Emma received the praise with a warm smile, her eyes crinkling in delight. "Thank you, sweetie. How is your mom? I didn't see her at the bridge club meeting last week."

Kim paused, her fork poised over her plate as she considered her response. Pushing her plate to the center of the table, she smiled and replied, "She was visiting her grandkids in North Carolina. You know my brother has two sons that she absolutely adores."

"Aww, that's so sweet. I can't wait to have grandkids," Mrs. Emma smiled and glanced at Isaiah.

The tension in the room mounted immediately and substantially.

Isaiah leaned back in his chair and let out a deep breath before standing and walking into the kitchen. The soft tap of his footsteps echoed in the silent room as he made his way to the kitchen, seeking a moment of solitude.

Kim looked from Mrs. Emma to Isaiah Sr. and with quiet resolve made her announcement, "I think I will go ahead and go home."

As she gathered her purse, she called out to Isaiah, "Isaiah, I'm leaving."

Isaiah looking at Kim with hooded eyes as he made his way back to the dining room from the kitchen. He waited patiently for Kim to hug his parents before he escorted her to the door.

"Isaiah, I wasn't trying to run your date off," she smirked as she opened the door.

Isaiah quiet and determined not to engage with Kim, simply nodded. Nonchalantly, he stated, "She will be okay. I am sure of it. I will call her later and make amends."

"It was good seeing you, Isaiah. Always is… ", her sentence faded off as he turned to walk back in the house. Closing the door gently behind him, he made his way back to the dining room and sat in the same chair where he sat before Charity left.

Concerned registered on the faces of Mr. and Mrs. King, as they watched their only son closely. Mrs. King was the first to speak, her voice gentle yet probing. "Isaiah, what happened? Charity seemed so upset."
Isaiah sighed deeply, running a hand through his hair. "Kim just showed up out of nowhere, Mom. I didn't know she was coming. And Kim likes to be messy. I didn't feel like having a huge fight in your home."

Mr. King nodded, understanding in his eyes. "We know, but Kim is like family to us. Maybe you should have been more upfront with Charity. Although In understand, it was a bit much for her to handle for another woman to show up at a dinner at your parents' home."

Silence filled the room for a moment, each King lost in thought. Isaiah's mind wandered back to the time he and Kim had spent together, recalling the easy camaraderie they once shared. But he also remembered why they had parted ways and decided that they were better off friends and how Charity had brought a new light, a new perspective into his life.

Finally, Mrs. King spoke again, her tone a mix of wisdom and encouragement. "Isaiah, you need to talk to Charity. Explain things to her and let her know where she stands. It's important for her to feel secure."

Isaiah nodded; determination settled in his eyes. "You're right. I need to make things right with Charity. I don't want her to feel pushed aside."

Mr. King smiled, a proud look crossing his face. "That's our boy. Just be honest with her. Communication is key, son."

As the family continued their dinner, the atmosphere slowly shifted from tension to ease.

∞ ∞ ∞ ∞ ∞ ∞ ∞ ∞ ∞ ∞ ∞ ∞

The drive to Misty's house was a blur for Charity. As she neared the house, the familiar landmarks of the neighborhood came into view. Charity parked her car in the driveway, the engine's gentle purr fading into silence as she turned off the ignition.

For the next thirty minutes, she sat in the quiet sanctuary of her vehicle, her eyes fixed on the neighborhood. Her mind wandered as her thoughts vied for her attention trying to make sense of the night's event.

Her phone, resting on the passenger seat, vibrated repeatedly. Charity glanced at it briefly, Isaiah's name flashing across the screen. It wasn't until the sixth call that she finally picked up, her voice carrying a hint of weariness.

"Hey," she answered flatly, her tone betraying the emotional fatigue she felt.

"Hey," Isaiah replied, his voice shaky.

"I wanted to make sure that you made it safely to Misty's house," he continued, his concern evident in the gentle whisper of his words.

"I did," Charity confirmed, her response clipped and succinct.

"Are you mad at me?" Isaiah's question hung in the air, with uncertainty.

"Should I be?" Charity countered, her voice defiant.

"You can't answer a question with a question," Isaiah chided gently, his tone playful, an attempt to bridge the distance between them.

"Oh, ok." Charity answered succinctly and then remained silent.

"Are you mad at me?"

"Dogs get mad, people get angry."

"We're in the fifth grade now, Charity?"

Charity continued to remain silent as she sat in her car staring out of the window at the towering oak at the end of the block and the vibrant flowers blooming in the neighbor's garden.

"So, are you angry with me?" Isaiah continued to prod, his voice growing stronger as he questioned Charity.

"I just don't have time to play games, Isaiah. I asked you when you started this courting thing, if you were sure you were going to be able to meet me where I am, and you said yes. But I swear you have me confused with those other women you are dating."

Isaiah stood outside of his parents' home trying to process this moment. Huffing, he said, "I'm not dating anyone."

"I know, and surely not me," Charity answered sarcastically.

"Really, Charity!" Isaiah raised his voice. "You are upset because of what?"

"Isaiah, really? To act like you don't know what I'm bothered about is ridiculous. You know what you did. You are a grown man. You know exactly what you did. I don't feel like playing."

There was silence on the line again.

Softening his frown as he stared into the night sky and surveyed the neighborhood, hearing the birds sing their night song. Isaiah asked, "Can I explain?"

"If you want. We are just friends, so it doesn't matter."

Ignoring Charity's sarcasm, Isaiah kept talking, "Family is important to me."

"Ok."

"And I didn't want to have a fiasco at my parents' home. It was easier for me to just let things happen as they did and not for me to escalate the situation."

Charity started gathering her things to go into her cousin's home. "No need to explain. I understand who you are and what you are about, and I just don't have time to play games with you."

She sighed heavily. "I know you enjoy playing games. Remember, you get paid to play games, but you can't play them with me. You need to find someone that likes to play."

"Can you give me one more chance? Please," Isaiah begged. "Charity, I promise I just didn't want any drama. I don't do drama well. Kim's mom and my mom are best friends, they have been trying to get us together since we were born. Kim is all in. I'm not. I knew my mom wasn't going to make Kim leave. She loves her like a daughter"

"I didn't want any drama either, and that's why I left."

"Charity, my parents liked you. My dad said you were a breath of fresh air, and I know what he means. You're not worried about material things or being all frilly and silly like these other chicks. You're so beautiful, smart and down to earth. I just want you to see me in a different light. I am not a woman chaser. I didn't want drama at my parents' home. Kim is only a friend. We've never dated, even though we have spent time together. I promise."

Holding the phone, Charity couldn't muster up any words to say to Isaiah. She was tired, mentally and physically and couldn't compose a sentence if she wanted to at this moment. Exhaustion and emotion held her tongue captive.

With a hopeful sincerity Isaiah asked, "Can I send you a ticket to the next game? It's called the Sports Bowl. I promise you, Charity. I will be all in and I'll start our courting process over."

"I'll think about it." Charity whispered softly into the phone.

Isaiah attempted to lighten the mood with humor, "The old folks say, think long, think wrong. "Yet, the usual laughter that would have accompanied his quip was absent, replaced by a silence.

Undeterred by Charity's silence, Isaiah continued. "Can you call me tomorrow afternoon and let me know so that I can get the tickets purchased?"

"I'll let you know." Charity gathered her things, eased out of the car and started making her way to the front door of Misty's home.

"I care for you, Charity. I promise I do. I want more with you." Isaiah sighed, holding the phone, now sitting on the steps of his parents' home, the cold stone cooling him off as he spoke.

Ringing the doorbell and signifying an end to the conversation, Charity murmured, "I'll let you know, Isaiah. I have a client that I have to meet in the morning. I'm going to prep tonight and then get ready for bed. Have a good night."

"You too, Charity."

Isaiah sat outside of his parents' home on the steps for another hour thinking. *How am I ever going to tear down the walls, if I giving her the bricks to build them?*

CHAPTER 25
THE THERAPY SESSION

Charity walked into Dr. Lesure's office, the scent of lavender mingling with the smell of freshly brewed coffee. The large windows offered a beautiful view of downtown Masters. The office overlooked the iconic Bank of Masters, housed within the historic Bell South building.

As Charity glanced out, she was momentarily transported back to her childhood, recalling visits with her mother and grandmother, their hands clasped tightly around hers as they navigated the bustling streets of Masters to pay bills.

Charity was still smiling when the receptionist called her name, Charity was still smiling, reminiscing about her childhood as she walked into Dr Lesure's office. A soft smile still played on Charity's lips as she took a seat.

The pastel blue walls of the office were adorned with serene artwork, each piece carefully chosen to evoke a sense of calm and reflection. The light blue loveseat she sank into enveloped her in its softness.

"Good morning," Charity greeted, her voice tinged with the warmth downplaying her wrecked nerves.

Dr. Lesure, with her kind eyes and gentle demeanor, radiated an aura of understanding and empathy. Her office was a sanctuary, a place where worries could be unpacked and examined in the safety of a trusted confidante. "How are you today, Charity?" she inquired, her tone a perfect balance of professional concern and genuine interest.

"I'm okay," Charity replied, her voice steady but carrying heavy undertones.

Dr. Lesure nodded, her pen poised over the notebook on her lap, ready to capture the nuances of their conversation. "So where do we start today?" she asked, her gaze shifting from her notes to meet Charity's eyes. The question was open-ended, an invitation for Charity to steer the session towards whatever weighed most heavily on her heart.

Charity took a deep breath. "Did you write the letter to Patrick?"

Dr. Lesure prompted, her voice gentle but probing, guiding Charity toward the heart of the matter.

"I did," Charity affirmed, her words carrying the weight of the emotions she'd poured into the letter.

"Would you like to share it?"

"Sure." Charity took the letter from her purse, leaned forward, exhaled sharply, and began to read. Her hands shook violently as she read the letter. She wore a pretty yellow cardigan with white flowers embroidered on the pockets and sleeves. Her messy bun hung to one side as usual. Her voice just above a whisper, she began to read.

Dearest Patrick:

Savage Garden wrote a song that I love. The lyrics said, "I think I loved you before I met you. I think I dreamed you into life." When I met you, I just knew I was dreaming. I remember studying your features in high school economics. Your teeth, your smile, your walk. I believed that you would be my forever love. I enjoyed spending time with you and just waking up knowing that you were a part of my life. I know towards the end, things were different—hard in fact, but the love I felt for you, never went away.

You were always my forever love. I never thought you'd leave without goodbye, but I'm sure you had your reasons why. I still miss you even though I beg my heart to be strong and not care, but I do. I honestly do. I struggle to know what to do with this level of pain. We have been best friends for so long that knowing that we can never be best friends again is heartbreaking. I'm proud of you and believe it or not I'm happy that you have found your forever love. I will always remember

and cherish our time together and I wish you nothing but peace and prosperity as you establish your life with your new wife.
May the force be with you. (Star Trek :)
Peace Out, Love In
Charity Love

Charity slowly folded the letter, placing it back into her purse. She steadied herself and smiled at Dr. Lesure.

"How have you felt since you wrote the letter?" Dr. Lesure stopped typing to look at Charity closely.

"I'm okay. It was short and sweet and to the point. I didn't ask any questions, and it was so hard for me not to ask questions." Charity laughed. "My mom used to tell us to ask questions all the time."

"Asking questions is not bad, but what would be the purpose of asking Patrick all the questions? The point I was trying to make is that even if you asked the questions and got answers, would it have made a difference in the long run?"

Charity shrugged. "I still think I need some type of closure."

Dr. Lesure tilted her head slightly. "The letter wasn't closure enough?"

"No, I think I need a face-to-face conversation."

"What would you say in a face-to-face conversation?"

Charity looked away and studied Dr. Lesure's painting. It was a picture of a sunset on a beach. The bluest of water marched the blue of the sky and peace exuded from the picture. It was like you were at the beach sitting in the midst of the sand. Returning to the present, Charity uttered, "I'm not sure."

"Think about it and let me know. So, what else is new?"

"I have a young man chasing me."

"Chasing? That insinuates that you're running."

"I am!" Charity's face brightened up.

"Why are you running? You don't want to be caught?" Dr. Lesure's question was gentle, yet probing, inviting Charity to explore the fears and hesitations that lay beneath her cheerful demeanor.

Charity hesitated, her smile faltering slightly as she considered her response. He's about six or seven years younger than me and he is a professional football player with a lot of women."

"But I don't know if you realized it or not, but your face brightened up the moment you started talking about him." Dr. Lesure's gaze was steady and encouraging, a silent reminder of the trust and understanding that anchored their sessions

"Really? "Charity's surprise was genuine, her eyes widening as she processed the revelation Dr. Lesure just laid on her.

"Yes ma'am. So, what's your plan?"

"I don't have one." Charity sighed, her fingers playing absently with the hem of her blouse as she pondered the question. Anxiety filled her eyes, shoulders slumping looking defeated before she even started playing the game.

"You're not going to let him catch you?" Dr. Lesure's wise eyes studied Charity briefly.

Charity cracked up when she made eye contact with Dr. Lesure. "Don't look at me like that, Dr. Lesure. I really hadn't planned on being caught. I think he is going to hurt me. He's a known player, on and off the field."

"Would you like my advice?" Dr. Lesure leaned forward slightly, her gaze filled with compassion and understanding.

"Of course." Charity moved nervously on the love seat, wringing her hands unconsciously.

"You're young, beautiful, successful—and if you want to be in a relationship you will have to be open to it. Relationships take work. All relationships whether they are friends, family, or lovers. The choice you must make is whether you want to try again. If you don't try again, what are your options?"

"I'm content with my books. I really don't mind being alone. I already have a retirement plan that includes a nursing home. It's not the worst thing in the world to be alone. I can travel and have a good life on my own." Her words were a declaration of independence, yet they carried the weight of solitude, an open display to the walls she had built around her heart. The same walls that Isaiah was determined to pull down.

"You are absolutely right. You can do all of that. Personally, I don't think we were meant to do life alone."

Dr. Lesure wrote for a moment in her notebook. After she finished writing, she gazed at Charity. "Here's your assignment, book a vacation and go by yourself. Take some time to see how it feels to do it alone and see how you feel about it. Evaluate how it makes you feel. And then decide if you want to do this forever or if you want to travel with someone else. Don't count out your friends and family either."

"I'm not, but everyone in my family is married or dating someone. I think my dad and my grandma have sweet things on the side." Charity laughed, her laughter a light, melodic sound that filled the room with warmth.

"I don't want to be a burden on anyone so that's why I had the nursing home added to my retirement plan."

"I get it, but don't count love out. You're too young to count out what God loves. You know God *is* love. Give Him your love life and see what He does with it. I bet He will wow you!"

"I'm sure of it."

"What vacation spot are you going to pick?"

"I think I'll go somewhere on the west coast. California is nice."

"I want you to relax and have fun." Dr. Leisure smiled.

"I plan on it." Charity assured, her resolve strengthening.

"When are you going to plan this trip?" Dr. Lesure asked, her voice gentle yet probing.

"I don't know but before our next therapy session in two weeks I will make sure that I have a date, time, and an overall vacation plan." Charity finally relaxed her shoulders as the visit with Dr. Lesure came to an end.

"Good. I'm impressed. I want you to write a list of everything that you want in a man. Also, I want you to make a list of the things that are deal breakers—the things you just cannot deal with at all. Smoking, cheating, lying—you make the decision, but I want you to work on that list as well. Also, next time your homework is to think about how closure

Dr. Taura M. Turner

looks with Patrick. Ask yourself if you should mail the letter, make the phone call, or schedule an in-person visit at the coffee shop."

Lowering her glasses and placing them on her desk, Dr. Lesure spoke encouragement to Charity. "Just know that I'm proud of you, Charity. I realize that growth and change are difficult, but it is so important to work through your issues."

"Thank you, Dr. Lesure." Charity picked up her purse. "I will see you in two weeks."

"Thank you, Charity, for trusting me with your pain and healing. See you soon."

Charity felt a little lighter this time leaving therapy. The letter to Patrick had provided a measure of closure, yet her thoughts now lingered on Isaiah King. With his enigmatic charm and undeniable presence, he was a puzzle she found both challenging and intriguing, but also a little leery. What was she going to do with Isaiah King? He was a handful, but she was captivated.

As she pondered her next steps, the path before her seemed filled with promise and potential, waiting for her to seize the opportunities that lay ahead.

CHAPTER 26
THE DELIVERIES

The sterile environment of the room buzzed with the hum of fluorescent lights and the soft murmur of conversations from the hallway. The air was cool, yet it did little to alleviate Lilly's discomfort. Lilly's expression was a mixture of frustration and determination, her brow glistening with beads of sweat.

Her hair, usually perfectly styled, was slightly tousled, a testament to the intensity of the labor pains that ebbed and flowed through her body like relentless waves. Despite the discomfort, her eyes held a fierce resolve, a silent promise to endure the ordeal with grace and strength.

"Lilly, why are you laying in this hospital bed naked?" She sat perched on the edge of the rigid bed without clothes, her face flushed with heat and exertion, as she attempted to find some relief by vigorously fanning herself with the flimsy cafeteria menu. The menu, a laminated piece of paper, flapped with every motion, creating a tiny breeze that did little to soothe the heat coursing through her body.

Lilly kept fanning herself vigorously. "I'm hot and in pain." Across from her stood Bertha Green, her mother, whose presence was as commanding as ever. Her voice, sharp and clear, cut through the hospital noise as she scolded Lilly. "Girl, if you don't put that hospital gown on—" Bertha's words echoed with the authority of a matriarch who had seen and weathered many storms in her lifetime. She wore a simple floral dress, its colors vibrant and lively, a reflection of her indomitable spirit. Her hands rested on her hips, a posture that spoke of exasperation.

"Ma, I'm so hot. I feel like I'm having a hot flash in between the labor pains!" She dropped her head back, letting it rest on the cool metal frame of the chair, and intensified her fanning, the menu flapping wildly in her hand.

"Lilly, you are the first lady of the church, you can't be laying up here showing all your goodies."

"Mom, I'm hot!" Lilly gasped between labor pains.

"Your husband is on the way in, girl. Cover up!" Bertha Green shook her head.

"Mom, he is the one that got me in this shape."

Just then Pastor Jeffries walked in about to check on his wife. He stopped in his tracks at the sight of Lilly lying in the bed naked. "Really baby?" He smiled at his wife. He knew at this moment, he wouldn't choose to be with anyone else in the world.

"Really." Lilly's voice was flat.

"You hot?" Pastor Jeffries asked jokingly and took the menu from her hand, taking over the fanning as she lay sprawled legs wide open, arms hanging off the side of the hospital bed.

"I'm burning up! Call somebody!"

"I'm not calling anyone with you in your birthday suit." Pastor Jeffries studied his wife of nine years. Her curls were pulled in a bun, and she still managed to keep on the string of pearls that he gave her for their 3rd wedding anniversary around her neck.

"Aww!" Lilly yelled. "This hurts so bad. Is it time for me to have something for the pain?"

"I thought you were going to have a natural birth?" Pastor Jeffries looked concerned.

Rolling her eyes at Ken Jeffries, she huffed, "Can you call a nurse?"

"I will," he said, grabbing her hand.

"I should have had kids when I was younger. Having a child at fifty is for the birds."

"Calm down, baby." Pastor Jeffries held one of Lily's hands and continued to fan with the other.

"Mom, can you call the nurse? I want an epidural!"

"Are you sure?" Ken asked.

"Yes, I'm sure. Stop asking me about whether I want something for pain!" Lily's eyes were ablaze; her normal demeanor replaced with a raging fire that was burning all who dared to enter the room.

"You're the one that said you wanted a natural birth," he reminded her while placing kisses on her salty cheeks as tears continued to stream down.

Lily groaned while turning her body to find comfort. Another labor pain hit her. "Have *you had a baby before?*" She stared at her husband as if she was really waiting on a response.

Bertha walked over to the bed and wiped the sweat from Lily's face. "Pastor, why don't you go down the hall and check on Sonya and Reggie. I'll get Lily situated and when you come back, she'll be all better."

"Alright." he said, releasing his hand from Lily's grip. He leaned in to kiss her, but she turned her head.

"Wow!" Pastor Jeffries looked hurt. He frowned at Lily and patted her arm.

"She doesn't mean it." Bertha rolled her eyes at her daughter.

Pastor Jeffries shook his head as he handed the cafeteria menu back to Lily so that she could continue her fanning. "You know I've heard the stories of how wives get mad at their husbands, but I still love you, my darling." He smiled.

Bertha hit Lily on the shoulder. "Say it back!"

"I love you, too." Her tone lacked enthusiasm.

"I know," Pastor Jeffries said with a smirk as he walked out the room.

"He's so arrogant."

"He's a man, darling." Bertha fanned Lily a little more giving her a reprieve from the heat.

"Mom, please call the nurse," Lily whimpered as another labor pain hit.

Bertha hit the call button, still fanning Lilly. When the nurse answered, Bertha explained that Lilly was in pain and needed an epidural.

Pastor Jeffries walked down the hall into the room where Sonya and Reggie were preparing for their fifth birth and tenth child.

"Hey, Family," Pastor Jeffries said excitedly knocking on the door as he walked into the Warren hospital room.

"Hey, Pastor J." Reggie stood to greet Pastor Jeffries with a handshake.

"How are you, man?"

"I'm good." He said with a hint of laughter in his voice.

"Why aren't you down there with my sister?" Sonya asked, her face twisted with concern.

"She put me out. She's been really mean today." Pastor Jeffries looked at Sonya suspiciously. "Why are you being so nice? You're not mad at Reggie?"

"I probably was the first time, but this is our fifth delivery. We are used to this now." Sonya leaned back in the bed casually looking at a television show that was playing. Unbothered, Sonya stated matter of factly, "I've had four spontaneous births, so I'm expecting this one to be the same."

"What is a spontaneous birth?" Pastor Jeffries inquired.

"When the babies just jump out, and their football dad just jumps up to catch them."

"Y'all are too funny. I wish my room was this much fun."

"Are you going back?" Reggie asked, laughing.

"Of course, I am! Bertha told me to give her a break and come pray for you. So here I am. Are y'all ready for some prayer?"

"We are," they said in unison and reached for each other's hands. Reggie grabbed the remote and turned the volume down as Pastor Jeffries reached for both of their hands and began to pray.

"Father, thank you for the Warren Family. We ask now that you bless this family and bless these babies that are preparing to enter the world. We pray that these babies would grow in stature and favor with God and with man. We ask that you touch the hands of the doctors, nurses, and anyone who enters this room. We bind anything that is not like you and release love, peace, joy, and comfort to the family. Touch their hearts and minds and allow them to be the parents that you have created them to be. May they walk in wisdom and love. In Jesus' name we pray, Amen."

Before releasing hands, they gave each other a squeeze. Pastor Jeffries then walked to the hospital room door. "Alright, good people. I'm headed back to see my queen."

"Reggie, let me know how things go. Text or call me when the twins get here."

Ken Jeffries walked back down the hall and back into the room to see that Lilly had calmed down.

"You better, my love?"

"I'm... I'm so sorry," Lilly stammered.

"You're ok, babe."

Bertha gathered her purse and Sunday School book. "I'm going to go to the waiting room to see who all is out there. I'll be right back. Y'all going to be ok?"

"Yes ma'am," Lilly said feeling better.

Bertha laughed. "That epidural worked wonders."

Lilly pursed her lips. "Whatever, Mom."

Bertha Green grabbed her purse and walked out the door singing Amazing Grace and made her way down to Sonya's room.

"I'm just peeping in. Are you all ok?"

"Yes, we are old pros at this, Mom." Sonya laughed.

"I see. Your sister is down the hall having a fit."

"Aww. I hate that I can't be down there with her."

"I'm going to the lobby to see who all is here. I hope we have some babies soon."

Reggie, looking at sports on his phone, raised his head for a moment. "Me too."

Bertha exited the Warren room and made her way to the lobby to see all her family. Leona, Diane, Mabel, Constance, Princeton, Dallas Jr., and Sam Love were all in the lobby waiting for the new Greens to arrive.

"Hey, Grandma," the Green grandchildren all yelled.

"Hey, family." Bertha looked at her family as if she was taking attendance. "Where is Charity?"

"She had a meeting," one of the Greens called out to Bertha. "She should be here soon."

Mabel looked at Bertha with anticipation. "How are the mothers-to-be?" About 15 Greens filled the hospital waiting room. Bertha smiled at her clan and continued, "Sonya is fine, but Lilly was having a fit until she got her epidural. She was cutting up back there with Pastor Jeffries. I didn't know you could talk to a man of the cloth that way."

Diane laughed. "My poor sister!"

"And then she said she was having a hot flash and had all of her clothes off while lying in the room."

"That's hilarious!" Mabel got up and walked towards the vending machine. "Y'all want anything?"

All the Greens started shouting their requests at once. "No, I'm good ... I could use a Coke ... Get me some chips, Mabel."

Mabel laughed as she made her way to the vending machines on the other side of the lobby trying to remember a few of the requests. She had no intention of getting everyone's request. *I shouldn't have asked,* she thought to herself laughing.

∞ ∞ ∞ ∞ ∞ ∞ ∞ ∞ ∞ ∞ ∞

The parking lot was filled as Charity maneuvered her Honda Accord, one of the last available spaces. As she turned off the ignition, Charity took a moment to center herself, closing her eyes for a brief, heartfelt prayer. "Please watch over the babies, the mommies, and grant them smooth, healthy deliveries," she murmured softly, her words a quiet plea to God.

She grabbed her laptop and cell phone realizing that she could be waiting for a long time and could probably get some editing done on one of her books. As she entered the lobby, her phone buzzed in her hand, pulling her attention back to the present. The screen lit up with

Joi's name, and Charity answered with a smile. "Hey big head," she greeted, her voice warm and teasing

Laughing, Joi responded, "Hey Char!"

"Are you at the hospital?"

"I'm walking in now." Charity's eyes scanned the bustling lobby as she replied

"Ok. I was just checking to see if the babies were here yet."

The Greens were a tight-knit family. They moved and operated like a well-oiled machine. There were instances when the entire family would show up for an event. They were present for the birth of a child, a graduation, a wedding, school programs, or a sporting event. They were in this thing together and they took family time seriously.

"Ok, Char, when you get settled, call me back on FaceTime so we can see everyone. "I sure will, my love." Charity promised, her heart swelling with sisterly love.

"Alright, sis. Thanks. I love you."

"Love you more. See you in a minute."

Distracted by her phone, Charity slipped it into her purse and, in her haste, collided with what she initially thought was a wall. "Oh shoot," she exclaimed, startled. But as she looked up, her surprise quickly turned into shock as she stuttered a greeting.

"Oh, hey," she stumbled over her words, her cheeks flushing slightly as she met the eyes of the man before her.

"Hey, Charity," Patrick replied, his voice calm and steady, a familiar warmth sparking between them.

The unexpected encounter sent a ripple of emotions through Charity, her heart skipping a beat as she stood face to face with a part of her past. The hospital lobby, with its bustling energy and constant movement, seemed to fade into the background, leaving just the two of them in a moment suspended in time.

CHAPTER 27
THE HOSPITAL

The hospital floor that housed the nursery was quiet. Charity could gather her thoughts here and finally breathe. Although she loved her family, there was very little silence when all the Greens were present. She'd snuck out and made her way to peep at the newborn babies. New life. She smiled as she turned the corner and saw a huge room full of new life. *What a blessing* she thought to herself as she stood gazing at the tangible favor of God.

Charity's aunts had two successful births, three beautiful new babies to add to the Green machine. As she stood by the nursery window and looked at all the beautiful bundles of blessings she whispered a prayer. "Father, thank you for the gift of life. Thank you for each one of these babies. Allow each to grow in your grace. Shield and protect each one and be with them all their days. In Jesus' name, Amen."

After her prayer she looked for their new babies. Her gaze lingered on the new additions to the Green family. Lilly's baby girl, Hanna Grace, lay peacefully, her tiny fists curled beside her sweet face. Next to her, Sonya's twin boys, McKenzie and Kensington, nestled together in a double crib, their breathing synchronized. A smile graced Charity's lips, her heart full of love and joy for her family.

As her eyes shifted to the other infants, one name caught her attention: Patricia Kilpatrick. Her heart skipped a beat, the name stirring a myriad of emotions within her. *Could this be Patrick's daughter?* The thought was bittersweet. She took a step back, the realization settling in, when a gentle touch on her shoulder pulled her from her thoughts.

Turning, she found herself face to face with Patrick again. His presence was a jarring reminder of a past she had tried to leave behind, and yet, here he was, standing before her in the quiet sanctuary of the nursery.

"Hey, Charity," he greeted, his voice carrying a note of discomfort that mirrored the awkwardness of the moment.

"Hey again." Her eyes darted to the wall behind him, seeking refuge from the intensity of his gaze. Her heart thumping with a plethora of emotions, felt like it was going to jump out of her chest.

Then came his words: "I don't think there has been a day that I have not thought about you since I left."

Charity turned her gaze back to the nursery and stood in silence. Patrick exhaled deeply. Charity could feel his breath on her neck. Her heartbeat began to race.

"Charity, I didn't know how to leave. I didn't know how to form the words to let you know that I was ready to leave. I tried to show you with my actions, but I saw you trying harder, and I didn't have the heart to tell you that I had fallen out of love with you."

How does one fall out of love with someone? Charity thought. To hold back tears, she kept her back to him and watched the babies in the nursery.

Patrick wanted to touch her shoulder, to turn her around, to see her face at this moment. He couldn't. "Charity, I was unhappy. And you were one of the good girls, so I didn't want to lead you on. But finding the words to say was hard. It was easier to just walk away." Patrick fidgeted with the ring on his finger, twisting it around over and over and looking at the vinyl hospital floors. He hated hospitals even on joyous occasions. The smell of disinfectant and sanitizer made him nauseous.

Charity continued to look at the bundles of joy in silence, thinking about the miracle of beginnings and the irony of endings.

Patrick placed his hand in the small of Charity's back. She flinched. He hurriedly removed his hand. "Sorry," he muttered. "Can you please find it in your heart to forgive me? I'm still really trying to forgive myself. I knew that it would hurt you, but I wanted to be free to live my life, my truth."

After at least a full sixty seconds, Charity spoke without offering any commentary on his speech or without turning around. "Your baby is beautiful. I see she is named after you: Patricia. That's sweet." Her fingers touched the glass.

Patrick looked down at his hands. At a loss for words, he simply answered the question. "Yes, she's my namesake. A beautiful baby girl."

"You better get that shotgun ready!" Charity laughed. It was genuine. If nothing else, she was truly a lover of children.

Patrick felt a weight had lifted; Charity was talking to him. "You still want kids?"

Charity thought briefly before answering, "Umm, I guess it's not a matter of what I want, but what God wants."

Patrick shook his head. "So you're still on *that*? See, that's part of the reason that I had to leave. You are more focused on waiting on God, but while you are waiting, others are living life."

Charity just laughed as she turned to face Patrick. She stared at his face for a moment. "Thank you, Patrick. I'm glad I finally know why you left."

"That's all you have to say?" He asked, frustrated by Charity and her nonchalant laugh.

"There's really not much else that needs to be said. I'm happy for you. You look happy and healthy. You have a beautiful daughter; a gorgeous wife, and you are prosperous. I think you have hit the jackpot."

Patrick turned his back to the nursery and leaned his back on the glass. He stared at Charity for a moment, though she made no eye contact with him now. Her gaze now lingered over the nursery. Patrick's eyes were a dark smoldering color that always made her think of a dark sky after a thunderstorm.

"I see that you are still running and avoiding your problems instead of facing them head on. You never confront anything and you're always putting your stuff off for another day." Patrick leaned his head on to the glass as he studied Charity waiting on a response. After waiting he turned back to the glass encased nursery placing his hands in his pockets.

Charity only smirked. Her days of arguing with Patrick were over. He was somebody else's problem now she thought to herself.

The tension between them was heavy, but Charity learned from therapy that sometimes you needed to sit in the uncomfortable places. She stood beside Patrick in uncomfortable silence. After a full minute, she spoke once again.

"The third baby from the left is Lilly's. That's Hannah Grace. She was named so because it was only God's grace that gave Lilly a baby at this age. She's beautiful. Can you believe Lilly is fifty and having her first baby? God is surely able. She and the Pastor didn't waste a day getting started trying to conceive and it finally happened! I'm so happy for them."

She moved her gaze to the twins. "And believe it or not, those two little boys over there in the corner, McKenzie and Kensington, belong to Sonya and Reggie. That's their final set of twins so they say." She smiled a bright smile, "but only time will tell. All these beautiful babies. All God's blessings. I once read somewhere that a baby is a sign that the world should go on."

Lost in the moment, Charity stopped talking to stare at the babies again. Tears filled her eyes. Babies represented new life, new opportunities, and new beginnings. They were the embodiment of dreams yet to unfold, of stories waiting to be told.

Charity shook herself, coming back to reality, and turned her attention back to Patrick. His presence was a reminder of the past, a reminder of a love once cherished and now lost. Yet, there was no bitterness in her heart, only a quiet acceptance of the journey they had taken together and the paths they now walked separately.

"I can concede defeat, Patrick," she began, her voice steady and sincere, carrying the weight of her truth. "I lost. I lost a beautiful man to a beautiful woman. Congratulations!" Her words were not laced with sarcasm or regret, but rather a genuine wish for his happiness.

The sincerity of her words hung in the air between them, giving them both closure. "I wish you and your wife nothing but the best. That's what you've always had and that's what you deserve!" Her gaze was unwavering, filled with a warmth and grace that spoke of her inner strength.

With that, Charity gave Patrick a brilliant, bright smile that held no resentment, no sorrow, no remorse, just peace. With a final look back, she walked away from her past and walked into her future.

CHAPTER 28
THE FIASCO

The airport buzzed with activity, people moving quickly from one location to the next, checking flight times, running to catch flights, dragging babies and bags. Travelers moved with purpose, their faces a mix of anticipation and eagerness.

As Sonya pulled into the airport drop-off area, Charity felt a pang of anxiety tighten her chest. The sleek, modern architecture of the airport terminal stood ahead, its glass facade reflecting the brilliant afternoon sun.

"Thank you for dropping me off at the airport, Sonya. I didn't want to leave my car here for an entire weekend." Her hands rested on her lap; fingers intertwined as she sought to steady her nerves.

"Girl, I understand. Those fees are ridiculous."

Charity sighed, her gaze staring at the flurry of travelers outside the car window

"I'm so nervous, Sonya. I don't feel like starting over again. I really thought Patrick and I were going to be together forever. I am not lingering in the past, I finally have closure, but I don't feel like starting over, that I can promise you."

Sonya's gaze softened as she looked at her niece, her heart swelling with empathy. "You know starting over is hard," she began, her tone gentle yet firm. "You can use all the jewels that you learned from Patrick and apply them to this new adventure with Isaiah." Sonya had always been a beacon of calm and wisdom, her presence reminiscent of

Charity's mother, Martha Love. In this moment, Charity felt the familiar ache of missing her mother, a longing for the comfort and guidance that only she could provide.

"I'm so nervous, Sonya," Charity repeated, needing more reassurance. "I just see him as a player and the last thing I want to do is to get played."

Sonya, always one to see the good in people, whispered in a calming voice, "I just think this is all new to you, Charity. He seems like a really good guy. He's God-fearing, handsome, and he's hilarious."

Sonya maneuvered into a parking space closer to the terminal. The car came to a stop, the engine's gentle hum fading into silence. Charity took a deep breath, the air filled with the promise of new beginnings and the warmth of her aunt's unwavering support.

Sonya grabbed Charity's hand in hers offering the comfort Charity needed. "You are such a planner and he's a free spirit. My advice to you for this weekend is just to relax and enjoy the time. Live in the moment; let it be what it's going to be. Don't think too much, too long or too hard. For once in your life, let go and go with the flow."

Charity wrapped her hand around her auntie and gave it a tight squeeze before she pulled her purse toward her and looked out the window. Her eyes held fear and apprehension. She exhaled deeply, releasing her pent-up tension. "I'm going to try my best," she said, gathering the rest of her things.

"Please do," Sonya laughed. "I think you'll enjoy it all. I bet he shows you a really good time in his city."

"Alright now, girl." Sonya leaned over and hugged Charity. "Be careful, have fun, and don't do anything I wouldn't do!"

Charity giggled. "Ok, I won't do anything *you would do*, but I promise to try to have a good time. Thank you so much auntie, I love you."

With that Charity hopped out the truck and walked into the airport to prepare for her flight to Isaiah's current home in Wisconsin. As she stepped out of the car, her heart drum cadence of emotions—nervousness, anticipation, and mixed with a little flicker of hope that perhaps, maybe Isaiah could be her next new beau.

∞   ∞   ∞ ∞ ∞ ∞ ∞ ∞ ∞ ∞ ∞

As the plane touched down at precisely 3:25 p.m., Charity felt a flutter of anticipation ripple through her. She'd slept most of the flight, the tiredness from weeks of going nonstop finally catching up with her.

The bustling airport terminal was a hive of activity, with travelers scurrying in every direction, their footsteps echoing through the expansive hall.

Feeling refreshed from her restful flight, Charity planned to go straight to the hotel, shower, change, and wait on Isaiah. He told her that he was sending a car. Charity navigated the throng of passengers with ease, making her way to the entrance of the valet service. A gentleman dressed in a black tuxedo lifted a sign that read: *Charity, My Love*! Isaiah was clever.

She loved the play on words. She dated many men who never knew that Charity was a synonym for love. Isaiah often teased her by calling her *Miss Love Love*. Charity walked over to the car, gave the gentleman her bags, climbed in, and leaned back on the soft leather seats. The seats cradled her like a gentle hug, their warmth a soothing balm to her frayed nerves. She called Isaiah's phone and left a voice message:

> "Hey, Isaiah. I've made it into town. I'm headed to the hotel. I'll see you a little bit later this afternoon. I'm going to shower, and I'll be ready by seven o'clock. I can't wait to see you. Take care. Bye! This is Charity." She added not thinking she needed to, but just in case. Charity was always the overthinker.

Isaiah spared no expense for the hotel accommodation. The penthouse suite was on the 44th floor. As Charity made her way to her room, she admired the gorgeous fixtures in the lobby. Everything in the suite was plush. The refrigerator and bar were stocked to capacity; there was no dollar limit on the room service. Charity was in heaven. There was an entire buffet area with coffee, muffins, water, sodas, juice, and a special section with wine and cheese.

She climbed into the bed slowly after taking a long shower. She planned to lay down for a couple of minutes just to rest her eyes again, but didn't wake up until 7:34 p.m.

Sitting up slowly, Charity glanced at her phone, half expecting to see a plethora of notifications. Yet the screen remained silent, no missed calls, no messages, no signs of Isaiah trying to reach her. A slight pang of disappointment hit her. She stretched and yawned, releasing the last remnants of sleep.

Determined to connect, she dialed Isaiah's number again, her fingers moving with practiced ease over the familiar digits. The call went straight to voicemail, his voice—a soothing baritone—offering a brief greeting before the soft beep invited her to leave a message. "Hey Isaiah, this is Charity again," she began, her voice carrying a note of eagerness. "Did I miss you? I fell asleep, maybe because of jet lag. Please call me back. I'm so excited to see you this evening. Call me back. I'll send you a text just in case you're in a place you can't talk now. Alright, take care, bye!"

Charity hung up the phone and sent Isaiah a text message before lying back down on the bed with a manuscript from one of her authors. Against all of Sonya's rules, she brought a little work to keep her occupied.

Another hour and a half went by and Charity still hadn't heard from Isaiah. Finally, at 10:30pm., he texted her and said he had an emergency and to order room service and he promised to see her tomorrow morning.

Charity texted back, "Ok, Isaiah, thanks for letting me know. I pray that you and your family are ok. Talk soon."

The next morning Isaiah sent a dozen roses to the hotel for Charity. Room service knocked on her door with Belgian waffles, a pitcher of orange juice, breakfast potatoes, bacon and eggs, muffins, and bagels—a delectable array of items. Charity ate breakfast and waited for Isaiah to call her back. At 11 o'clock she got up and took a shower.

Dressed and refreshed, Charity tried calling Isaiah again, her fingers tapping out the familiar number with practiced ease. But once more, the call went straight to voicemail, the silence on the other end growing louder with each attempt.

"Hey Isaiah, it's Charity," she began, her voice steady despite the flutter of nerves in her stomach. "Just checking on you. Thank you so much for the beautiful roses and the wonderful breakfast. I just got out of the shower and I'm available whenever you're available. Can't wait to see you. I hope all is well; talk to you later. Bye."

The hours stretched on, each one marked by the quiet ticking of the clock and the gentle hum of the city outside her window. Charity sent a text. "Hey, is everything ok? I left you a message, just to make sure you're good. Let me know. I'll talk to you later."

Yet, as time passed with no reply, her mind began to wander down familiar, unsettling paths. The echoes of her past with Patrick resurfaced: memories of unanswered calls and unmet promises whispering through her thoughts. She felt herself spiraling, the weight of uncertainty pressing on her chest.

She started—slowly and deliberately—pacing the floor, reciting her favorite mantra: "Blessings on Blessings."

An hour went by. Charity called his phone again; left another voicemail:

"Hey Isaiah, it's me again, just checking on you. I'm trying to figure out what's going on. Listen, if you had other plans, if you had other things to do this weekend, you didn't have to invite me out here. It's kind of rude that I've been here almost twenty-four hours and I've yet to see you. Hopefully, everything is ok. Please call me back."

By 7:30 that night, Charity felt defeated. She contacted the airline and changed her flight to 10:00 o'clock. She left Sonya a message and told her she was heading back to Masters:

"Hey Sonya, it's Charity I'm calling to let you know I'm headed back to Mississippi. Isaiah was a no-show. I never

*heard from him other than text messages. He never returned
any of my calls. I'm taking an Uber to the airport and then
boarding a flight to Masters. It'll be late when I get in, so I'll
catch an Uber home. I just wanted to let someone know what
was going on. Love you much, auntie. I'll talk to you later."*

Charity's flight landed in Masters, at 1:43 a.m. She made it home, took a long shower, and hopped in the bed. She was exhausted mentally, physically, and emotionally. *This was the last time I put myself out there being vulnerable and coming up short*, she thought.

Her mind replayed snippets of the weekend—Isaiah's absence, the unfulfilled anticipation, the echoes of past heartaches—and she felt the familiar pang of defeat.

Slipping into bed, the cool sheets embraced her weary body, offering comfort. Her heart was heavy with the echoes of unmet expectations. Before surrendering to the lull of sleep, Charity whispered a heartfelt prayer into the darkness, her words a tender plea for healing and strength. "Father, thank you for traveling grace and mercy," she murmured, her eyes closed in reverence. "I ask that you heal my heart and help me to love what you love and to hate what you hate. Help me to be the woman that you've called me to be. Give me strength. I pray this prayer in Jesus' name, Amen."

∞ ∞ ∞ ∞ ∞ ∞ ∞ ∞ ∞ ∞ ∞

The early morning sun poured through the sheer curtains in Charity's bedroom, she lay awake, her eyes tracing the familiar lines of the ceiling, lost in thought as she processed the events of the past weekend. Her heart still felt heavy, weighed down by Isaiah's absence and the unfulfilled promise of their time together.

At precisely 6:00 a.m., the silence was broken by the shrill ring of her phone, its insistent call piercing the tranquility of her room. Charity glanced at the screen, her heart twinging at the sight of Isaiah's name flashing insistently. She hesitated, her fingers hovering over the device before letting it slip back to the nightstand, the call unanswered. Isaiah, of course, left a message.

"Hey Charity, I'm sorry I missed you. I promise it was an emergency. I would never do this if it weren't. Please call me back. I apologize. I'm so very sorry. Please call me back. Let's talk. Please Charity, call me back."

Not bothering to answer or reply, the phone fell silent for a moment, allowing the quiet of the morning to settle back into place like a comforting blanket.

Three hours later, the phone rang again, its persistent sound pulling Charity from her thoughts. Once more, Isaiah's name illuminated the screen, Charity's resolve remained firm, her decision clear as she watched the phone vibrate softly, then still. The voicemail icon blinked at her, a reminder of the multiple messages he'd left. She'd spent the morning cleaning then went to her office to work on a couple of new books.

∞ ∞   ∞ ∞ ∞ ∞ ∞ ∞ ∞ ∞ ∞

On Tuesday morning, the digital clock on the nightstand glowed with the time: 7:30 a.m., a soft vibration bringing her awake. Charity lay in bed, momentarily confused, as the phone buzzed insistently on the bedside table. Each ring brought her further out of her sleep. She ignored the calls at first, her resolve firm as she focused on her to do list for today.

As the morning wore on, the calls continued with unrelenting regularity, every fifteen to thirty minutes. By 11:30 a.m., Charity gave in, reaching for the phone with a sigh of resignation. "Hello," she answered, her voice held an emptiness that mirrored the emotions in her heart.

"Hey, Charity," Isaiah's voice came through the line, warm and familiar, yet carrying a note of uncertainty.

"Hey," she replied, her tone guarded.

"Are you okay?" he asked, the question loaded with concern.

Charity paused, considering the complexity of her answer. Her mind was a whirlwind of thoughts of the past few days colliding. "Yes, I'm fine," she replied, the words dry yet measured.

"I just called to apologize," Isaiah continued, his voice sincere, a gentle plea for understanding.

"No apology is necessary. I get it," Charity replied.

"You get what?" Isaiah questioned, his tone filled with confusion.

"I get that you had me fly across the country and never called to talk to me. You only sent text messages and left voicemails. I find it amazing, but I'm not surprised. Just a little disappointed. But it's okay. It's par for the course," she explained, her voice steady but carrying the weight of her disappointment.

"Par for the course, huh? Do you know I miss you?" Isaiah's voice was like molasses—smooth, slow, heavy, and sweet, wrapping around her like a comforting embrace.

Charity felt a flutter in her chest, a reminder of the connection they were building. Yet, she pushed the feeling aside, her defenses rising to the surface. "Oh, ok," she replied, her voice steady.

"Oh, ok? So, you don't believe me?" Isaiah's inquiry was gentle, a soft nudge against the walls she had erected.

"No, I sure don't," Charity affirmed, her resolve firm.

"Can I explain?" he persisted, his voice carrying a note of urgency.

"Ha," Charity laughed, the sound a mix of disbelief and amusement. "Go for it!" She held the phone loosely, poised to end the call if necessary.

"I want to explain in person," Isaiah insisted, his tone earnest.

"The phone will suffice," Charity countered, her voice a blend of determination and self-protection.

"I don't think it will," he replied, his insistence a gentle challenge.

"I do," she retorted.

"Don't be like that, Charity," Isaiah pleaded.

"Like what? Truthful?" she challenged.

"No, mean!" he replied, his voice a soft reprimand.

"Ok," Charity conceded, the word holding a plethora of emotions.

The doorbell rang, its sound cutting through the tension like a knife. It was a welcome interruption, a reprieve from the emotional tug-of-war unfolding over the phone. "I have to go; I have a visitor," Charity said, her voice carrying a note of finality as she ended the call. A sense of relief washed over her.

Charity went to the door and peeked outside. "What are you doing here?" she asked, holding the blinds on her front door open.

"Open the door." Isaiah knocked and simultaneously rang the doorbell. "I need to see you and talk to you."

"We could have talked over the phone, or better yet we could have talked in Milwaukee last weekend."

"Charity, please open the door!" Isaiah begged, leaning his forehead on the glass portion of her front door.

"I don't think this is a good idea."

"Charity, *open-the-door!*"

And she did—but slowly.

Isaiah stepped in and grabbed Charity's hand. "Can I have a hug?"

"Nope, not at all. Nope, not at all," Charity repeated, her words firmly.

Isaiah shook his head, a wry smile tugging at his lips. "You're so stubborn," he observed, his gaze meeting hers with a mixture of frustration and affection.

Charity crossed her arms, a protective barrier against the emotions his presence stirred. "What can I do for you, Mr. King?" she inquired, her voice cool and composed.

"You can stop acting like a jerk." She realized that must have been Isaiah's favorite word for her.

"Oh really? A jerk?" Charity, dressed in her mother's lounge set and hair wrapped in a printed fabric, looked like an African princess. She stood while Isaiah walked over and took a seat on her gray leather sofa accented with red pillows.

"You're the one that invited me to dinner and your ex showed up, but I'm a jerk? And then flew me to Milwaukee and never came to see me, but I'm a jerk?"

Charity stood her ground, her posture firm and unyielding, as Isaiah walked sprawled out on her gray leather sofa. The room was filled with heavy tension between them. Her mother's chaise lounge, that she'd inherited after her death, sat in the corner, a vibrant mixture of colors.

As Charity's words hung in the air, she folded her arms across her chest again, her expression a mixture of hurt and defiance.

"I didn't invite her to dinner, and I told you she wasn't an ex of mine. She's my mother's best friend's daughter. We thought about trying to date because that's the natural progression when your parents are best friends. It didn't work out; end of story." Isaiah still lounging on the sofa lowered his gaze and stared at Charity.

"But you didn't stop me from leaving." Charity paced the room, walking a hole into the pathway that led from the door to the sofa where Isaiah sat calmly observing her intently.

"She would have caused a major scene, and it just wasn't worth it."

"Like I said, oh ok." Charity continued her walk from one end of the living room to the other.

"Oh, ok." Isaiah stood and reached for her. Charity moved out of his way.

"Remind me again why you are here?" Charity moved back to the door and turned the knob preparing to open it and invite Isaiah to enjoy the weather outside.

"One, I want to apologize for everything! For dinner and your trip to Milwaukee." Isaiah walked to the door, took Charity's hand off the doorknob and held it gently while he gazed at her.

"Will you please let me explain?" Isaiah's posture was that of a young boy trying to explain his report card to his mom.

She shrugged. "Go for it."

Taking a deep breath, Isaiah started explaining. "My little sister surprised me the night you came to town. I didn't know she was coming. I couldn't just leave her by herself and hang out with you. She broke up with her boyfriend and was in a terrible mood. I kept trying to get her together, but she just kept crying."

So, I'm not worth meeting? Charity thought to herself, the unspoken question was a silent accusation that lingered in the air. Her lips pressed into a thin line, a reflection of the disappointment and disbelief that simmered beneath her calm exterior. "Oh, ok. That's all you got?" she replied, her voice steady filled with hurt that she struggled to hide.

"Charity!" Exasperated, Isaiah started pacing the floor, using Charity's route. The room felt smaller, the walls closing in as he retraced the path Charity had paced just a few minutes before. Her stubbornness was a force to be reckoned with.

"Listen, Isaiah. I flew all the way across the United States. My flight was not a surprise to you. We have planned this weekend for weeks and yet your sister drops in and you can't even pick up your phone. I spent the weekend calling and texting you with very limited responses from you and I had to take an Uber back to the airport. You are delusional if you think I'm ok with any of that."

Charity tapped the doorknob with her fingers. "And on top of that, the next day when I get home, I see you plastered all over the Sunday afternoon newspaper. You had time for another woman, but not for me. I know you never said we were exclusive, but why pursue me so hard without telling me you're still seeing other women?"

"I hear you." Isaiah stopped walking and stopped in front of Charity. He wanted to grab her hand but knew that she would not be open to that based on her closed off stance.

"Oh, ok." was her frigid reply.

"Can you let me explain?" Isaiah looked weary. His normally nonchalant demeanor was tense.

"Sure, if you'd like. But your explanations are falling short, sir."

"The woman you saw me with was my former agent. She wanted to see about getting me back as a client." Isaiah moved to the recliner nearest to Charity. She remained standing near the front door. "The meeting was at the hotel. I'm not seeing her or sleeping with her. I'm interested in you, but you seem to have this wall built up all around you. So, what do you want me to do?"

"Don't try to blame this on me. I only wanted to be friends. You kept trying to pursue a relationship. And you're a part of the walls that I am building up. You're heling me build more with all this foolishness. But I don't think you're ready or mature enough. You're young."

"Really? Age is only a number."

"You keep saying that, but you act like you're a teenager when it comes to communicating."

"I'm a well-known football player. Do you know how much my phone rings? It's nonstop. Sometimes, I just turn it off."

"It sounds so convenient, Isaiah." Charity stared at him without emotion.

Opening the door as she continued to speak, Charity said, "However, I'm big on communication. I'm a writer. When I can't figure something out, my imagination goes wild. I need you to be honest with me."

"Charity, it's not that serious. Damn! I see why you are alone. This is too much pressure." With that Isaiah got up and walked out the door.

Charity's breath caught as she closed the door behind him. She was exhausted. She headed to bed. Tomorrow she'd deal with her feelings for Isaiah and work through this nonsense.

∞ ∞ ∞ ∞ ∞ ∞ ∞ ∞ ∞ ∞ ∞

At 6:30 the following morning, Charity's doorbell rang. Charity sighed, her eyes fluttering open to the soft light that permeated the room. She knew, without a shadow of a doubt, who stood on the other side of the door. With a feeling of reluctance, she rose from her bed.

Just as she suspected, it was Isaiah. "What do you want?"

"Charity, I'm sorry. Listen, can I talk to you? Please open the door. I apologize." Isaiah's voice was earnest, his eyes reflecting a sincerity that tugged at her defenses. He stood with a quiet humility, his figure framed by the gentle glow of the morning sun.

Without a word, Charity turned away, exhausted and frustrated. She went back to bed. Sleep overtook her. By the time she woke up again, the clock on her bedside table read 10:37 a.m. She had a business meeting at one o'clock but needed to go by the cleaners to drop off clothes and stop by Sonya's to show her the proof of the books she was working on for the new babies. She got out of bed and got ready for her day.

∞ ∞ ∞ ∞ ∞ ∞ ∞ ∞ ∞ ∞ ∞

As she stepped out the door, her thoughts focused on the tasks at hand, she collided with the solid presence of Isaiah. The unexpected encounter sent a jolt through her, her heart skipping a beat as she looked up into his familiar eyes.

"Hey!" Isaiah greeted, his voice carrying a mix of heaviness and hope.

"Hey," Charity replied, her tone cautious and untrusting.

"I sent you flowers yesterday," Isaiah continued, his gaze searching hers for a flicker of connection.

"I got them," she acknowledged, her voice steady and firm.

Looking off into the distance, Isaiah continued, his words a confession wrapped in vulnerability. "I left you like a thousand messages."

"I got them," Charity replied.

"Charity, I apologize," Isaiah began, his voice earnest and sincere. "The day you arrived in Milwaukee; I received a call that I was cut from the team, and I was in a bad mood all day. That's why Denise wanted to meet with me. I'm a free agent again and needed to discuss my options. Then in the midst of that, my sister showed up and it was all downhill from there."

"Ok." Charity remained unwavering.

"Charity, please forgive me. I'm honestly crazy about you. I know you don't believe me. I know I messed up by walking out yesterday and speaking so harshly to you." His voice trailed off as he looked at her like a five-year-old explaining why his school clothes were covered in dirt.

"Apology accepted."

"Can I have a hug, and a kiss?"

Charity offered a half-hearted hug, her embrace tentative and restrained. The contact was brief, a gesture that spoke of her lingering reservations.

"So, I guess you really are still mad," Isaiah observed, his tone a mixture of disappointment and understanding.

"No really, I'm not," Charity replied, her words frank. "I seem to have the worst luck with men. You're young and fly off when you don't get your way, and I can't handle that. We haven't really dated, and you're already upsetting me beyond measure. You really need to know how to communicate with me."

Isaiah's posture was one of quiet humility, his hands resting at his sides as he absorbed her words. "I'm apologizing now," he noted, his voice a gentle reminder of his intentions.

"I told you I accept," Charity reaffirmed, her gaze steady, yet her heart a swirl of conflicting emotions.

"But you don't want to deal with me anymore," Isaiah surmised, his tone carrying a note of resignation.

"I can't," Charity replied, her voice firm yet tinged with regret. "I'm protecting my peace. I also think the age difference is a problem, and you've still got a lot of growing to do."

Isaiah nodded slowly, his expression thoughtful as he reached to touch Charity's cheek, a tender gesture that spoke of his affection. "Hmm. Ok," he murmured, his voice a quiet acknowledgment of the gulf between them. "I miss talking to you."

"Oh, really?" Charity's tone was tinged with sarcasm.

"Yes, I do," Isaiah insisted, his eyes earnest.

"Oh ok," Charity responded, the familiar phrase slipping from her lips, a well-worn shield of protection that she wore well.

"You've said 'Oh ok' a thousand times and I don't like it," Isaiah challenged gently, his frustration tempered with a desire to understand.

Charity let out a genuinely hearty laugh, the sound a release of the tension that had built between them. "'Oh, ok' is my defense mechanism," she admitted, a hint of self-awareness coloring her words. "I say it when I'm angry, upset, sad, or just processing and need more time before I speak."

Her laughter was infectious, a moment of lightness that bridged the gap between them, for only a moment. Exhaling, Charity walked over to Isaiah and gave him a quick hug, the contact a small offering of peace. "I have a meeting in a couple of hours. Take care of yourself," she said, her voice warm and final.

Charity repositioned her messenger bag on her shoulder and pulled her sunglasses from her purse, placing them over her eyes. With a gentle side-step, she moved past Isaiah and walked to her car, the soft click of her heels a steady rhythm that echoed her resolve to move forward, one step at a time. Charity continued her walk. That strong steady walk.

CHAPTER 29
LEONA GREEN (MONROE)

Jason Baxter stepped into the cozy, beautifully decorated home shared by Lee and Monroe. The living room, with its soft beige walls and plush furniture, exuded an air of warmth and comfort. A large in the living room window allowed the golden afternoon sun to pour in, displaying fun patterns of light across the room. The scent of fresh lilies, filled the air from a vase on the coffee table, mingled with the faint aroma of freshly brewed coffee, creating an inviting atmosphere.

"Hey, Leona," Jason greeted as he entered, his voice carrying a note of familiarity and ease. Monroe, visibly unsteady, clung to Jason's side with an air of desperation, his grip firm yet unsteady as he leaned heavily on his friend. He explained to Leona,

Leona, hearing Jason's voice, appeared at the top of the staircase. Her expression was one of concern, her brow furrowing slightly as she descended the polished wooden steps. Her eyes, sharp, took in the scene with a mixture of anger and apprehension. "Monroe, gave me the key to open the door."

"What's going on, Jason?" she inquired, trying to maintain a steady tone. Her gaze shifted to Monroe, whose demeanor seemed dulled by an unseen weight.

Jason adjusted his hold on Monroe, steadying him firmly. "Monroe had a bit too much to drink," he explained, his voice carrying a hint of embarrassment. "I didn't want him to drive home and have a wreck or anything."

Leona's expression hardened, "Umm, ok," she replied, her voice thoughtful as she processed the situation.

Leona, arriving at the bottom of the step, gestured toward the plush sofa in the center of the living room. Its warm, inviting cushions seemed to beckon Monroe with the promise of comfort and rest. "You can leave him on the couch," Leona instructed, "Thank you for bringing him home safely."

Jason nodded, a shy smile touching his lips as he helped Monroe settle onto the sofa. The room was quiet, except for the rustle of fabric and the soft hum of the ceiling fan overhead.

"You're quite welcome," Jason replied, his eyes meeting Lee's with empathy. "I think he has something to tell you. But please take it easy on him, Lee." Jason stated, using Leona's nickname. "He is really trying."

Leona's brow furrowed slightly, a hint of skepticism creeping into her expression. "Trying to do what, Jason? Give me a heart attack?" she retorted, her voice carrying a playful edge, though her eyes held a depth of concern for her partner.

As Jason gently helped Monroe onto the sofa, Leona's mind raced with a mixture of emotions. A familiar feeling of disappointment settled in the pit of her stomach, yet she remained outwardly calm. Her eyes lingered on Monroe, taking in his disheveled appearance and the faint smell of alcohol that clung to him like an unwelcome reminder of their past struggles.

Leona's gaze softened momentarily as she recalled the turbulent early years of their relationship. She had been a young lawyer, full of ambition and dreams, while Monroe had been the charismatic charmer who swept her off her feet. Their love had been a whirlwind of passion and conflict. The late nights, the arguments, and the broken promises had all left their mark on her heart. Broken in so many pieces, she wondered how it was still beating.

With a sigh, Leona turned her attention back to Jason, who stood awkwardly by the door. She appreciated his efforts to ensure Monroe's safety, but her mind was already racing ahead to the conversation she needed to have with her fiancé.

"No, he's really trying to be a better man."

"Really? And you think he's going to do that by coming into the house at eight o'clock in the morning, twenty-four hours from the time he left here yesterday headed to work?"

"Look, I'm not making excuses for Monroe, but he's going through a lot at work, and he got into some trouble and started trying to work his way out. All I'm saying is that I have known Monroe for over twenty years. I remember when you all first got together. I remember the torture and the turmoil. All I'm saying is that I see him working hard trying to be a better man and it's for you. It's all for you."

Lee stood silently, tears rolling down her pretty brown face.

"Listen, call my wife, Chante. She will tell you about all the things that we went through in our marriage. Marriage is hard work. Relationships are hard work. It takes a fighting spirit. It takes a spirit that refuses to give up. This man is crazy about you. The worst is over; he's striving for better. I have seen him do a complete one-eighty. Most folks don't work that hard, but Mon loves you and wants to make it work." Jason looked at Lee with compassion and understanding. "Mark my words, you are going to be fine. The best is yet to come."

Jason leaned in and hugged Lee. Monroe and Jason had worked together for over twenty years. Jason understood the type of man that Monroe was and the type of man that he was becoming. He was proud of him. Five years his senior, he took Monroe under his wings years ago and saw him really trying to be a better man. He knew that Monroe was crazy about Leona Green. Jason just hoped the two could survive this current trial.

"When he wakes up, just listen with an open heart and an open mind. Extend him some grace." Jason walked toward the door and turned to Leona again. "I love you, Lee. Tell Mon to call me later and we can go get his car."

"Where is the car, Jason?"

"I'll let him tell you where it is," he said, walking out the door. "Thank you, Jason," she said, her voice steady yet deflated, despite the storm of emotions within. "I'll take it from here."

Exhausted and tired of thinking, Leona just said, "Ok" and closed the door softly behind Jason.

As Jason left, Leona's thoughts drifted to the therapy sessions that had helped her reclaim her sense of self-worth. Those sessions had been a lifeline, teaching her to set boundaries and recognize her own strength. She had learned the importance of self-care and how to navigate the complexities of her relationship with Monroe.

Leona knew that Monroe's drinking was not just a lapse in judgment, but a symptom of deeper issues. She had seen him work tirelessly to change, to be the fiancé she deserved. Yet, moments like these reminded her that the journey to healing was not a straight path, and that trust, once broken, took time to rebuild.

Leona approached the sofa, her footsteps deliberate and measured. She sat down beside Monroe studying his features. His locs had grown considerably since he first started growing them a few years ago. They rested on his shoulders and hung freely into his face. His chiseled features made him look like a Greek god. Brushing a lock of hair from his forehead, her touch was gentle, but her determination was unwavering. She knew that this was a moment that required patience and understanding, but also honesty.

"Monroe," she whispered softly, her voice a mix of tenderness and firmness. "You promised me, remember? We talked about this."
Monroe stirred, his eyes fluttering open to meet hers. There was a flicker of remorse in his gaze, a silent acknowledgment of the promises he had made—and broken.

"I'm sorry, Lee," he murmured, his voice thick with regret. "I didn't mean for it to get out of hand." He slumped back on the sofa and fell asleep.

Lee leaned back on the sofa and let her thoughts drift. Their first few years together were fun but toxic. They were young and both hot-headed. Though their intimacy was unmatched they couldn't get along. Monroe was dating multiple women and wasn't doing a good job of hiding his affairs. Lee was trying to hold on and make their relationship work.

Over and over Monroe promised to clean up his act and each time he failed, Lee would get angry, and a fight would break out. Police would be called, and they'd separate before starting the cycle again a few years later. After Martha' death, it seemed that they both calmed down and started trying to make their relationship work.

Maturity set in and they were doing well. Monroe started applying for better jobs, received a promotion and started taking Lee on nice vacations and fancy dinners. Ultimately, he asked her to marry him, and the rest was supposed to be history. But here they were again, Monroe staying out late at night or coming in days later. Lee was totally over it.

She stared at Monroe again. She loved this man with all of her being. He was the ham to her burger and the French to her fry. She needed him in her life, *but at what cost Lee* she thought to herself. She rested her head on the pillows of the sofa for another minute, taking deep breaths, begging her emotions not to overwhelm or overtake her. She was anything but a crybaby, but lately she was crying more. She finally got her breathing in check and opened her eyes staring out the large window in their living room.

With a final look at Monroe lying on the couch, Leona shook her head and walked up the stairs. She had a heavy caseload this week including going through files from her own nephew's case, but she was mentally and physically exhausted. She took off her pink robe and matching slippers and climbed into her big bed alone wondering what Monroe had to say to her. Sleep soon found her and before she knew it, she had drifted off.

∞ ∞ ∞ ∞ ∞ ∞ ∞ ∞ ∞ ∞ ∞

"Hey, my love," Monroe greeted, his voice a gentle caress that wrapped around her like the morning sun. He perched on the edge of the bed, his fingers lightly tracing the bottom of her feet, eliciting a sleepy smile from Leona.

Leona blinked to clear her vision as she focused on Monroe's face. His presence was always comforting, a reminder of the bond they shared. Yet, as her mind replayed Jason's words from the earlier in the day, a note of caution tempered her warmth. She knew the importance of grace—how often she herself had been the recipient of God's grace — and she resolved to extend it to Monroe, who deserved it just as much as she did.

Leona wiped the sleep from her eyes. "Hey Mon."

"How are you?" he asked, his voice carrying hints of uncertainty, turning to face Lee. The question was simple, yet it held a depth of meaning.

Leona could tell Monroe was timid. He looked down at his hands, studied the quilt on the bed, and looked off into the distance instead of looking at Leona directly in her eyes. The tension in his body was palpable, a silent plea for patience and understanding.

"I need to talk to you about something." He spoke quickly, not wanting Leona to interrupt. "I need you to just listen—not judge me, not yell at me, and please don't leave me."

"Ok, I'm listening." Leaning back into the headboard of the bed, surrounded by a slew of pillows, Leona closed her eyes and said, "Lord, help," as Monroe started to explain his issue.

"Lee, the stress at the job has been so high for the last few months. I needed something to take my mind off it. One night the guys were going to the casino and I tagged along. I didn't think anything of it. You know I'm not a gambler, but I just wanted to relieve some stress." Monroe looked at the wall behind the bed, studying the painting that Mable created for them when they got engaged a few years ago.

Lee sighed, waiting on Monroe and leaning into the headboard of their California king bed.

"I uhh, drank a little, ate a little, and then got on the tables and started playing. It took my mind off the stress. So that first weekend, I won big. That's when I put all that money into our savings account. I thought, *man, I relieved stress and then made some money too! How great is that?*" He smiled a timid smile hoping Leona was proud of his big money windfall.

"Wow!" Lee interrupted. "So that's where the extra money came from in our account? I remember asking you and you never told me. You just said it was a deal that came through." Lee repositioned herself in the bed to study Monroe's face.

Monroe dropped his head and rubbed his hands together. "Yep, that's where the money came from. I started going back every Friday night. At first, I could leave and come home with a few extra dollars, and we were good. But I guess my beginner's luck ran out.

"And a couple of months ago, I ran through the savings so fast that I almost lost my mind, and I have been trying to get it back." His voice began to crack. "I thought you would notice by now, but you never said anything. I knew that you were busy with Markus' court case and working long hours, so I decided to just wait until you noticed." He paused to check Lee's temperature; he wanted to know if she was hot or cold. She looked like she was in complete shock. So, Monroe continued, "It was easier to replace the money in the checking account, but I couldn't win enough to replace the savings." As he spoke, his voice quivered slightly, each word a hesitant step into the unknown.

"Monroe!" Lee looked around the room.

"What are you looking for?" he asked, following her gaze.

"My cell phone, I need to check the balance."

"No, you don't. Lee, there is nothing in the savings account."

"Monroe, that was our wedding money. That was our honeymoon money! That was our rainy-day cushion! All of it is gone?" Lee placed her head in her hands and leaned down touching her knees. She was sick to her stomach. She felt as if she would throw up all over their king-sized comforter set. Clutching it for dear life, she fought back every emotion that was trying to surface. Trying to maintain her composure, she stared at Monroe in disbelief!

"Lee, yes! But can you *please* let me finish?" his words tumbling out in a rush as if fearing the consequences of his silence.

"What more is there to say, Mon? What else could you have done?" Head still down on her knees, she started crying. It was as if an avalanche erupted and ran down the side of a mountain. Her tears wouldn't stop flowing.

"Lee, listen!" Monroe raised his voice. "Last night was the worst loss I had. I ran out of money and apparently—we got new cards, so I couldn't use the checking account. I tried everything to get to that account but because the cards were expired none of the tellers would allow me to get any money. And oh, how I tried. I was so tunneled visioned and focused that I asked someone how I could get money, and they recommended using credit cards to get balance advances or finding a bookie. After our financial class with FINFIT, I stopped carrying credit cards, so I found a bookie and sold my truck to him."

Monroe stood up, hands on top of his head, looking defeated. "I lost the truck. I called Jason to come but before he got there, I just started drinking to ease the pain of it all. Lee, I'm sorry but to get the truck back I need $5,000."

Lee sat quietly. *It's definitely over with Monroe*; she thought to herself. *I can't do this anymore.* It was time to consider her options.

Monroe moved to stand beside her at the head of the bed. "Can you say something?"

She shrugged. "I have nothing to say." The look in her eyes was scary. They were dark but otherwise devoid of emotion. She rocked back and forth almost as if she was having a panic attack.

"Nothing at all? I need you to say something, Lee."

After several minutes, her voice heavy with tears, Lee held the throw pillow tight, still rocking. "I have nothing. I have nothing left. I've tried for twelve years to make this thing work and when we finally get through the women and the affairs and the joblessness, in comes the casino and gambling and you taking all the money that we have worked for in a matter of months."

"Lee, I'm sorry! If there was something more I could do, I would."

"You've done quite a lot, too much." Lee pressed her face into the pillow allowing it to catch her tears and screamed a soul jarring scream that held Monroe's feet captive. "Monroe, why would Jason tell me that you and he were going to get the car?" She thought about the fact that the truck would cost $5,000 to get back.

"I told him that I would see if you'd give me the money to get it back."

"You've got to be kidding me." Lee started to laugh, hysterically almost as if she had lost her mind. "You've taken all the money out of our savings and now you want the money in the checking?"

She shook her head in disgust. "I guess the blessing is that you didn't have the new card with you. You don't know how many times I tried to call you Thursday when the cards came to tell you that I was activating them. But every time I reached for the phone, something happened. A client called, Constance called, Princeton called, Mom called. I was frustrated but decided to just tell you later. I'm so grateful that I didn't."

Lee looked Monroe in the face. "*No.* Figure out how to get the truck back on your own and the wedding is officially off." She took her ring off her finger and tossed it on the bed. "Maybe you can pawn this and get your truck back. Use what's left and find a place to live. Monroe, be out of my house by Friday. That gives you about a week."

Monroe's eyes widened in disbelief, his heart a cacophony of emotions – regret, desperation, and a little flicker of determination. He watched as Lee moved to the end of the bed, her movements fluid as she stood, stretched, and walked into the bathroom, her departure leaving a deep void in the room.

Left alone, Monroe remained seated on the edge of the bed, his posture slumped with the weight of his own mistakes. He cried quietly, vowing to himself that he was going to win her back and right this wrong. He knew what he needed to do, and he was willing to do it. He hated that he was losing in life and in love.

CHAPTER 30
THE ART SHOW

"What time is the show supposed to start?" Constance asked Sonya. The two were wrapping up decorating the convention center for Mabel's art show and Bertha Green's fundraiser.

The Masters Convention Center was the most popular place in town for event hosting. Weddings, baby showers, parties, concerts—just about every type of gathering was held there. Today the Greens hosted their annual fundraiser.

Bertha was a socialite and philanthropist to her heart and dedicated to giving back to a community that gave so much to her and her family. Helping people and seeing their progress were the highlights of her life and she was creating that same value in her children. Not all of them had her heart or passion, but they all wanted to make sure she was well taken care of. She was their queen, and they treated her as such.

"I think it starts at six," Sonya replied. "But I have pregnancy brain. I can't remember anything."

Laughing, Constance agreed. "Yep, that pregnancy brain can last for a year after the baby is born."

"Well, I carried two babies, so I have a double loss."

"How are the babies doing?"

"They are doing well—keeping me and Reggie up at night. But I wouldn't change it for the world. Babies are such a blessing."

"Indeed, they are. Even the big ones."

Sonya glanced over at her sister. Constance was an example of constant growth. Over the past year, she really tried to make amends with Markus after the whole jail fiasco. They were now in a much better place.

"How's Markus?" Sonya asked cutting her eyes towards Constance.

"He's good. He's still in anger management, but he's doing well."

"Well praise God for that."

They continued to decorate. Green and white effects, balloons lined the stage, and red carpet covered the walkway at the front entrance of the convention center.

"Have you heard that Mabel has a man?"

"What! Mabel? Girl, stop gossiping." Constance giggled. "Mabel has been so focused on the art show and growing her business that I doubt if she has a new man. Men are hard work!!" They looked at each other and laughed, thinking of their husbands, Reggie and Princeton.

"Well, let's just see what the night holds; Ms. Mabel may have a surprise for us," Sonya winked.

Sundays in the Green household were always sacred. Those times were used to reflect, to fellowship, to love on one another, and to just enjoy life. It's always about family. But this particular Sunday, everyone was attending Mabel's art show. It was the talk of the town. Mabel's art was displayed throughout the city of Masters and beyond. She started creating paintings with Granddad when she was just a little girl but never really pursued the craft until she got older. Now people from all over the world, definitely all over Masters and other parts of Mississippi, were coming to see Mabel at her art show.

After spending the day decorating, the Green sisters were ready to welcome guests. The decor was impeccable. Markus' band performed background music and held the audience captive with their musical selections. There were surprise selections and guest solos that included Sam Love and Leona Green. The people of Masters were so excited to see Lee and Sam in action. The ohhhs and ahhhhs filled the crowd as Leona scatted for what seemed like an hour. The night was shaping up to be a grand ole affair.

Mabel's paintings were displayed throughout the ballroom of the convention center. There was a crowd of about two hundred people gathered in the foyer waiting to behold her pieces. Bertha Green showed up with her mingled-gray hair and a sassy suit to match. A handsome gentleman dressed in a black and white seersucker suit accompanied her.

Leona turned around and noticed Bertha and her beau and as loud as she could said, "Who is that man with Mom?"

Sonya chuckled. "You guys are late. Mom has been dating Mr. Turner for a while now."

"Ladies, it's time to shine. Let's take our places." Mabel walked over and signaled for the Greens to start welcoming guests.

Charity took her place at the entrance greeting patrons as they walked in. To her surprise, Isaiah King walked in with Reggie.

"Hey, Charity," Isaiah whispered hesitantly.

"Hi, Isaiah," Charity replied, her tone nonchalant.

"How are you?"

With a smile plastered on her face, Charity offered him a program. "I'm well. How are you?"

"Can we chat a little later?"

"Good evening, welcome. Thank you for coming," Charity said, looking around Isaiah to speak to the next guest.

Isaiah greeted the guest as well.

"Hello, Charity," Isaiah said again standing directly in front of her making sure that she couldn't ignore him. "Can we talk?" Their last conversation was held on Charity's porch the week after the Wisconsin Fiasco as Charity liked to call it.

"Hello. I'm busy right now. As you can see, I'm greeting guests."

"Can we chat later?" he repeated starting at her, his eyes penetrating her soul.

"I don't think we have anything to chat about."

"Looking past Isaiah again, Charity motioned for the next guest to enter. "Welcome. Thank you for coming; refreshments are in the rear."

"Charity, I *need* to talk to you." His whisper was louder, and his voice was heavier with much more than a request but a plea. Charity had to admit that Isaiah looked like fine wine in that suit but looks were on the lowest rung of the ladder of the qualities that she looked for in a man. Patrick was handsome as well and look where that got her.

"I don't think tonight is the time and this is certainly not the place."

"You won't return my texts or calls, so *when can* I ever talk to you?"

"I don't know. I don't think we have anything more to talk about."

Staring at her for a full 30 seconds while she continued to ignore him, he whispered in dismay, "Bye, Charity."

With that Isaiah walked away to network throughout the room.

Charity greeted the next guest. Her mouth was dry, her hands wet with sweat. "Good evening, Sir, and welcome. Thank you for coming." She struggled to maintain her smile and keep her composure. She breathed slowly and welcomed the next guest.

"Good evening. I'm looking for Mabel," an unfamiliar gentleman said. He looked at Charity with the confidence of an unqualified politician. *He's fine for an older man*, Charity thought to herself. Dressed in a dark mid-tan suit with a white dress shirt and a red bowtie, he was the cat's meow.

"Let me see if I can spot her for you." Charity scanned the room. "There she is over there in the red dress." Charity caught herself before she mentioned that it was quite a coincidence that Mabel and the gentleman were matching this evening. She smiled a sly smile as the gentleman walked over to Mabel and placed his hand on the small of her back.

Next, in walked Ryce, Diane's wayward husband. "Hey, Charity."

"Hey, Ryce!" Charity embraced him in a hug. "How are you? We sure have been missing you!"

Ryce grinned at Charity. "I've missed you guys as well."

"I know Diane and the kids miss you as well."

Ryce emitted genuine joy. "Are they here?"

"Yes, the kids are probably doing a little work. Diane oversaw the silent auction, so she may be at the long tables in the back of the room."

"Thank you, ma'am. How have you been?"

"I'm superb or as my mom used to say, 'I'm better than great.'"

"You look great. Good to see you Char."

"You too Ryce."

Reverend Ryce strolled away headed to greet his wife.

The next guest arrived: Monroe. "Hey Char. Is Lee here?" Monroe was one of the most handsome men Charity had ever seen. He stood six feet even with dark skin that reminded her of dark chocolate. His long locs fell gently over the side of his face; he walked with the swagger of Denzel and the confidence of Michael Jordan. Tonight, he was dressed to the nines in a black tux and a bright sexy smile.

"Hey, Mon." Charity tried not to stare. "Yes, she's in the back helping with the hors d'oeuvres."

Monroe walked back to the buffet area where the Green sisters were setting up the snacks and hors d'oeuvres for the evening. Since the Greens owned their own bakery, they delighted in cooking and baking for every event. Even though Mabel insisted that they hire caterers so they could wholly enjoy the festivities, the Green sisters declined and decided to handle their own affairs. Mabel conceded but reminded them of their decision and that she wasn't going to help. It was her big day, and she wanted to enjoy it!

"Hey, Lee," Monroe said timidly. "Can I talk to you for a minute?"

"Now is not a good time, Monroe. We are in the middle of getting refreshments ready for the guests."

"Lee, it won't take but a minute. Please."

Sonya looked at Lee with a stern face, eyes hooded and mouth turned in a frown. "Could you please go check on your fiancé? We can handle things until you get back."

Leona hadn't told her sisters that Monroe had moved out and the wedding was canceled.

"Lee," Monroe ushered her into a corner near the back of the ballroom. "I want to apologize for everything. I have taken on extra shifts at the plant, and I want to repay the money."

"Ok thanks," Lee said, moving to walk away. Monroe grabbed her hand.

"I still want us to get married and try to work things out. I've been staying at the Masters Inn. I didn't get my truck back, but I purchased a car using cash. Lee, I know I messed up. I've even started in Gamblers Anonymous. I'm so sorry. I should have come to you when the problem got out of control."

"Yes, you should have."

"Honestly, I was just afraid, Lee. I didn't want to keep it from you, but I didn't realize how far gone I was."

Silent, Leona stared at Monroe.

"I love you, Lee. I started counseling, too. My therapist wants you to attend a session with me one day if you want to, but no pressure. I'm not going to pressure you to be with me, but I just want you to know that I love you and miss you."

After a few more minutes of silence Monroe said, "I want my baby back." Seeing that Leona was half-heartedly involved in this conversation, Monroe cut his losses, "Lee, I know you need to get back to work. Just think about it."

"I will think about it. I love you Monroe, but I just don't know how to handle all of this."

"I know, but if you come to therapy with me then maybe you can figure out a solution together. I know I messed up big time, but I honestly can't imagine a life without you. The last few weeks have been hell."

The Masters Inn was nice but nothing to compared to the home he and Lee shared together. The beds weren't comfortable, the food was always cold, and stale and he missed Lee's warmth, her inner sunshine that woke him up challenged him to be better.

"I'll think about it." Lee's response was curt and short as if she didn't even know the man standing in front of her.

"See you soon, Lee, I love you," he whispered and kissed her on her cheek before she walked away.

As Monroe stared at Leona as she walked away, he couldn't help but to admire that purple ball gown that hit every curve of her body. As he stood smiling at God's beautiful creation, Ryce made his way to the silent auction tables. "Hey beautiful."

Diane turned around quickly and bumped into her husband. Tears gathered in her eyes. "We haven't heard from you all week", she turned fussing at her husband.

"I know," Ryce replied softly. "I wanted to surprise you and the kids."

"Well, we are surprised. I think we made up our minds that you were gone again."

"You all have no faith in me? None?"

"We're trying, Ryce," Diane looked at him sympathetically.

"I'm here in the flesh, in living color. I told y'all I was coming back. He took his phone out of the breast pocket of his tuxedo jacket and handed it to Diane. "Look at this picture on my phone."

Taking the phone and studying the picture, Diane smiled, "This is a nice house, Ryce."

"That's all you have to say. It's a nice house, Ryce?" he said, mimicking her with that perfect smile that always melted her heart.

Diane snickered, "It's a beautiful house!"

Moving closer to Diane, Ryce took the phone and whispered in her ear, "You think you can make it into our forever home?"

"It's ours?" Diane screamed! "It's ours!" She could barely contain herself or catch her breath. Her heart was racing as if it was going to explode in her chest.

"Yes!" Ryce, beamed. "I told you I was going to get us set up and come back to get you and the kids. I see you doubted me." He smiled, embracing Diane in a tight hug, planting soft kisses on the top of her head.

Tears ran down Diane's face as she took the phone from Rye again and asked, "This is *our* house?"

He leaned down and gave Diane a kiss. "Nope, it's our home. Our forever home."

"Oh Ryce!" Diane screamed again unable to control her emotions. She was surprised by her joy.

"Shhh, woman, you are going to get us put out of here." He said laughing as he held her tight and lifted her about a foot off the floor.

"I'm just so grateful."

"I love you, Diane. Don't ever doubt the power of God. It's only by His grace and mercy that any of this is possible."

"Amen, Reverend Ryce, Amen. Let's go find the kids and share the good news."

"Diane, who's going to man the auction table?" He stated looking at all the amazing gifts that companies and sponsors donated to the silent action.

"I will only be gone for a moment. It'll be okay."

Ryce laughed and pulled her over to where their kids were standing assisting their grandmother, Bertha. "Come on my lady."

The patrons loved Mabel's art. It was flying off the walls. Bids were growing higher and higher at the silent auction table once Diane returned to man her station after finding her children and telling them about their new life and home in Memphis. The evening was progressing nicely. Another Green event down in the books.

"Speech! Speech!" The audience called for Mabel to make a speech after the emcee announced that all the paintings were sold and the silent auction ended with every piece being sold.

Mabel made her way to the stage wearing a bright red dress and yellow pumps–a combination that would look crazy on anyone else, but Mabel made it look incredible. She was surely an undercover fashionista.

"Thank you all for coming out to my art show and fundraiser. Each year I pick a nonprofit or a small business to assist. This year, along with Green's Goodies, we chose a nonprofit founded and run by my brother-in-law, Reggie Warren. He is founder of The Boys to Men Mentoring Program. He supports the young men in the community and today, we are giving him a check for $10,000 to keep his vision alive. I know that he uses much of his own money and influence to keep his organization going, but we'd like to give him a little rest. Thank you for impacting our community, Reggie."

The audience erupted in applause. Reggie blushed, leaned over, kissed Sonya's hand and hugged her.

"Come on up, Reggie!" Mabel clapped, beckoning for Reggie to come to the stage.

Reggie looked overwhelmed and shocked. As he approached the stage, he hugged Mabel. "Wow. Thank you, ladies. I really am at a loss for words. I never thought I would be selected. It gives me joy to know that there are people who truly support the work I do. I just want to give these young men great role models and real-life education from tying ties to building a strong work ethic to lessons in love and operating in integrity."

"How do you know anything about operating in integrity?" A voice yelled from the crowd.

Reggie recognized the voice and immediately turned to look for Sonya. He wanted to make sure that she was okay. Reggie wasn't worried about the person behind the voice because he knew he hadn't had any dealings with her since she'd acted out at the church homecoming ten years ago. All that resulted in Tammy being arrested and sentenced to prison. His eyes met Sonya, and she nodded, reassuring him that she was okay. He nodded back.

Tammy's voice rang out, clear and defiant, cutting through the murmurs like a bell. "None of the men in Masters are worth a dime, a quarter, or two nickels rubbed together!" she exclaimed, her words a bold declaration echoing off the vaulted ceilings. Her eyes flashed with a deep fiery hatred.

The security guards, alerted by the commotion, began to move towards her, their expressions a mix of professionalism and concern. Their uniforms were crisp and orderly, but they were prepared for any type of trouble the night may hold. They brought an assurance of order and safety.

"Get back! I don't want any trouble! I just came to drop off a package for the good reverend!" Tammy shouted, as the guards approached her. Her audacious statement carried over the crowd as she held the baby carrier aloft, its contents a mystery that piqued the curiosity of onlookers. Tammy strolled slowly through the crowd carrying the baby carrier. The security guards moved toward her making sure to push the crowd towards the exists of the room just in case she carried something other than a baby in the carrier.

"Pastor, here is your package." Tammy walked directly in front of Pastor Jeffries and tried to hand him the baby carrier. Failing initially, she tried to place the baby carrier in Pastor Jeffries hands again.

Pastor Jeffries turned from talking to one of the church parishioners to look at Tammy with a face filled with dread and fright.

"What?" Pastor Jeffries asked, walking towards Tammy and the baby carrier she held as she took a step back with each of his forward movements. Reggie came down from the stage to stand between Tammy and Ken. "Ken," Reggie said looking at Pastor Jeffries, "please don't give her the time of day. You know her routine. She lies to cause a scene because she can. Don't let her."

"Reggie, *you* shut up!" Tammy screamed.

Tammy's eyes narrowed, a defiant smirk playing on her lips as she locked eyes with Pastor Jeffries, the baby carrier still cradled protectively in her arms. Her voice was a low, sultry drawl, each word laced with a challenge that hung in the air like a taunt. "Pastor, I want what I was promised. Now give me what you owe me and take this baby!

"Ma'am, I don't know what type of sick joke this is, but please leave me alone, You and I both know that this is not my baby." Pastor Jeffries implored, his voice steady yet mingled with an edge of frustration and disbelief. His gaze was unwavering, his posture a reflection of his inner strength, even as he faced the storm that Tammy had unleashed.

Tammy's lips curled into a sly smile, her eyes dancing with a mischievous glint as she leaned in, her words a whisper that carried through the hushed room. "It *is* your baby! Don't be scared, Pastor. Tell all the good people of Masters that you are in love with me, and I had your baby," she declared, her voice sweet, yet venomous and loud that sent a ripple of shock through the conference hall.

Gasps echoed around the room; the disbelief evident as whispers spread like wildfire among the gathered patrons. Pastor Jeffries stood firm, his expression calm as he faced Tammy's bold accusation.

The air was thick with anticipation, the patrons holding their collective breath as they awaited his response. His eyes met Tammy's with a steady intensity that demonstrated his integrity and the truth he knew.

"I'm not telling these people any such thing, young lady!" Pastor Jeffries voice rose above his normal calm, comforting voice that the people of Masters had grown to love.

Lilly made her way to the front of the room where all the commotion was taking place. "What's going on, Ken?"

"Nothing Lilly. This delusional lady is trying to give away a baby."

"What?" Sonya made her way to the front by now and looked at Tammy. Tammy was dressed in a two-piece outfit that was gasping for breath as it tried to remain on her body. "Tammy, will you ever quit? Will you ever just leave people alone? Your goal is just to keep up a ton of mess and that is so unfortunate."

"You shut up and leave me alone, you hussy! You stole my man and my life. I was supposed to be Reggie's wife."

"Girl, *gone on* with that foolishness." Sonya responded vehemently.

Tammy, with a swift and decisive movement, placed the baby carrier on the polished wooden floor. Her eyes held a rebellious glint as she surveyed the room, her posture one of defiance and determination.

"Listen, I didn't come for no problems," she declared, her voice carrying a thread of urgency and finality as she started backing away from the baby carrier. "Like I said, I'm just dropping off this package for the First Family. Y'all enjoy. And don't forget you owe me *big*, Pastor Ken!"

With that, Tammy turned on her heel and made a swift beeline for the front entrance of the ballroom, her footsteps echoing in the hushed silence. The conference hall was so silent, you could hear feathers falling from heaven. Everyone watched in stunned silence; their eyes glued to the baby carrier now resting alone on the floor. No one moved to stop Tammy as she slipped out the double glass doors that led in and out of the convention center. Her departure as abrupt as her arrival.

As the patrons looked on, the emcee trying to get order back in the room and graciously bring the night to a close, called everyone's attention to the big screen. "Thank you all for joining us tonight. As you can see on the screen, we have more than doubled our contributions from last year. Thank you all for a phenomenal year and we wish you all nothing but the best. On your way out, please pick up a souvenir bag that contains a Green's Goodies cupcake. See you all next year! Same bat time, same bat channel. Good night."

As the emcee's final announcement echoed through the ballroom, the initial shock of Tammy's abrupt departure began to dissolve, leaving a room full of murmurs and curious glances directed at the baby carrier.

Ken Jeffries bent down and removed the cover off the baby carrier, revealing a brown baby little girl about the same age as his daughter with a head full of thick curly black hair and dimpled cheeks. She quietly assessed Pastor Ken as he assessed her. A note attached to the front of the baby carrier read: *My name is Anna Rae Jeffries*

Lilly stood in bewilderment and shock staring at the baby that lay in the carriage and the note that her husband held in his hand. The other Green sisters went to work cleaning the venue and packing boxes. Mabel came over and walked Lilly to the bathroom.

The presence of little Anna Rae Jeffries had cast a shadow over the evening's celebratory atmosphere.

The festive mood was gone. The crowd had turned silent and most began to leave. Guests walked to the front entrance, greeted by the Green grandkids as they handed out departing gift bags.

"Come on Lilly, it looks like you are in a state of shock. Let's get you to the bathroom and wash your face." Mabel brought her sister into an embrace and ushered her away. Tears flowed freely down Lilly's face. She slowly walked to the restroom with her sister leaning in for support.

Back in the ballroom, Reggie looked at Pastor Jefferies. "I'm so sorry man. I cannot believe that this has happened."

"What is wrong with that lady, man?" Pastor Ken Jeffries stared at Reggie, looking like he'd fought the good fight but lost terribly.

Reggie shook his head and frowned. "At this point, I honestly think she is crazy. I can't imagine her just leaving her baby here and walking away."

"Man, I can tell that Lilly doesn't believe me. We got a letter in the mail about six months ago about a baby, but I thought nothing of it. I should have paid more attention. Lilly was upset then." Pastor Jeffries took off his glasses and said, "Lord please give me direction," as he shook his head. He bent down to talk to the baby. "Hey, Anna Rae." The caramel-colored baby girl with fluffy cheeks looked up at him.

Pastor Jeffries took the note with the baby's name off the side of the carrier and read it to Reggie. "It says she's three months old, that's the same age as our babies. Man, what are we going to do?" Pastor Jeffries asked Reggie.

"Listen, tonight take the baby home and tomorrow morning get up and go to the department of child services and find out what you need to do."

"Reggie, this is not my baby."

"Man, I believe you."

"I know from experience that Tammy is crazy."

"It's as simple as taking a DNA test. I'm sure they can do all of that at DCS."

"Wow, man. This night has totally taken a wrong turn."

Bertha Green walked over to the Reverend. "Hey Pastor, are you ok?" concerned itched in her face as she stared down at the cooing baby.

"I don't know what to think; what to do. Lilly probably hates me, but I promise this is not my baby, Mamma Green."

Bertha Green rubbed Pastor Green's back before she bent down and picked up Anna Rae. "I believe you. We all know Tammy's history." She turned her attention to the baby.

"Hey pretty girl. Let's check your pamper and see about getting you some milk." Anna Rae cooed and murmured as Bertha patted her back. "I'll go get Lilly," she said, looking at Reggie and the pastor. You two help clean up so we can get out of here."

Bertha walked in the restroom with Anna Rae. Mabel and Lilly stood at the sink chatting about the evening. Lilly saw Bertha and screamed, "Mom, *don't* bring that baby near me!"

"Lilly, this baby has done nothing to you. You are a first lady of the church. In times like these you have to show yourself strong in the Lord. The devil is busy, but you always have to have your armor on. So, you have to shape up and get it together. This baby has to go home with you tonight. She is just as innocent in all of this as you are."

Bertha looked down at the baby. "She doesn't even know that her mother has abandoned her. Get yourself together and let's get out of here. I will meet you and Ken at the house in the morning and we can go to DCS and work out a plan. This is the time to show your strength, baby." Bertha Green had spoken with finality. The Green sisters present nodded in agreement.

"Lilly," Sonya said walking in, "you cannot believe anything that Tammy says. As a matter of fact, believe the exact opposite of anything that she says."

Constance walked in and bossily stated, "We have the ballroom all cleaned. Let's go."

Bertha continued to hold the baby as they walked to their cars. "Pastor, put her in Hannah's car seat and y'all drive safely. I'll see you in the morning."

Lilly and Ken drove home in uncomfortable silence.

Finally, Pastor Jeffries asked, "Are you going to talk to me?"

"About?" Lilly whispered.

"Really? The passive aggressive stance, Lilly?" He blew out a deep breath as he took in the sights that led to their home

"I don't have anything to say at this moment. When I tried to talk to you six months ago about that letter, you blew it off. Now we will talk once the DNA test results come back."

"So that's it. You take the word of a deranged woman who tried to break up your sister and her husband, over me?"

"Just remember, Ken, I told you about the letter months ago and you swept it under the rug. And now look at this mess. You didn't even try to address it"

"Do you hear yourself?" Pastor Jeffries asked as they pulled into the driveway of their home. "What was I supposed to do? I'm telling you I have never slept with Tammy. The last time that I have seen her is when she acted foolishly at the homecoming years ago."

"Are you sure?"

"*Am I sure?*" Pastor Jeffries paused and looked at Lilly in awe. He pressed the garage door opener and drove the car into their three-car garage, opened the car door, and removed the baby from the car seat in one swift movement.

"Yes, I'm sure."

"You have a prison ministry," Lilly bawled forcefully. Her eyes ablaze with anger.

"No, *the church* has a prison ministry. You think that when I go to the prison, I'm having conjugal visits with the inmates?" Pastor Jeffries' shoulders slumped as he bent down in the car to stare at Lilly in disbelief.

Lilly rolled her eyes and opened the car door. "It sure looks like it."

"Lilly, you know women visit the women inmates and men visit the men. The only time that Tammy could have ever seen me is when I have preached to the whole population and that has happened maybe two or three times in the whole year that we've been going there."

"Ok."

"That's it? You're just going to believe the same woman who stole money from Reggie, tried to keep Reggie and Sonya apart, and break up their marriage?"

Lilly was silent.

"Hello! What is this all about? How can you not trust me?"

Changing the subject, Lilly questioned her husband. "What are you going to do with your baby tonight?"

"*My* baby?" Pastor Jeffries shook his head in disbelief.

"Lilly, you cannot go to sleep angry." Pastor Jeffries opened the garage door to their home, maneuvering the carrier through the door gingerly, making sure not to bump Anna Rae.

"Then I'll stay up all night," she said as she climbed the steps to the nursery to check on their daughter, Hannah Grace.

Pastor Jeffries walked behind her to the door of Hannah Grace's room. She stood at the door, Lilly whispered forcefully, "I don't want that baby in here with my daughter."

"You're being so unreasonable."

Opening the door to Hannah Grace's room, Miss. Deborah, a mother of the church, greeted them holding Hannah Grace in her arms. "Hey Pastor and First Lady. How are you?" Not pausing for an answer, she continued, "Hannah Grace was her cute, adorable self. She gave me no problems."

Lilly reached down to the shorter lady and took Hannah Grace in her arms. "Thank you so much, Miss Deborah."

"We appreciate you; I'll walk you out and pay you," Pastor Jeffries offered, his voice warm and sincere.

"Whose beautiful baby is this?" Mrs. Deborah asked as she stood to put her jacket on and noticed the baby in the carrier that Pastor Jeffries held.

"Hannah's got a little friend." Pastor Jeffries replied with a strained smile, his eyes flicking to see Lilly's expression. Where once there had been joy and trust, now there was a stony facade that left him feeling uncertain. The sight of Lilly's tears, glistening in the dim light, pierced his heart.

As he escorted Mrs. Deborah to her car holding Anna Rae after taking her from the carrier, he thanked her with a gentle nod, his words sincere despite the heaviness in his heart. "Thank you for everything, Mrs. Deborah," he murmured, his voice a quiet echo in the night.

Returning to Hannah's room, Pastor Jeffries resumed the conversation. "I just didn't know that we had no trust between us. I thought that we were good. I never thought that you would instantly believe anyone over me. Have I given you reason to believe that I'm a cheater? All I do is work in the church and come home," his voice steady yet colored with a quiet desperation. The words were a plea for understanding, a search for the connection that had once anchored them both to this marriage.

Lilly remained silent, her gaze fixed on Hannah as she gently laid her down in the crib. Her heart was a storm of emotions—hurt, betrayal, and a longing for the certainty that had once defined their love. Tears streamed silently down her cheeks.

"Lilly, you have to know that I would never do anything to hurt you, our baby, or our marriage."

Lilly didn't respond. She cried silently as he spoke.

Frustrated Pastor Jeffries conceded, "Alright then. I'll take Anna Rae to the guest room, and we'll sleep there. I love you, Lilly. I just wish you loved and trusted me so we could get through this without you shutting me out."

Still no answer from Lilly as she stared into Hannah's crib. This hurt was too deep for words. Making a sound seemed impossible for Lilly. In an instant her world was flipped upside down. Pastor Jeffries watched her with a heavy heart, his own eyes glistening with unshed tears.

"Good night." Pastor Jeffries said as he took Anna and walked out of the room defeated.

∞ ∞ ∞ ∞ ∞ ∞ ∞ ∞ ∞ ∞ ∞

At precisely 8 a.m., the sound of the doorbell rang through the house, a cheerful chime that announced Bertha Green's timely arrival. She was a woman whose presence commanded respect and admiration.

"Good morning, sunshine," Bertha greeted warmly as she stepped over the threshold, her voice a welcome relief to the tension that filled the Jeffries household. Her presence brought warmth to the home. Her eyes, sharp yet compassionate, took in her daughter's weary demeanor with a mixture of concern and understanding.

Lilly opened the door and stepped aside allowing her mother room to enter. Her posture tense, her eyes shadowed with the remnants of a sleepless night. Her hair was slightly disheveled, evidence of a restless night contemplating her next move. She managed a weak smile, though it did little to mask the fatigue etched into her features. "Come on in the kitchen. I'm fixing Hannah Grace a bottle," she said, her voice carrying a note of exhaustion.

∞ ∞ ∞ ∞ ∞ ∞ ∞ ∞ ∞ ∞ ∞

Hannah Grace lay in her bassinet sleeping peacefully.

Bertha laid her purse down, walked over to the bassinet, and smiled at her granddaughter. "She's so beautiful."

Lilly beamed with joy; it was her first real smile since yesterday afternoon. "Yes, she is, she looks like her glamma!"

"Ohhh Glamma! I like that name 'cause Bertha Green is glamorous!"

Bertha watched her daughter with quiet empathy, her heart aching with the knowledge of the burdens Lilly carried. "How are you holding up, darling?" she asked gently.

Lilly sighed, her hands moving with practiced ease as she prepared the bottle. "I didn't sleep much," she admitted, her gaze fixed on Hannah Grace, a soft tenderness in her eyes. "There's just so much on my mind."

Bertha nodded, her expression was one of understanding. "You know I'm here for you, whatever you need," she offered, her words, a promise of support.

Pastor Jeffries walked in the kitchen with Anna Rae in his arms and said a low *good morning*. He too was up all-night thinking and praying. He was afraid to lose Lilly. She was his best friend and his true love. After Melia, his first wife died, he never thought he would find love again. But in Lilly he found true love, joy and peace.

Bertha greeted him warmly. "Hey Pastor. Hey Anna Rae."

"Are you doing alright today, Mamma Green?" Pastor Jeffries asked as he tried to open the refrigerator door while holding Anna Rae.

"I'm better than you and Lilly, that's for sure. You two look like zombies."

"Hey, my love," Pastor Jeffries looked at Lilly who failed to respond. He shook his head and walked over to the coffee pot.

"Are you all ready to go to DCS?" Bertha asked as cheerfully as she could. Sensing the tension in the room, Bertha's goal was to remain lively and cheerful until they could get some answers.

"I'm not going," Lilly said, folding her arms. "You all can go by yourselves."

Bertha turned and looked at Lilly with fire in her eyes. Her plan to remain cheerful, flying out the kitchen window. "You *are* going! We are *not* going by ourselves. Get yourself together." She turned to her son-in-law. "Pastor, grab Anna Rae and Lilly, grab Hannah Grace and come on. This is not the time or the place for you to lose heart. Satan is busy and you're giving him your power. God works in mysterious ways. Let's go. You don't know what plans he has in store for you or these babies." Bertha grabbed her purse and walked out of the room towards the front door.

∞ ∞ ∞ ∞ ∞ ∞ ∞ ∞ ∞ ∞ ∞

The drive to the Department of Children's Services (DCS) was tense; the air was heavy in the car with unspoken fears and uncertainties. The city streets slipped by as the car was covered with heavy silence. Each mile brought them closer to the moment of truth, the weight of the situation pressing heavily on their hearts.

As they arrived at DCS, the building loomed ahead. The doors swung open with a soft hiss, welcoming them into the sterile interior where the day's business was just beginning.

The waiting room was lined with informational posters and brochures. The air was filled with the faint scent of antiseptic, a reminder of the clinical procedures that took place within its confines. The seats were arranged in neat rows, their plastic surfaces cool and unyielding. The ticking of the clock on the wall marked the time and the heaviness of the decisions they awaited.

As they sat in the waiting room, the tension continued to mount. Lilly's face was a mask of frustration, her eyes flicking to the clock with increasing frequency as if willing the minutes to pass more quickly.

Pastor Jeffries sat beside her, his posture tense yet resolute, his thoughts a chaotic swirl of trepidation.

When his name was called, Pastor Jeffries followed the nurse and submitted to the DNA test with a quiet determination, the swab brushing against his cheek a symbolic gesture that held the weight of their future. Anna Rae, cradled gently in his arms, was swabbed as well, her tiny form a picture of innocence. She let out a loud cry when the nurse opened her mouth.

Mrs. Thompson, the case worker, offered them a choice that hung heavily in the air. Her demeanor was professional yet compassionate, her eyes reflecting the gravity of the situation. They could either keep Anna Rae in their custody until the test results were returned in a couple of weeks or turn her over to the care of DCS.

The decision was both simple and complex. Pastor Jeffries, his heart filled with a deep-seated compassion, chose to keep the baby with them, unable to bear the thought of leaving her in the uncertainty of foster care. However, he knew his choice could potentially ruin his marriage and create more shadows of doubt for Lilly.

As they left DCS, the tension between Lilly and Pastor Jeffries was tangible, a simmering undercurrent that threatened to erupt. Lilly's expression was fire hot, her emotions a maelstrom of disbelief and frustration. Yet, Pastor Jeffries held firm to his decision, his gaze meeting Bertha Green's as they walked behind Lilly toward the car.

"It's going to be a long couple of weeks," he murmured, his voice a quiet acknowledgment of the challenges that lay ahead.

"Indeed, indeed," Bertha Green replied, her eyes reflecting a deep concern. The drive home was completely silent. The decision to keep Anna Rae drove another wedge between Lilly and Pastor Jeffries, but he was still determined to keep his family together.

CHAPTER 31
GREEN GOODIES III

It was the Wednesday following the fundraiser for Mabel's Marvels. The Green sisters gathered in the cozy, wood-paneled conference room of Green's Goodies. The room exuded an air of quiet elegance, its rich mahogany table gleaming under the soft glow of the overhead chandelier. The walls were adorned with framed photographs of past family gatherings and successful events, the legacy of the Green sisters. The scent of freshly brewed coffee mingled with the faint sweetness of freshly baked cinnamon rolls laid out on the table.

As the sisters settled into the plush leather chairs, there was a sense of anticipation that filled the room. The fundraiser for Mabel's Marvels had been a resounding success, and the time had come to discuss the event. Diane, ever the practical one, wasted no time diving into the heart of the matter.

"How much did we raise, Lilly?" Diane demanded, her fingers tapping lightly on the table as she awaited an answer.

"Mabel's art pieces were flying off the walls last night," Sonya chimed in, her voice bright with enthusiasm. "I know we must have raised a hefty amount."

"I know, right?" Leona added, her eyes sparkling with pride as she glanced around at her sisters. "Good job, Mabel. I was impressed."

Mabel, ever the modest artist, blushed slightly at the praise. Her art had captured the hearts of many at the fundraiser, and her sisters' support meant the world to her.

Sonya caught Constance's eye and winked, a silent acknowledgment of the unspoken excitement that lingered from the event. Constance needed no further prompting to join the conversation.

"Oh, so who was that the man in the nice gray suit with the red tie that perfectly matched your dress, Mabel?" Constance teased; her voice laced with playful curiosity. Her eyes danced with mischief.

Without skipping a beat, Constance continued, "He was quite handsome. He said he was purchasing prints for his home and his businesses. *Businesses*," she repeated with emphasis, "meaning more than one."

The sisters exchanged knowing glances, their laughter filling the air with a lightness and camaraderie. The mention of Mabel's friend, Anthony Dawkins, a distinguished art collector with a penchant for Mabel's work, had added a delightful twist to the evening's success. His presence had been a highlight.

As the conversation flowed, the sisters reveled in their shared success, their hearts buoyed by the knowledge that their efforts were making a tangible difference. "Wow. Alright Mabel!" Leona laughed at the Green Girl's shenanigans.

"We cleared $57,000, but we have to pay for the venue and the setup of the tables and chairs, which comes to about $5,000." Lilly looked over the books as she spoke.

"Wow, we made far more than we did last year?" Diane did a little dance in her seat. "I'm so excited! My sisters are the best sisters."

Lilly held onto Hannah Grace while Mabel held Anna Rae. Pastor Jeffries had to officiate at a memorial service, and Mrs. Deborah was not available for short notice. So, Lilly had to act like an adult and take care of both babies. She was not happy about it, but she knew her husband's first responsibility was to God and the parishioners he served.

"So how is everyone doing?" Mabel put on her big sister hat to make sure her younger sisters were good.

"I'm good," Diane yelled across the room. "The kids and I are moving to Memphis in about a month."

"I'm so happy for you, Diane. But why are you yelling?" Sonya chuckled.

"I'm just excited. I didn't mean to yell."

Constance grinned. "Ryce made good on his promise. But I'm sure going to miss you. I need to come and get some recipes before you go. Princeton likes everything you cook."

"I can send you recipes whenever you'd like, Constance. And I will be home often. Memphis is just two hours away. You know the kids are going to want to see the family. I can't keep them away from their aunts and cousins and especially not Bertha Green."

They all laughed in unison.

As the sisters shared a moment of laughter, the room's warmth embraced them. Mabel, ever the voice of reason, leaned back in her chair, her eyes twinkling with amusement. "So true," she agreed, her voice carrying a note of playful camaraderie.

Turning her attention to Lilly, Mabel's expression softened with concern. "Lilly, how are you?" she inquired, her voice gentle yet probing. Lilly, her posture tense and defensive, forced a smile that didn't quite reach her eyes. "I'm fine, Mabel. Thank you for asking," she replied, trying to keep up a false calm facade.

Mabel, catching the strain in her sister's voice, snickered softly. "Who are you trying to convince? Me or you?" she teased, her words a gentle nudge.

A flicker of anger igniting in Lilly's eyes. "Well Mabel, how do you think I should feel with you holding my husband's baby in your arms?" she retorted, her voice rising with hurt and anger.

Sonya, hoping to make peace, interjected with a soothing tone. "Now you know good and well that is not Pastor Jeffries' baby," she assured, her voice a calming presence. "Why are you acting like this? Everyone knows that Tammy is a liar and a deceiver. When the DNA results come back in a couple of days, you will have your answer. It will be negative."

Constance, her demeanor poised and authoritative as usual, added her voice to the conversation. "And since all of us know it, act like it and stop treating that man so badly. You are the first lady, govern yourself accordingly," she advised, her words a gentle reminder of Lilly's strength and grace. "And another thing, Constance continued, that baby don't look nothing like Pastor Ken, and you know it."

Always truthful Constance hit the nail on the head. She said what everyone else thought but didn't dare say. She had no filter at all! The outburst served its purpose and had all the Green sisters laughing. Even Lully joined in momentarily.

After the short comedy break that they all needed, Mabel, returned her gaze, back to Lilly. "That man looks like he has lost his best friend and you're around here giving him the silent treatment. He has no more been with Tammy than I have been with Denzel Washington or Idris Elba," she declared, her voice carrying the weight of truth, love, and laughter.

Lilly, her defenses crumbling, looked around at her sisters, her eyes glistening with unshed tears. "How should a first lady act then, Constance?" she asked, her voice a whisper of vulnerability.

"With grace," Constance replied, her voice soft and reassuring. "You know Anna Rae is innocent in all of this. And I would be willing to bet my home and my car that Pastor Jeffries is too. Extend grace, child, and save your family."

Overwhelmed by emotion, Lilly let out a cry that rose from the depths of her soul, a raw expression of the pain and longing that had been building within her. Her sisters, united in their love and support, gathered around her, their presence a comforting embrace showing their unbreakable bond.

"I wanted my baby to be his first baby. I wanted it to be special," Lilly confessed, her voice choked with tears.

Leona, her voice filled with gentle humor, giggled softly. "Hannah Grace is his only child. Rejoice and be glad. We all know that" she assured, her words salve to Lilly's aching heart.

Lilly slowed her crying and grabbed Leona's hand. "Thank you." She then cleared her throat. "We need to go over the books again. We need renovations and we need to look at increasing salaries again and finding new help since Diane is moving."

With a deep breath, Lilly shifted the conversation back to the business at hand.

Turning to Lee, her expression thoughtful, Lilly continued, "Lee, can you look over the contract with the bookstore and the coffee shop and see what we are looking like going forward?"

"Of course," Lee said half-heartedly.

Sonya noticed the change in her sister's demeanor. "What's wrong, Lee?" she asked, her voice gentle as she rocked McKenzie to sleep, his twin brother Kensington already slumbering peacefully in the baby carrier.

Lee, her eyes focused on her cell phone, avoided making eye contact with her sisters. "Nothing," she replied, her voice a whisper of uncertainty amongst the warmth and love that surrounded her.

"I saw Mon at the art show looking good as ever," Sonya drooled.

"You good, Sis? When is the wedding?" Mabel asked.

"The wedding is off," Lee replied flatly.

"Wait! What happened?"

Lee waved her hands dismissively. "I don't want to get into it. It's just too much." Her definitive tone brought an end to the conversation or so she thought.

"We won't talk about it now, but Mabel has some explaining to do as well." Sonya winked at Constance.

"Sure do, Mabel! Let's get into the man with the gray suit who was buying up everything."

"We are just friends. I met him at a coffee shop in New York last year and we've stayed in touch. When I told him about the show, he told me he owned a few businesses and would love to display my work in some of his locations."

"Well alright, Ms. Fastee Mae. You better not get pregnant!" Sonya laughed. Pregnancy at sixty plus was not an option for Mabel. Her grown kids would lose their minds, and she would join them. She was through raising kids other than her nieces and nephews.

"I think we have enough babies in the Green clan to last for a while," Mabel added, rolling her eyes playfully at Sonya.

When the meeting closed, Constance walked with Lee to her car. "Lee, I want to thank you for everything you did for Markus. I was so nervous about what would happen—but leave it to my baby sister to save the day." Constance, not one for a lot of sentimental interaction, held Lee's hand.

"You're welcome, Constance. Tell Markus next time he has as much right to call the police when he's been wronged as the person who wronged him. Never take matters into his own hands. It's just not worth it."

"He's a good man, just a little hotheaded," Constance said.

"I wonder where he gets it from," Lee mocked as she made her way to her sleek Jaguar.

"Okay! I can admit that he got it from his mother." Constance laughed out loud.

"Listen, Lee. I don't know what's going on with you and Monroe but try to work it out. You have been through the worst. He loves you. I could see it at the art show. He was looking like a sad puppy dog," Constance said with a small, reassuring smile. Her words were a gentle reminder of the bond that still existed between Lee and Monroe, despite the challenges they faced. "I don't want to interfere, but marriage and relationships are hard work. Pray about it and take some time to be by yourself. Monroe has changed since you were fighting and calling the police in the early days. When a man is trying, just support him. I learned that the hard way."

Lee's heart ached with the truth of her sister's words, each one resonating with the depth of her own feelings. "I don't know, Constance," she replied, her voice catching in her throat as tears welled in her eyes. "I just don't know." The admission was a release, a crack in the armor she had built around her heart.

Before she knew it, she was sobbing, the sound a raw, unfiltered expression of the pain and confusion she had been holding at bay. Her tears fell freely, each a display of vulnerability she felt in the face of her uncertain future.

Constance jumped in as the protective older sister, wrapped her arms around Lee, drawing her close in a hug that spoke of unconditional love and unwavering support. Lee rested her head on Constance's shoulder, the familiar scent of her sister's perfume, a comforting reminder of the bond they shared. "You're going to be okay, Lee. I promise. It's going to work out," Constance murmured, her voice a soothing lullaby that calmed the storm within Lee's heart.

They remained embraced for a long time, the world outside fading into a gentle hum as they shared the moment of connection and solace. When they finally parted, Constance offered Lee a warm smile, her eyes filled with reassurance. "My phone is always on. Call if you need me."

"Thank you, Constance," Lee replied, her voice filled with gratitude and a newfound sense of hope.

Lee sat in her car contemplating her next steps. *Life sure is like a box of chocolates*, you really never know what you will get, she thought to herself. She pulled her Jaguar out of the Green's Goodies parking lot and drove off.

CHAPTER 32
THERAPY SESSION

Charity entered Dr. Leisure's office, her movements deliberate and subtle with heavy tension. Her eyes, usually bright with curiosity and determination, now carried a hint of weariness, a reflection of the emotional journey she had been navigating the past few weeks. She settled into the chair opposite Dr. Lesure.

"Good afternoon, Charity," Dr. Lesure greeted, her voice offering a soothing reassurance. Her eyes, framed by stylish cat-eyeglasses in orange today, held a depth of empathy and understanding. She adjusted the glasses slightly, their frames catching the light of the sun beaming in the office.

"How are you today, Dr. Lesure?" Charity inquired, her voice carrying a note of gratitude for the familiar sanctuary of the office.

"I'm well, Charity. Thank you for asking," Dr. Lesure replied, a gentle smile touching her lips. Her presence was a calming anchor, a steady force amidst the tumult of emotions that Charity carried with her.

As the session began, Dr. Lesure leaned back in her chair, her long gray hair cascading in soft waves down her back. Her attire was impeccably stylish, a tailored suit paired with comfortable flats both elegant and practical. The subtle sophistication gave a sense of Dr. Leisure's remarkable style.

"Here we are again," Dr. Lesure noted, her voice a gentle invitation to Charity to share her thoughts. "How are you doing this week? Any new developments you want to discuss?"

Charity hesitated, her fingers tracing the armrests of her chair as she gathered her thoughts. "I honestly don't know where to start. So much has happened that I'm still trying to process," she confessed, her voice heavy.

Dr. Lesure nodded, her eyes studying Charity. "Well, tell me everything. That's what I'm here for," she assured, her laptop poised on her lap, ready to capture the conversation.

Charity took a deep breath, the soft rhythm of the air conditioner providing a soothing backdrop to her words. "I don't know where to start. It's all been quite devastating. I know I missed a few appointments because of work, but mentally, I have been on a roller coaster," she admitted, her voice a whisper.

"Start at the beginning. What happened?" Dr. Lesure prompted, her gaze steady and encouraging. "Is it the young man who is chasing you or is it Patrick?"

"How about both of them?" Charity replied, a hint of wry humor lacing her words.

"Ummm please tell me what happened," Dr. Lesure encouraged, her fingers poised over the keyboard, ready to document the unfolding narrative.

"My aunts both delivered their babies the same day at the same hospital," Charity began, her voice gaining strength as she recounted the events. "I bumped into Patrick there twice: once walking in and the other at the nursery."

"Patrick? Really." Dr. Lesure had to work to keep the surprise out of her eyes. Normally she could retain her composure, but this new revelation from Charity was quite interesting.

"Yes, Patrick. He had a daughter born there that same day; named her Patricia. She's a beautiful baby girl with sweet little fat rosy cheeks."

"How did that meeting go?"

"I didn't say much. I tried not to ask any questions and just let the moment happen. I think it was the closure that I needed."

"What did he say?"

"Some of what he said was mean and was uncalled for, but I never let him take me out of character." Dr. Lesure smiled. She was proud that Charity remained in character and not allowing Patrick to take her power.

"I'm glad to hear that, but what kind of things did he say?"

"Basically, that I was a holy roller and that I was always too caught up in church to have a real relationship."

"How did that make you feel?" Her eyebrows furrowed with concern.

"Honestly, I was indifferent. I mean I was hurt, but not as hurt as I thought that I would be when I saw him after our breakup."

"Do you think you handled it well?"

"Yes, I remained cool. I didn't raise my voice. As a matter of fact, I didn't really address any of it. I realized it wasn't necessary to say anything. He's married with a child so really there is no explanation."

"Good job! How is your heart?"

"I'm healing. I'm on the road to a great mend."

"It seems like you handled yourself well. What else happened that derailed your road to healing? Something to do with the guy that is chasing you?"

"Why of course," Charity said with a smirk. "I finally let my guard down and it backfired."

"Don't be so hard on yourself, Charity."

"But let me tell you what happened first. I had a speaking engagement in Memphis. His parents live in Nashville; he planned a dinner so I could meet them. I thought it was too soon. But I decided to do something I never do: take a chance and live on the edge of spontaneity. Can you say total backfire?"

"What happened?"

"*Dinner* went great. But another woman showed up and he just invited her into the room and started back eating like nothing was going on."

"Who was she?"

"He said an old friend."

"I told him I was leaving, and he said, 'ok.' I left. He called my phone six times before I could get to my cousin's house. He said that he didn't want the drama, so he just didn't say or do anything to disrespect his parents' home. Then he had the audacity to invite me to a game in Milwaukee."

"He was trying to make amends, at least that is what it sounds like," Dr. Lesure emphasized.

"He tried. But he failed!"

"How did he fail?"

"He had me fly out to Wisconsin and I never saw him when I was there. He claimed his sister came and distracted him from coming to see me. I flew in on a Saturday morning and left on Sunday night. I never saw him the entire time I was there."

"So, have you heard from him since?"

"He came to my house to apologize after the Wisconsin Fiasco as I like to term it, and he texts me every week but nothing personal. He sends positive messages, words of the day, verse of the day, or a funny joke."

"And do you reply?"

"I have found saying nothing works best for me."

"You say absolutely nothing?"

"Yes, exactly that is what I say. I don't want to get involved with someone so careless and find myself vulnerable again and eventually heartbroken."

"It sounds like you have a problem with confrontation, so you avoid pressure. You just need to set boundaries and stay in them. We will continue to work through those issues as we meet." Dr. Lesure paused to type notes into her laptop.

"I gave you an assignment last time. Tell me what you came up with for the qualities you want and the deal breakers."

Charity took her paper out of her purse. In Charity style, she had typed her responses. She read from the list of qualities she wanted in a man and those that were deal breakers.

Qualities: God-fearing, Kind, Loving, Handsome would be nice, Caring, Funny, Smart

Deal breakers: Smoking, Drinking, Drugs, Mean, Domestic Abuse

"What's the gentleman's name who is chasing you?"

"His name is Isaiah."

"Does Isaiah have any of these qualities?"

"I'm not sure. I haven't thought much about it."

"Take a few minutes and think about Isaiah and tell me if he has any of the qualities that you are looking for."

"He's definitely funny." Charity contemplated her list again. "He makes me laugh. He is VERY handsome and fine."

"He *seems* caring. He cared enough about your feelings to offer you a free trip to see him. And even though it was a disaster, you continue to get text messages, and he still seems to care because he's reaching out to you."

"I guess."

"No pressure from me, Charity. The list should guide you. It is not an end-all-be-all list. It serves to put you in the right frame of mind. You are so hard on yourself when it comes to issues of the heart. You don't have to make all the rules yet. You can take your time."

A tear slowly crawled its way down Charity's face; she swiped it as quickly as she could.

"There's no dishonor in crying, Charity." Dr. Lesure handed her a tissue.

"Have you decided to take a vacation?"

"Yes, I sure have. I'm planning to go to Santa Monica, and I plan on staying for a week.

"How are you feeling about taking your first solo vacation?"

"I'm quite nervous and a bit apprehensive, but I'm looking forward to it."

"Why the apprehension?"

"Safety is my biggest concern. I just want to make sure that no one kidnaps me." Charity smiled. "I wouldn't be a good victim."

Dr. Lesure laughed, "Well at least you know. Here are a few tips: make sure you give your hotel phone number to your family, befriend the concierge, and turn on your phone's location sharing. In case you go missing, your family can track your phone."

"Those are great tips. I'll definitely do all of them."

"When do you leave?"

"I'm pretty excited, but I haven't chosen a date, maybe in about a week."

"Don't forget to plan some fun activities as well as get some very good rest."

"I will, definitely." Charity looked admiringly at Dr. Lesure. "I'm so happy that I chose to come to therapy. I honestly feel like my load is getting lighter."

"That makes my heart smile," Dr. Lesure folded her laptop down. "This week's assignment is just to have fun! When you get back, make sure that you have a detailed report." She smiled. "I'm just kidding, but I'm looking forward to our next meeting and to hear about your vacation."

"Me too!"

"Enjoy your vacation, Miss Charity and try not to take anything work related with you."

Charity thought that was impossible for a workaholic like herself. She made it to the door then turned and said, "I'll do my best."

Leave work behind? That was probably the hardest assignment Charity had in her entire life. There was no way she would go anywhere without her phone or laptop. That just wasn't the Charity way.

CHAPTER 33
DIVINE INTERVENTION

The airport terminal was a hive of activity, with travelers bustling about, each on their own journey.

As Charity disembarked from her delayed flight, the urgency of the situation hit her like a wave. The overhead PA system crackled to life, its announcement slicing through the noise with an edge of finality: "This is the last call for Flight 3554 to Santa Monica. The doors will close in two minutes. Thank you for flying with Sky Airlines."

Her heart leapt into her throat, panic tightening her chest as she absorbed the reality of her predicament. "What?!" she exclaimed, her voice a blend of disbelief and desperation. The connecting flight from Masters had been a full forty-five minutes late, leaving her with a daunting trek through the maze of the Chicago O'Hare airport. Her eyes darted to the signage overhead, mapping the distance from Gate C3 to Gate C32—a span that felt insurmountable in the time remaining.

How in the world am I going to get to the door in two minutes when it's at least a five-minute walk? Maybe I could catch a ride on one of the carts, she told herself. She quickly decided to make a run for it.

By the time Charity reached Gate C32, her lungs burned with exertion, and her heart hammered in her chest like a relentless drummer. But the sight that greeted her was one of finality—the door was locked and sealed.

Tears stung her eyes, but she wouldn't allow them to come. She recited her mantra, "Blessings on Blessings, Just make it through this moment, I will not cry!" She was determined that the crying spell that had overwhelmed her for the last few months would end NOW!

Taking a deep breath, she went to the counter and inquired about the next flight. "Excuse me. How are you?" Without allowing the customer service representative to speak, she continued: "My connecting flight from Masters was late. I just missed my flight to Santa Monica. When will the next one depart?"

The customer service representative looked pained as she checked the screen. "I'm so sorry, ma'am, but it looks like the next flight doesn't leave until 8:45 this evening." Clicking on the keyboard with precision and ease, she continued. "And that's our last flight out today."

"Are you serious?" Charity leaned onto the desk as if catching her balance. One more blow and she was sure she was going to fall. She looked so lost at that moment. "It's just 3:55. That's almost five hours!"

The young customer service woman looked at Charity with care. "I'm sorry ma'am. We have been running fewer flights during the week than we run on the weekend."

"It's not your fault, I'm just frustrated." Charity blew a breath and leaned on the counter exasperated.

Tapping on the screen and looking at the keyboard, the young lady said, "Listen, I can bump you up to first class and give you a food voucher. Since you have such a long wait until the next flight, you can at least grab a late lunch or an early dinner at any one of the restaurants on this concourse. I'll give you some money so that you can grab snacks as well. Sound fair?"

"Sounds great! I truly appreciate it!" Charity smiled for the first time since leaving her home that morning and she breathed a sigh of relief.

The young lady looked warmly at Charity. "You know everything happens for a reason. Maybe God just wanted you to get some much-needed rest. You seem like a real busy lady." She handed Charity the voucher and her first-class boarding pass.

"How'd you get that I was busy just looking at me?"

The woman looked at Charity and smiled. "You have a bag on your arm that I'm sure holds a laptop or a tablet, if not both. You have two phones—one in your hand and one on the side of your laptop bag. To me that's pretty busy."

Charity started laughing. "You are so right. I'm actually taking me a much-needed vacation."

The woman crinkled her face. "Are you sure?"

"Yes, I'm sure, why do you ask that?" Charity asked surprised by the candor and the facial expression of the young lady.

"Because most people don't take all their gadgets on vacation with them. I would have thought you were going on a work trip."

"To Santa Monica?" Charity asked with a frown.

"You know they have businesses out there. People go to conferences, job interviews, and meetings in Santa Monica all day long."

"I thought the destination would let you know that I was going on vacation."

"Ma'am, the destination means nothing if you are taking the work with you. You could be going to Hawaii. If you take work, it's just a beautiful place to work." She shrugged.

"Umm that's true. Such wisdom for a young lady thought to herself. "Thanks, what's your name?"

"I'm Monica. Moni for short. Have a great day and please find time to enjoy your vacation."

"Moni, I sure will try. Thank you and enjoy the rest of your day." In that moment and by a perfect stranger, Charity was schooled.

∞ ∞ ∞ ∞ ∞ ∞ ∞ ∞ ∞ ∞ ∞

Her mind was preoccupied with the anxiety of nearly missing her flight, and she was focused on her phone as a text message dinged through.

Lost in her thoughts, Charity didn't notice the obstacle in front of her until it was too late. She collided with what felt like a brick wall. *I have to stop doing this*, she thought, her mind momentarily distracted from her rush.

"Funny running into you here," a familiar voice said, as strong arms gently steadied her.

Charity looked up, her eyes widening in surprise as she met Isaiah King's gaze. Her mind raced with disbelief and confusion. *Was this a dream?* "Hey," she finally muttered, finding her voice.

"How are you?" Isaiah asked, his grip still firm as he held her.

"I'm good. How are you?" she managed to get out, her words filled with a mix of emotions.

"I'm great now that you are in my arms," Isaiah replied with a warm smile, his eyes twinkling with a playful light.

Charity attempted to wiggle free, her cheeks flushed with embarrassment. "Stop struggling," he whispered softly. "You don't want to make a scene at the airport. The federal agents would be here in a heartbeat."

"What are you doing here?" she asked breathlessly, grappling through a myriad of emotions—happiness, apprehension, and a hint of irritation.

"I guess, like you, I'm at the airport to catch a flight," Isaiah replied nonchalantly.

Charity took a step back, regaining her composure. "I know that. It just seems strange that you would be at the same airport at the same time as me."

"Oh really. So, you are trying to say that I'm a stalker?" Isaiah teased, raising an eyebrow.

Charity considered the notion for a moment, but she hadn't shared her travel plans with anyone except her assistant. "No, I'm not saying that. I just think it's a total coincidence that you are here while I'm here. Where are you headed?"

"To Santa Monica. It's the off-season, and I decided I wanted to head to Santa Monica—enjoy a little fun and sun at the beach."

"Oh wow. Wow! I guess it really is a coincidence. That's exactly where I'm headed."

Isaiah's expression softened, a hint of sincerity in his eyes. "Charity, I don't believe in coincidences. I believe in blessings. I believe in fate. I believe in divine intervention."

"Divine intervention?" Charity asked pointedly.

"Yes. That means that God steps into an equation and intervenes."

"Why would He do that?" Charity challenged playfully.

"Now you're asking me to know the mind of God? You know His thoughts and His ways are not our ways." Isaiah feigned a serious expression before breaking into a goofy grin. "You're such a comedian."

"Yes, I've been told that a time or two, and believe me, I know that you don't know the mind of God."

Ignoring her little sarcastic barb, he continued his conversation with Charity. "So, then you know that He divinely orders things to happen. It's called the Providence of God."

"Isaiah, I know about all of that!" Charity replied, rolling her eyes.

"Well, do you believe it?" Knowing a thing and believing a thing were two completely different things.

"I don't have time to sit through a Bible study right now. I'm headed to get something to eat before my flight."

"What time is your flight?"

"It's at 8:45 p.m."

"We are on the same flight! Come on, I'll treat you."

"No, I have a voucher, and I would prefer to eat alone."

"Why?"

"Because" Charity hesitated, searching for a reason to decline. Her heart whispered fears she wasn't ready to voice. She was afraid of getting attached again, afraid of falling for someone who might leave her brokenhearted, afraid of all the negative possibilities.

"Because what?" Isaiah pressed Charity, his gaze unwavering.

"Look, Isaiah, I just think we are two people who are unsuited for a relationship of any kind."

"I didn't ask you for a relationship. You've already told me that you don't want any dealings with me. I can take a hint—your bluntness when I was in Masters was hard to misread. I know that you don't want a relationship with me. I get that. I simply asked to treat you to a meal in an airport."

"Wow. You place all of this on me and don't accept responsibility for yourself and your actions." Charity shifted her carry-on bag from her arm to the floor.

"I have apologized a thousand times, and I've tried not to bother you."

"I can't tell—you still send text messages at least once a week."

"They are just positive text messages, funny memes, and jokes, nothing serious or personal. I want to make sure I keep myself on your mind. There's a connection between us, Charity. There was something there the day you interviewed me almost a year ago, and there is still something now."

"You think so?" Charity pondered his statement. She liked Isaiah that was true, but nothing had gone right since the time they met. One interference after another told her to move forward, not stay put.

"No, I know so."

"I just want to be your friend. My texts haven't been forward or suggestive, and they haven't even been returned."

Charity laughed softly. "I see you are straightforward, too."

"Charity, I have nothing to lose, and you know I'm an athlete. I play to win, but if I lose, I just practice longer, pay more attention, study my opponent, and win the next time."

"I see."

"So, are we eating or not?" Isaiah asked again, his tone lighthearted.

"I can eat."

"Can you eat with me, Charity Love?"

"Yes, Isaiah King."

"Thank you, Charity," he said, gently taking her arm, leading her towards the food court, a shared meal marking the beginning of what could be a new chapter between them.

∞ ∞ ∞ ∞ ∞ ∞ ∞ ∞ ∞ ∞ ∞

"Thank you for dinner." Isaiah walked close to Charity as they made their way back to the terminal. They'd enjoyed some chicken and waffles and even stopped by Garrett's popcorn to grab a bag of the famous Chicago mix.

Hurriedly, before Isaiah could interject, Charity blurted out, "I'll see you on the plane. I have some calls and emails to return." Charity tried to make a quick exit when they arrived back to the gate for their plane departure.

"So, you just eat and run, eh?" Isaiah started laughing.

"Isaiah, I have to make some calls."

"I thought you were on vacation."

"I'm on vacation."

"I see, maybe you should act like it."

She threw her hand up in a dismissive gesture. "Bye, Isaiah!"

"Bye, Felicia!" Isaiah started laughing as he made his way to the gate to grab a seat. There was only about a twenty-minute wait until they started boarding.

He looked over in Charity's direction and studied her features. He said to himself: *She's so pretty. She doesn't even know how beautiful she is. She has so many walls up. Am I willing to put in the work to knock them down and replace them with love—my love?*

Isaiah knew that he kept messing up, but he thought about her all the time. Maybe this just wasn't the right time or the right person. In his heart he knew she was, but she was making it awfully hard. He also realized that they had gotten off to a very rocky start thanks to him.

Isaiah was no longer interested in girls who only cared about how their hair looked, what name brand they rocked, what they would post on Facebook, Twitter, Instagram, or TikTok. He wanted someone with substance; a woman with a heart of gold even if it was broken. He wanted Charity.

In his mind it was divine intervention that she missed her flight.

He felt God was working the details of this relationship. But he was also wise enough to know when to give a person space and time. He was going to do just that. But he sure wanted to know why God had placed them in the same airport, on the same flight, and heading to the same place. All he knew to do was to pray.

He refused to chase her. He had done so much chasing in his younger years that he was willing to wait on the right person. He thought that was Charity. If it was meant to be, it would happen. He was a man of faith. He knew that God orchestrated all things. He didn't mind waiting on the Lord. *Lord, if it's meant to be, you work out the details*, Isaiah prayed as he unlocked his cell phone to make a call.

"Good afternoon, Sky Airline passengers. We would like to start boarding now for first class. If you have boarding passes for first class, please come up to the counter to begin the boarding process."

Isaiah made his way to the boarding door and looked back at Charity, who was still on the phone. He waved a goodbye wave. He doubted that he would see her after they boarded, when they landed, in Santa Monica, or ever again after today. He wanted to say goodbye or better yet, see you later. She'd made herself perfectly clear. She wanted no dealings with him, and he'd respect her wishes.

She caught his eye and waved as he boarded.
Charity shook her head when she saw him board. He looked helpless. She had to admit that she liked him, though. He was right about there being something about him and something between them, but she was still hurting from Patrick and didn't want to take that hurt into another relationship. Besides, nothing was going right with them.

After the dinner fiasco at his parents' home and the trip to Milwaukee, she had decided to put him on a shelf marked for *Another Day*.

Taking a vacation alone and spending time learning to love herself fully and completely was a big step for Charity. She was determined to learn who she was before she ventured into the arms of another man. She was hell-bent on being the best Charity before she became a part of a dynamic duo. So, she would make sure that she waved now, because she had no intentions of seeing him during, after, or anytime while she was learning and loving herself on her Santa Monica vacation.

"Last call for boarding flight 3554 to Los Angeles." She wanted to make sure she didn't miss this one. As she prepared to board the flight, Charity said a prayer. *"Lord, please grant me traveling grace and mercy and please don't let me be sitting anywhere near Isaiah."* Approaching the counter, she looked at her seat number, 2B. She stated it out loud, committing it to memory. Then she took a deep breath and walked onto the plane. She immediately locked eyes with Isaiah.

"Are you seat 2B?" he asked.

"Yes," she answered, wanting to slap that arrogant smirk off his face.

He stood to allow her access to the second seat in first class. She sighed. Her first time having a free first-class seat, and this happens. Her second prayer hadn't been answered, so she prayed again for traveling grace. *Lord, please hear this prayer* she said to herself, looking up to the ceiling of the plane.

Isaiah looked over at her as he eased his tall frame back into his seat and radiated with pure joy. He looked up toward Heaven and offered a silent *"thank you."* God was working.

As the flight attendant gave her spiel, he leaned over to Charity and whispered, "Divine Intervention."

ABOUT THE AUTHOR

Teacher, Author, Speaker, Nonprofit Founder, Writer, and Blogger are some of the titles that Dr. Taura Turner Jefferson holds. Her work across multiple disciplines broadly addresses various topics of interest. Taura is an author's author. Though she loves to write poems. books, and blogs, she also loves helping others reach their dreams of being an author.

In 2021 she founded SansScripts to help authors find their voices and write their stories. Taura started writing in fifth grade and has yet to stop. A self-proclaimed people watcher, she gets much of her inspiration from studying people in random places like grocery stores and malls.

Taura calls the Memphis area home. You can reach her online at *www.sansscripts.com* or follow her on Instagram (@taura_jefferson).

ACKNOWLEDGEMENTS

To my husband, Keith, thank you for your unconditional love and unwavering commitment. I am so grateful to God for him bringing you to my life and for the way you love me. I soar with you. I am forever grateful that our hearts synced.

To my sister Tiayra, and my nephews, Jeremiah, and Jaxson, I draw so much strength from you. You are my love, my joy, my sweet inspiration. We are San's Legacy!

To my grandmother, Mrs. Ernestine Marie Madden Hunt. I am so happy that God made you, my grandmother. You are simply the best!

To my family... There are way too many to name, but I love each of you in a very special and unique way. Thank you for supporting, listening, and encouraging me to DO THE WORK! You all give me so much love, support, entertainment, and content. In each of you, God is with me.

To my friends, I love you. You are just an extension of my family. The family that I chose, to walk this journey of life with me.

To God, I owe for the gift of writing that serves as my love, my talent, and my therapy. Everything that I am or will be is because of the Most High. Without God, I am nothing.

Special shouts out to EVERYONE who ever said a positive word to me or taught me anything. I have felt loved and seen by you.

All the Best
~ Dr. Taura

ALSO BY THE AUTHOR

*Laid to Rest

*Still Sleeping with the Lights On

*Our Giants Are Falling Asleep Grief Journal

*Addicted

*FINFIT Financial Journal and Workbook

*San's Child Affirmation Journal and Coloring Book for Boys

*San's Child Affirmation Journal and Coloring Book for Girls

*My Prayer Journal

*Living In the Red Devotional and Journal

*Available on Amazon

Made in the USA
Columbia, SC
09 February 2025

53295128R00141